REPRISE
OF 2 THE
SPEAR
HERO

Aneko
Yusagi

HI, EVERYONE! IT'S ME, RAPHTALIA, FROM THE LAST BOOK. THIS IS MR. NAOFUMI, THE SHIELD HERO.

THANKS FOR THE INTRO. WELL, IT'S A PAIN, BUT I'M GOING TO EXPLAIN SOME IMPORTANT THINGS THROUGHOUT THE STORY.

Motoyasu Kitamura

The protagonist of the story. Twenty-one years old. Summoned from Japan to serve as the Spear Hero.

Intensely earnest and devoted, Motoyasu is a self-proclaimed Love Hunter. Even though he died in battle, thanks to his spear's ability "Time Reversal," Motoyasu is summoned to begin the adventure again with his stats unaffected by the reset. He loves Filo and filolials to a worrying extreme.

Naofumi Iwatani

Twenty years old. Summoned to serve as the Shield Hero. In Motoyasu's first go-around, he was Filo's master.

When he was initially summoned, Naofumi was an inquisitive and energetic young man with a gentle disposition. But after going through a traumatic experience, his personality got all twisted. Motoyasu is making sure that Naofumi doesn't encounter any "circumstances that bring back Father's bad memories." At the moment, Naofumi is still a regular, pleasant young man.

One of Motoyasu's filolials. A thoroughbred filolial, Yuki is worth much more than the others. Bred and born with elegance and a sense of responsibility, she's the leader of the flock.

Yuki

A female filolial. Naive and honest. In Motoyasu's first go-around, he fell completely in love with her, but after the time loop reset, they have yet to meet.

Motoyasu's objective is to ensure she becomes the filolial queen.

Filo

One of Motoyasu's filolials. Hatched from a cheap egg.
She's happy-go-lucky and loves attention. She's the filolial who most reminds Motoyasu of Filo. Quite attached to Naofumi.

Sakura

Kou

One of Motoyasu's filolials. Along with Sakura, he's a regular filolial hatched from an egg thrown in as a bonus. Lively, curious, and loves to eat. He's not so great at reading the room.

I'M NOT SURE WHAT'S GOING TO HAPPEN TO THEM ALL, BUT LET'S FIND OUT ALREADY.

LET'S SEE THE SECOND VOLUME, PLEASE!

ABOUT FILOLIALS (KINGS AND QUEENS)

Stomach (digestion):
The stomach of a filolial is a bottomless pit. Filolials love eating. Especially when they're still growing, they devour a terrifying quantity of food. Although it may seem cute at times, their physical strength is connected to the intensity of their hunger.

Head (thought):
Typically filolials have gentle personalities and they often become attached to humans. They tend to love eating, singing, dancing, and running. In this world, they're used like horses to pull carriages, so they also love to help carry things.

Now we can all better understand the incredible power of filolials!

Back:
You can tell regular filolials apart from filolial queens by their backs. Filolial queens have far more feathers than other filolials. Their figure can appear to be a perfect circle, but this is a misperception.
With pompom like soft feathers that run along their backs, their shape is more like that of an unusually plump ostrich. How one can possibly ride on the back of such a creature remains a secret.

Feathers (touch):
Fluffy. Despite their remarkable softness, filolial feathers are firm and sturdy. Motoyasu uses them as a material for making clothes. The color of the feathers greatly varies, but generally they are monochrome. Supposedly, there is no other filolial that has the exact same coloring as Filo.

A true hero is able to power up majestic filolials into a filolial queen or king! As leaders, king and queen filolials have boosted strength and value and can even transform into angels. You can really tell these filolials apart from the flock!

Feet (speed):
Since filolials are used to pull carriages, they have a lot of confidence in their leg strength. Sometimes they even compete in filolial races. Since filolials take such pride in their running ability, they put immense effort into these competitions.

Table of Contents

VOLUME 1 SUMMARY

College junior **Motoyasu Kitamura** died when he was fatally stabbed with a knife for seeing too many women at the same time. He awoke in a strange place—a world strikingly similar to an online game he often played. He had been summoned to save the world as the **Spear Hero**.

Many months passed, and Motoyasu eventually faced death as the Spear Hero once again. As the world was fading to black, Motoyasu recalled Filo—that angel from heaven who was there for him in his darkest hour, when an evil witch had deceived him. Just when he began to lose consciousness, Motoyasu prayed with all his might: "All I want is to save the world for Filo-tan and all filolials! Please let me help Naofumi, for all he's done for **Filo**!"

Motoyasu, who probably should have died this time, mysteriously came back to life. When he opened his eyes, he was back at the altar where he had first appeared when he was summoned to another world. He confirmed that his stats were as high as they were at the moment of his death. Motoyasu was back for a **new adventure in god mode**.

Reflecting on everything that happened in the first go-around, Motoyasu worked hard to help Naofumi and sent him off to Siltvelt, which Motoyasu considered to be safer than Melromarc. However, all of a sudden, Motoyasu was flung back in time to the first day that he arrived yet again. It appeared that the time reversal occurred **whenever one of the four heroes died**. Motoyasu regretted ever leaving Naofumi's side. He resolved to guard Naofumi closely so he could achieve his goal of meeting Filo again.

Motoyasu promptly informed his allies of his new plan to successfully get Naofumi out of Melromarc. This time they traveled together, Motoyasu protecting Naofumi at every turn.

Along the way, Motoyasu bought three filolial eggs. After all, it would be much faster to ride to Siltvelt on the backs of filolials. Filolials hatched from the eggs, and Motoyasu named them **Yuki, Kou, and Sakura**. Raised by the hand of a hero, the three quickly grew, and Motoyasu and company at last arrived safely in Siltvelt.

Going to Siltvelt brings back some bad memories. What exactly do they think I am, anyways?

They only act that way toward you because their whole religion is based around the Shield Hero.

In Siltvelt, I was attacked by hordes of women and paraded around the country. I'm not some breeding horse!

They did make some tough demands of you. In a sense, you only got through it thanks to Atla.

It didn't make it any easier on me that you looked so over the moon during the parade.

That parade was necessary to raise morale! Plus, I happen to remember that you were the one who forced me to march in the front.

You hold quite a grudge.

ABOUT SILTVELT

In order to prevent a plot against Raphtalia's life from being carried out, it became necessary to travel to the country of Q'ten Lo. The only way to get there was by a boat that departed from the demi-human nation of Siltvelt. So Naofumi and company set out for Siltvelt.

As the people of Siltvelt have a religion that revolves around the Shield Hero, Naofumi's gang was met with a preposterously warm welcome. The people of Siltvelt proclaimed and demonstrated their loyalty to the point where Naofumi felt pretty uncomfortable.

What happened next was a nightmare. Without any regard for Naofumi's protests, the people of Siltvelt tried to force him to stay in their country by using women to entice him. In the back of his mind, Naofumi remembered how he had been deceived back in Melromarc.

Soon after, Naofumi and his friends were served poisoned food. While they used their poison-sensing abilities to detect it, the experience made them aware that **Siltvelt had a dark side**—the lion therianthrope Jaralis. Jaralis decided that there was no reason that the Shield Hero, who had been close with the enemy nation of Melromarc, could have any value to Siltvelt. But Atla, the female hakuko, raised objections to the leadership in Siltvelt about Jaralis's declarations.

Jaralis, furious upon hearing Atla's protest, challenged her and her brother Fohl to a duel.

There, Fohl learned his father's final secret: that Jaralis had killed his father. The sinister Jaralis took a mysterious potion to recklessly boost his strength, but Naofumi managed to help unlock Fohl's true power so Fohl could defeat Jaralis. The Siltvelt legend of **Unleashing True Power** was born on that day.

Thus diverting a bloody civil war in Siltvelt, Naofumi and company received the strong support of the entire nation and continued on to Q'ten Lo.

Jaralis

Lion therianthrope

A lion therianthrope. In the first go-around, he did all that he could to topple the Shield Hero, including poisoning his food. In his battle with Fohl, he took a suspicious potion to grow more powerful and, underestimating the potion, flew off the rails.

THE SHADOW OF SILTVELT.

Werner

Shusaku demi-human

A representative demi-human of the shusaku, one of the four holy beasts of Siltvelt. He demonstrated goodwill toward the Shield Hero. Previously, he looked down on Atla and Fohl, who aren't purebred hakuko. But after Naofumi unleashed Fohl's true power, Werner reconsidered his attitude toward them.

A SERIOUS BUT TRUSTWORTHY PRETTY BOY.

Prologue: The Heroes' Arrival

At long last, Father, Éclair, my filolials, our Siltvelt escort, and I approached the Siltvelt castle town. The weather was still miserable. It was a torrential downpour.

"Father," I repeated, "I insist, why don't we blow away this rain with some magic?"

"I wish you would stop suggesting that. The townspeople are going to think we're gods or something and end up worshipping us."

My name is Motoyasu Kitamura. I am the Love Hunter, the Spear Hero. The call of fate summoned me here once again to save the world in god mode, with my stats unaffected by the time loop! The man I was speaking to at the moment is the father of my true love and devotion, Filo-tan. His name is Naofumi Iwatani, and he's like the holy mother: merciful, compassionate, and an amazing cook. Filo-tan inherited her angelic compassion from Father, no doubt about it, I say!

"You don't want that?" I asked.

"It's not that I don't want to stand out," Father said. "It's just that every time we do something it seems to backfire. I mean, getting here was a complete wreck."

"Fair enough," Éclair said, nodding. "It was a long and dangerous road."

Yes, Éclair! Her last name, was it Seaetto or something?

Oho? For some reason she always pronounced her name incorrectly, but it wasn't anything to worry about. Anyways, Éclair had been held in an underground prison in Melromarc for punishing a demi-human-hunting soldier. When she heard about how Father and I were deceived by Trash and the crimson swine, she decided to accompany us out of righteous indignation. According to Father, she's a pretty serious character.

"Still, I'm relieved we managed to make it to a big castle town like this," Father said. "Maybe we won't get attacked anymore."

"Even the Church of the Three Heroes will have trouble attacking us here in Siltvelt," Éclair said. "They worship the Shield Hero here."

"That makes sense," Father said. "And even if there's a revolt or attack, Siltvelt should be able to suppress it immediately."

I copied what Father was doing and looked around the castle town. The buildings looked vaguely Chinese, but there were Western-style buildings too. It gave me the impression of a developing country. There were even flying demi-humans. It looked completely different from Melromarc!

"Each race has its own architectural style," Éclair said. "You can tell which buildings belong to which race by the architecture."

"Huh! So there's no single race or culture here," Father said.

"Apparently the previous Shield Hero once said, 'Multiculturalism should be a cause for cooperation, not war,'" Éclair said.

"Wow," Father said. "Those are pretty words, but if everyone remembers them, that means if I say the wrong thing, they'll remember that too."

"Well, that's generally true," Éclair said. "Please be careful, Mr. Iwatani."

"I, too, pledge my undying allegiance to Father!" I declared.

"Mr. Iwatani, do you understand?" Éclair asked.

"I know," Father said. "I can't afford to say anything stupid."

Was it just my imagination, or was Father even more determined than he was when we warned him about Siltvelt before?

"Now that you mention it, when is the wave coming?" Father asked.

"The Melromarc wave of destruction?" I asked. "I think it's in about one week."

"Hm. Then that was dangerous," Father said. "We were summoned right to the location of one of the waves."

Yes, we had definitely been in danger.

"The dragon hourglass was in one of the lands we visited on the way here," said Éclair. "Based on what Mr. Kitamura told us, I think we should've stopped there."

"The dragon hourglass?" Father asked. "Why didn't we have Yuki and the other filolials drop by there?"

"It was too dangerous to stop there on the way," Éclair said. "There was a good chance it would have been a trap."

Father nodded. Naturally! The Church of the Three Heroes would do something like that.

"At the dragon hourglass there's also a ceremony called level reset, which we can use to class up," Éclair said. "But I have no idea how it will turn out if we try to class up in a country we can't trust."

Hm? In the back of my brain, Father appeared.

|| The Dragon Hourglass ||

Silky red sand slides down this towering hourglass. Those that have reached their maximum level can break the cap by classing up. A person's level can also be brought back to level 1 in the ritual "level reset."
When the sand finishes falling through the dragon hourglass, the four heroes and their companions are flung to the location of the next wave of destruction. It's a useful facility, but its abuse can lead to trouble.

"So? Is there also a dragon hourglass in Siltvelt?" Father asked.

"That's what I heard, but I'm not too sure," Éclair said. "They also speak a different language here. I think I know enough for everyday conversation . . ."

Now that she mentioned it, I remembered that the heroes' weapons have a translation function. It helps the hero understand what the other person is saying in their language, but you can't use it for reading or speaking. I never learned Siltvelt's alphabet from Father, so I couldn't read at all. We'd be able to get by in simple conversations, but I couldn't handle any written communication at all.

"So when will Siltvelt's wave happen?" asked Father.

"Last time, it was about two weeks after Melromarc's wave," I said.

We were nearly at the entrance to the castle.

"Which means that there was also a wave at about the same time we were summoned, right?" Father asked.

"I'm guessing that the next Siltvelt wave will happen in three weeks," I said.

"Three weeks, huh?" Father said. "I wonder how strong I can get in the next three weeks."

"But won't you be forced to take part in a bunch of public ceremonies?" Éclair asked.

"Public ceremonies?"

"Mr. Iwatani, the Shield Hero did a lot to treat demi-humans well, so the people of Siltvelt worship him. You're a god to them."

Father gave me a bewildered glance.

"What's wrong?" I asked him.

"Well, I was wondering if maybe you had heard about . . ."

"I've certainly heard something of the sort."

The people from Father's village told me something about it. At the time, I was in the middle of taking care of a suspicious bunch that had been approaching Father's village. Meanwhile, Father and his companions had gone to Siltvelt and seemed to get caught up in their own troubles.

"I heard there was trouble," I told Father, "but since I wasn't there, I don't know the details, I say!"

Just then, the carriage stopped. "We're here!" called Yuki.

"Ugh . . . We're already here?" Sakura rubbed her eyes. She had been sleeping in the middle of the carriage.

"Looks like it," I said.

"This is a fun-looking town," Kou said, who had been peering around the area as well. "I bet they also have tasty food."

"Oh, now that's something I'm interested in," Father said. "I wonder if they have good food."

"Hm . . ." Kou tilted his head in thought.

Yuki, Sakura, and Kou were the filolials I had bought and hatched on the way to Siltvelt. Yuki was a graceful and refined thoroughbred. Merry Sakura was a beautiful pink color like cherry blossoms. And Kou was the curious and lively black-feathered male of the group.

"Well, let's talk more about that later," Father told me. "Let's go!"

ALL ABOUT THE PHOENIX WAR

The Phoenix, like the Spirit Tortoise, is one of the four benevolent animals. In order to investigate the Phoenix, Naofumi and company went to a shrine in the mountains, but when they arrived, they found the statue of the Phoenix already destroyed. With the stone monument destroyed, they realized that the **Phoenix had in fact come to life**.

On the day of the Phoenix battle, a pillar of fire rose from the middle of the mountain and two gigantic birds appeared. With no choice but to defeat both the Phoenixes at the same time, Naofumi realized that cooperation was indispensable. The four heroes and their followers began their battle against the Phoenixes.

They launched a simultaneous offensive. But even as they battled and managed to weaken the high-altitude Phoenix, the low-altitude one would heal itself. They had to find a way not to give the Phoenixes a chance to recover. Just as Naofumi began pressing for an answer, a beam of light fell from the sky and struck the high-altitude Phoenix. All that remained were the Phoenix's feathers, scattering and dissolving in the sky. The four heroes were taken aback and quickly turned their attention to the low-altitude Phoenix. They heard a groaning sound. The Phoenix was rapidly healing its wounds and swelling larger than ever—signaling a **self-destruct attack**. If they couldn't stop the Phoenix at once, there was no saving any of them. Naofumi, risking his life, charged to the front.

At that very moment, as the Phoenix unleashed a blast of fire at Naofumi, Atla raced in front of him and, using all her life force, diverted the blaze. It was then she became the **shield** that saved Naofumi's life. The rest of the companions then launched a dual attack on the Phoenixes and, defeating them both, closed the curtain on the Phoenix battle.

Atla

Naofumi's slave

In the previous go-around, Naofumi received Atla in a package deal when he purchased Fohl, Atla's older brother, in Zeltoble. She was a demi-human hakuko. Through her strong devotion to Naofumi, she was a perfect representative of the citizens of Siltvelt.

When Naofumi first met Atla, she suffered from an incurable disease and seemed like she was going to die. But after Naofumi gave her medicine, she got better in the blink of an eye—so much better that her liveliness became almost overbearing.

After her recovery, she trained with Naofumi, somehow managing to learn the challenging Hengen Muso martial arts style, even if she didn't truly understand the essence. In other words, she was a prodigy.

IN LOVE WITH NAOFUMI.

Fohl

Naofumi's slave

A demi-human hakuko that Naofumi purchased in Zeltoble. Atla's older brother. From time to time, Atla knocked him around a bit.

While Naofumi purchased him for his military prowess, he seemed to be about average in that department, with Atla actually having turned out to be the soldier with better potential. In Siltvelt, Naofumi helped unleash Fohl's true power and Fohl transformed into a therianthrope in combat.

After the battle, he displayed immense pride in his power.

Like any older brother would, he did not approve of the way Atla fawned over Naofumi.

SISCON.

We got off the carriage and a group of demi-humans took it to the stable. The heavy rain kept on falling. I still wanted to blast it away with some magic, but I resisted the urge for Father's sake. We wanted to stay under the radar, after all.

As for the state of the castle? Although the surrounding castle town expanded out of sight with identical Chinese-style buildings, the castle itself was made of stone and had a medieval appearance. Melromarc's castle was also pretty large, but Siltvelt's definitely topped it on all fronts. The castle bridge, doors, and gates were all enormous. Cranes crept slowly around the castle grounds.

A representative from the castle came to greet us as we arrived at the throne room. "Welcome, Shield Hero and Spear Hero." It was a male shusaku. "You must be weary from your long travels. I am Werner, and I serve as the leader of the shusaku. Pleased to make your acquaintance."

What were the different races again? Shusaku, hakuko, aotatsu, and genmu? I remembered that in the future Father had hakuko subordinates, but I couldn't recall the details. I was pretty sure that I met them in the Phoenix battle. But they didn't have much to do with me, so whatever.

"Ah, nice to meet you!" Father said. "I'm Naofumi Iwatani, summoned here as the Shield Hero."

"It is I, the Love Hunter!" I proclaimed. "Motoyasu Kitamura, I say!"

"Motoyasu, shouldn't you mention that you're the Spear Hero too?" Naofumi said.

"Should I? Well, that's me, the Spear Hero."

"The Spear Hero!?" Werner looked completely taken aback.

"Nice to meet you. Anyways . . ."

Werner looked over at Éclair expectantly.

"That's the daughter of House Seaetto," Naofumi added.

"Oh!" Éclair gasped. "Yes, I'm Eclair Seaetto. I've been serving as the escort of the Shield Hero in place of my late father."

"That Éclair fellow, she's got her own name wrong!" I whispered to Naofumi.

"No, Motoyasu, you're the one who can't pronounce the name of the person we've traveled all the way from Melromarc with."

Really? Well, whatever. If I called her Éclair, I figured she'd respond.

"We would like to applaud your noble efforts, undergoing such a harsh journey here in the hope of ending discrimination against demi-humans in Melromarc, with hardly any regard for your own safety," Werner went on.

"No, no, we only did what was right," said Naofumi, and Éclair nodded.

I did hear that they enslave demi-humans in Melromarc. In the previous world, Father and even Éclair's dad had slaves, though they took the effort to treat them well.

"Heeey, Naofumi," Sakura said, "I'm bored!"

"Just wait a little bit longer, Sakura," Naofumi said.

"Fiiine!"

Naofumi and Sakura seemed pretty close.

"Are those new comrades you met on your way here?" Werner asked, looking at Sakura, Yuki, and Kou.

"So . . ." Naofumi started.

"They're filolials!" I declared. Since for some reason Father was being all vague about it, I decided to set the record straight. I can't stand beating around the bush.

"Filolials?" Werner asked.

"Precisely. Thanks to them, we made it to the castle safely. They can take the form of legendary godlike bird creatures," I said. "Now, come on, everyone!" I called. "Show your true forms!"

With a powerful *boom*, Yuki, Kou, and Sakura turned into their filolial forms. The shusaku took a step back.

"I—I see . . ." he stuttered. "It's reassuring that we have such legendary creatures at our side."

Reassuring, huh? I couldn't help but feel suspicious about his reaction.

Father spoke up. "So what can we do while we're here to prepare for the wave?"

"Before that," Werner said, "I thought that we might be

able to provide you with some delightful rest and relaxation."

His tone hinted at another meaning—a meaning I was very familiar with from my experiences with insensitive pigs. I wish that Father could recognize that he doesn't have a good awareness for this sort of danger!

"We've also prepared an offering of our gratitude for the arrival of such great heroes," Werner continued. "Wouldn't you all like to relax your bodies and enjoy yourselves?"

"Okay, sure," Naofumi said. "Thanks for taking care of us."

He then showed us to the rooms that Siltvelt had prepared for us. Father was in a separate room, but since Sakura was going to watch over him, I refrained from insisting that we stay together. Father hugged Sakura tight and told me to leave it to her. I was so proud of them!

Oh, by the way, Father's room was insanely big and beautiful.

"Hey, Motoyasu," Father called.

"What is it, Father?"

"Well, you've been such a big help to me, and so I thought I at least should say thank you," Father said.

"Say what? Father, you should know that I would never ask for you to thank me for anything."

"I know that. But still, thanks."

What a perfect expression of gratitude!

"I also figure I should talk with you to discuss a couple different things from before," he added.

"Such as?"

"Let's talk in your room, not out here. And let's have Sakura, Kou, and Yuki stand guard to make sure no one is eavesdropping."

"Of course."

At Father's direction, the filolials stood outside the room and we went inside.

"So does this work? What did you want to talk about?" I asked.

"What we were talking about before. The trouble in Silt-velt—you were saying you didn't remember what happened."

I vaguely remembered an incident in Siltvelt that Filo-tan had mentioned to me. She said something about how Father got caught up in a rebellion.

"It was all hearsay and very vague," I said. "I just know that there was a duel or something like that."

"A duel?" Father said. "Now that you mention it, I feel like Eclair said something about how people in Siltvelt have the urge to show off their strength, a sort of sense of righteousness. Well, if you don't remember specifically, we'll just have to be on guard."

While Father spoke, I was deep in thought.

"Was it that if we lost the duel, I had to be used as a breeding stud?" Father asked.

"It's not impossible," I said. When you think about it, people in this world had strange ideas about the heroes. Even though the Church of the Three Heroes was definitely evil, if someone told me that a different religion was better, I don't know if I'd believe them.

Everything that happened in the previous go-around was full of gaping holes in my memory, so I really didn't know anything about Siltvelt besides the fact that they worshipped the Shield Hero, which I already knew from the online games I played.

"What's the right way to put it . . ." Father said. "You've taught me a lot of helpful things, but it seems like you can't remember anything unless I ask you about it directly. I want to be careful moving forward, so I'm trying to figure out the right thing to ask."

Father believed what I told him about him dying, and now he's taking superb care to not die! Which means that I, Motoyasu Kitamura, must continue to protect Father with all my heart and soul!

"Let's try sorting out the possibilities," Father said. "In novels or manga, didn't anyone ever try to keep the hero trapped, powerless in one place, or something like that?"

"Novels and manga?"

"Oh, so you're not that kind of person?"

Well, I didn't know what he meant by "that kind of person,"

because unfortunately I was only familiar with online games and this one small part of a console game. It was a great game where you crushed on angels called *Evil Earth*, which I started playing because I bought this so-called "suite" of games.

Now that I thought about it, in that game, it had also been my fate to meet Filo-tan and filolials. I started to feel the workings of destiny. Thank the heavens for the hands of fate!

"By the way, I'm curious what kind of life you had in your world, Motoyasu," Naofumi said.

"When I was in high school, I was always chasing around pigs, pretty much."

"Right." Naofumi paused. "I don't think we discussed it in great detail, but didn't you have a lot of trouble with women for some reason? It was so much that the filolial I raised named Filo would always chastise you for it, right?"

"That never happened! In fact, according to Filo, I opened her eyes to the meaning of true love!"

"Right. Well, anyways, back in your world you were always trying to get close to pigs, right?"

"I suppose so. When I look back, they were filthy characters, but yeah, stuff happened."

"Really? Such as?"

Humph, such as, he says? I don't really want to remember those pig companions I had, but if Father was asking, I better do my best to answer him. The first pig I remember was from back in middle school. I couldn't believe I had let myself get worked up over her lies.

What happened was . . .

"Since my parents were out on long-term business trips abroad, I was pretty much living by myself in middle school," I began.

Chapter One: Soulmate

"Can a middle schooler really live by themselves?" Father asked. "Practically, not to mention legally?"

"There wasn't really an issue. A neighborhood pig always came to wake me up. And a different pig, the landlord's daughter, took me to school. And just when I thought my parents were coming back, I got transferred into this weird backcountry school."

"That's crazy. It's like you're a character in a gal game."

It seemed like my story was catching Father's interest. I had his undivided attention! In the last round, Father always had a glint of discernment in his eyes that sent a shiver down my spine, like he saw right through me. No wonder a man like that raised Filo.

"So even though things were fairly settled, did something happen?" Father asked.

"With the pigs? This is no time for joking around!"

Repulsive, vile things happened, I say, things that I never want to remember. Pigs, my God!

"No, I'm just interested in what happened in your life at the time," Father said.

"When I was about to enter college, I decided to move

to Tokyo to polish up my manhood. The pigs saw me off graciously."

"No kidding."

Yup. And then I set off into the world, freely traipsing around for more than two years. I admit that I was a bit of a selfish pig myself. When there was something that I didn't like, I easily got upset and it was almost impossible to cheer me up. I was probably just trying to get people to do what I wanted. There was no end to my annoyances.

But pigs took problems that were so easy to solve and made them dire. At the time, I used all of my strength to solve those problems. As to why the pigs took such a trifling issue and made it into such a disaster . . . even now I have no idea, so there's nothing I can do about it. Yup, nothing to be done. If I had to think of anything useful that the pigs taught me, it would be online games, and that's about it.

Still, if all of that hadn't happened before, I may have never met Filo-tan. So I'll give them credit for that.

"So you don't want to go back home?" Father asked.

"Not in the slightest. Even without me, I'm sure the pigs have found someone else to butter up. That's just what pigs do."

"I can see why you don't like women who do that."

"By now they're definitely over my death."

"You do have a businesslike side to you, Motoyasu."

"Do I? Well, that's what it takes to deal with pigs and love." To a pig, a hero is little more than a slave, I say.

But I was different from how I was before. The "me" that left those pigs behind had never known true love. Oh, how love can bring out the sunshine on a cloudy day!

To keep your true love happy, I thought, it's necessary to keep up a good appearance. Still, someday you'll get worn out. And it's an undeniable fact that pigs only wanted to date me for my good looks. I won the trust of most pigs easily by telling them sweet nothings. But Filo . . . Filo was the one curious creature that didn't care at all about my looks. She was the only one who cheered me up without any regard for my appearance!

But those pigs! Pigs took advantage of my weaknesses and taught the other pigs how to do the same. Filo-tan didn't have that kind of twisted heart. Therefore, I, Motoyasu Kitamura, resolved to love Filo-tan and all filolials with all of my soul!

"We're off topic again," Father said. "Okay, let's try one more time. Is there anything else you can think of about how Siltvelt treated the heroes? We know that we need to take precautions. Remember what happened back in Melromarc."

Just what you'd expect from a genius like Father. He had the prudence to look before he leapt and the boldness to lose a battle to win the war. I didn't sense that piercing glint of discernment in his gaze, but when I saw how deep his care and caution ran, and when I realized just how much he had grown,

I couldn't help but burst into tears.

"Why are you crying, Motoyasu? Is it something I said?"

"Motoyasu, what's wrong?" cried Yuki from outside the room.

"I'm fine, I say!" I wailed. "Your caution simply moved me to tears, Father!"

"You're not making fun of me, are you?"

"Don't be absurd!" I sobbed.

"Well, I guess you must actually feel that way," Father said. He let out a deep sigh. "I suppose what we should worry about for the time being is what I talked about with Eclair on the way here—about marriage proposals in Siltvelt."

I also had plenty of marriage proposals when I was last summoned here! The pigs that wanted me in their pants just because I was the Spear Hero had disgusted me. I may have liked pigs back then, but at least I despised promiscuity! I somehow managed to turn away the crimson swine.

Back then, I wanted to have sex with pigs that I trusted and that were my friends. I even dreamt about having a harem. I believed that playboys were the most resourceful men. I went so far as to imagine that the day I saved the world, all of the world's good pigs would join my harem. Now, it made me nauseous to think about.

Thinking that much about pigs was making me feel disgusting.

"Motoyasu, can you please stop changing your expression so much? It's making me pretty uncomfortable."

"Understood!"

I decided to silence my thoughts and listen only to Father.

Yes, that was how my world used to be. Always full of pigs.

"So like I was saying, it seems like from tomorrow on we'll be called to all sorts of meetings and dinner meetings and marriage proposals," Father said. "Even though we were summoned here to save the world, I'm just being paraded around like some sort of prized breeding stud." He sighed. "Well, I am still a virgin, and I *would* like to be able to experience it at least once . . ."

I wasn't thinking. I was listening only to Father.

"Motoyasu, are you listening to me?"

Not thinking . . . listening . . .

"Motoyasu!"

"What is it, Father?"

"If you're not going to listen, why don't you just go back to your room?"

"I was listening! But since you told me to stop changing my expression, I decided to listen to you without thinking any thoughts of my own!"

Father stared at me blankly.

Hm. It seemed that Father was pretty embarrassed by his virginity.

"So let's get back to our discussion," I told him. "To remain a virgin is to be pure, I say. You must not feed your virginity to the pigs. Even thinking about it now gives me the chills! To have your first experience with a pig, my God, I'm going to vomit!"

"No! My God, Motoyasu, not now! I think I chose the wrong person to talk to."

"Thank you for those words of praise, Father." I was nearly overwhelmed with gratitude!

"I'm not praising you! I—I . . ." Father trailed off and started again. "So, Motoyasu, if I have a soulmate in this world, do you know who it is? I just thought maybe you'd have a guess."

A soulmate? The first person Father had as his companion was Filo-tan's older sister, so maybe her? But even though Father was with Filo-tan's sister for a long time, I had hardly heard anything about it.

Before, back when we lived in the village, I heard the filolials talking about something like this. Maybe Filo-tan's older sister's older sister was also a good prospect? Since Filo-tan and Father together would be nothing short of incest, at the very least, I had to stop that pairing at all costs.

"I heard that in the future," I told Father, "you try to sleep with a man."

"What?" Father's face twitched.

Most definitely he had. Since Father disliked the idea of sleeping with a woman, he had made Filo-tan's sister and the others stand guard outside. Then he had tried to sleep with a man.

"Because I was betrayed by women, I went for men instead?"

"Yes. In fact, I'm pretty sure it was a white-tiger man. He was a slave." I started to recall what the filolials had been talking about. Father had tried to sleep with a man, but the man ended up running away. At the time, Father was in charge of a lot of things, so I had no idea exactly what kind of relationship he had with who. Still, I got the sense that it had been a pretty rough time for Father. I wouldn't let Father experience that ever again!

"I don't know if I like the idea of doing it with a man . . ." Father held his head in his hands, looking troubled.

This was quite the predicament.

"Nevertheless," I declared, "I'll say it loud and proud to both virgins and maidens alike: don't recklessly throw your virtue down the drain!"

"That's what you're trying to say?"

"Being a virgin is the way to go, I say!"

"That's the first time I've heard anyone say that," Father said. He sighed and hung his head.

Why in the world was he so upset? Virginity is like a treasure that you can only lose once. Although for men there's no physical evidence, like there is for maidens, losing your virginity still cuts into your very soul. And what I mean by all that is this: you must be able to tell your soulmate honestly that you have a pure body!

It struck me as wrong that only maidens get to be recognized as special. When people talk about female virgins, they get called "pure as snow" and all that, so why don't male virgins get to be pure as snow as well? Well, either way, there was no going back for me, as much as I would've liked to dedicate my chastity to Filo-tan.

"I regret talking to you about all this in the first place," Father said.

"What do you mean?" I cried. "This is important! What will you do if you lose your virginity to some pig and end up with an STD? Look at the options here—remain a virgin or get an STD! Which one is better *now*?"

"But maidens can't have STDs, right?"

"In the last round, a pig went so far as to lie to me about her virginity," I explained. According to the queen, the crimson swine was no virgin.

"They'd go that far?" Father looked terrified. "I'll keep that in mind. I don't want to have sex with a guy, so I'd like to at least try a marriage proposal."

I supposed that was the best option. Easy sex is far from satisfactory, I say.

"If we act too carefully, we won't get anything done," Father said. "Good luck, Motoyasu."

"Good luck, Father!" I said. "Please rest up!"

"Yup, see you tomorrow. Okay, Sakura, let's go."

"Cooooming!"

With that, Father went off to his separate room. I, Motoyasu Kitamura, shall endeavor with all my might to be of assistance to Father. To that end, I need to do some more digging.

"Mr. Kitamura, what's wrong?"

"What are you doing?"

Yuki and Kou were calling to me. I noticed that Éclair seemed to be talking to somebody in a different room.

"I'm going to head out for just a bit. Yuki and Kou, you should continue to act as if I'm here while I'm gone and keep watch for me."

Somewhere in this castle, there could be some sort of dastardly scheme to take out Father. Trash and the crimson swine were undoubtedly putting together dark plots. And I was determined to be the one to uncover them!

"We'll take care of it!" Yuki said. "Should I imitate your voice from behind that partition there?"

"That would be marvelous," I said. "Incidentally, I do believe that's called a folding screen."

"Wow! You're a genius, Motoyasu," Yuki said. "I'll act exactly like I'm you and talk to Kou, I promise!" With that,

Yuki hid behind the folding screen and started to talk to Kou in an imitation of my voice.

"I'm off!" I declared. "Activate Cloaking Lance X and Liberation Fire Mirage!"

Activating a stealth condition with one of my skills, as well as a composite concealment ability with some magic, I swiftly leapt out of the bedroom window. Moving with my typical stealth and swagger, I swept across the castle on my reconnaissance mission.

My stealth condition engaged, I embarked on a thorough search of the castle interior. Surely there was some foul plot afoot. I had to be careful. And I had to be doubly careful, too, since demi-humans and therianthropes might get a whiff of me even while I was in stealth mode.

I recalled that Filo-tan's older sister noticed me in stealth mode a number of times. Wait? Was it her sister? I had an inkling that there *may* have been times besides where I was discovered as well, but I didn't remember in the slightest.

And as I thought about those sorts of things, a lion therianthrope passed by me. He had bad posture and looked pretty self-important.

A lion, huh? When I thought about it more, didn't Filo-tan tell me she fought a lion like that? Rather than just aimlessly wandering around, I thought it might be more efficient just to follow this guy.

With that, I followed him. He went across the castle and entered a dismal, poorly lit room that appeared to be a meeting place of sorts and closed the door.

How could I infiltrate the room? If I made my typical grand entrance, they might happen to notice me.

Hmm. Before I came to this world, I used to know a pig that studied ninja techniques. I tried to remember what she had told me. If there were any ventilation shafts, I could use those to sneak in, but I didn't see any. Plus, I had absolutely no idea what the layout of the castle was like.

That would appear to limit my options.

I looked around and noticed a nearby shelf exhibiting fancy weapons. It would be a gamble, but I could break the shelf with my spear to stir up some commotion. That way, when the people in the nearby room came out to check what had happened, I could infiltrate the meeting room. I decided to give it a shot and broke the shelf with a stab.

"What the hell?" I heard a voice say.

Say what now? Someone was coming out of a different room a bit farther away from the one I had set my sights on.

"The shelf broke?" The person simply fixed it with some magic.

Well, that was a failure. And if I did it again, they'd almost certainly suspect foul play. Unless . . . surely that lion was the type who wouldn't be able to rest easy until he came and checked what had made the sound.

Just then, a wide hippo-like therianthrope came plodding sluggishly across the hall. This could be my chance, I thought, so I followed them from behind. Just as I suspected, they opened the door to the very room I had been after! They had to open the door as wide as possible in order to fit their tremendous girth through the door, so I was able to slip into the room behind them.

With that, I successfully infiltrated the target destination.

With a few entering at a time, before long a large group of demi-humans and therianthropes had gathered in the meeting room. Perhaps this was some sort of important meeting. But I didn't see that shusaku man that had greeted us earlier.

The lion spoke up, addressing the group: "Now we'll begin the meeting concerning the Shield Hero," he said.

Everyone nodded in agreement.

What on earth? The room was dim, lit only by candlelight, which meant that this meeting surely had to do with wicked deeds. If they were going to discuss Father, then I had arrived at exactly the right time.

"Now the Shield Hero rests easy with his idiotic grin," the lion said, "pleasantly recuperating after a long journey."

How dare they.

"I can't believe a kid like that is the legendary hero!" someone in the room shouted.

"Why they would summon a pathetic creature like him is

beyond my understanding," another said.

They were disrespecting Father! Should I kill them all at once or let the slander continue for a little longer? Perhaps this was just them strategically preparing to praise him all the more, so I decided to remain patient.

After all, I used to say bad things about Father too. When the crimson swine first betrayed me, I said so many terrible things. I'm ashamed of what I said then. I should emulate the mercy of Father, who forgave me for my insolence. Since Siltvelt's citizens worship Father, after all, I should try to respond to them with Father's generosity.

"However," the lion continued, "according to legend, the Shield Hero will give birth to a special child. We ought to at least try to make that child. The Shield Hero falling right into our lap is great fortune for us."

"That's right," another demi-human chimed in. "We need to try to bring the legend to life. In order to prepare for the coming holy war, we'll use the Shield Hero like a breeding stud!"

Now that he said that, couldn't the same thing apply to any of the heroes? That was why so many pigs had gathered around me, surely. I, Motoyasu Kitamura, have a lot to think about, I say.

"When I saw him, he looked so innocent," one said.

"The knights we sent out reported that his personality is exactly what it seems," the lion said with a sneer.

A demi-human seated near the lion started to laugh. "Then we can persuade him to do whatever we want. He'll be easy to deal with. Looks like all of our precaution was unnecessary."

"While that may be the case, he did manage to escape from Melromarc and make it all the way here," another added.

"The Spear Hero at his side has supposedly displayed god-like strength," the lion said. "But at the same time, the Shield Hero isn't particularly strong himself."

"Shouldn't we take that with a grain of salt? There's no use in being paralyzed in fear of some Spear Hero."

"In any case, are the preparations complete?" the lion asked.

Naturally, our prudence turned out to be necessary. Since Father and I discussed being careful already, there wouldn't be any problems at all.

"We're nearly ready," someone in the crowd responded. "We've already taken out Werner's group and substituted one of our own in its place."

"Excellent. Then we can easily lure the Shield Hero," the lion said. "That so-called hero . . . We'll seduce him with our scheme, and then it will be simple to infiltrate his ranks. By then, Werner will be powerless to stop us. Our time has come!"

A powerful clap of thunder sounded from the small window, followed by flashes of lightning. That was the final proof I needed to determine that this unsavory lot is up to unsavory deeds. But no matter how underhanded their devious plots may be, they're powerless against Father!

It all made sense. When Father died before, he must have gotten caught up in a trap like this. Well, as did I, long ago. When I remembered that pig with a false accusation in hand, ready to share a few days of romance with Father only to turn on him, I nearly puked. That pig bath I had been trapped in had damaged my very spirit.

I heroically managed to hold in my vomit so they wouldn't notice I was there.

"So who are we going to use to seduce him?" someone asked.

"Isn't it obvious by looking at his companions?" the lion said. "We're going to use someone who looks young."

He must be referring to how Yuki and Sakura are traveling with us. How dare those villains lay their eyes upon my majestic filolials!

"We can't show our hand now," the lion explained. "It will be troublesome if they find out who it is."

I couldn't wait to tell Father all about this.

"So what do we do once we've captured the Shield Hero and produced his child?" someone asked.

"Isn't it obvious?" someone cackled. "We'll dispose of him."

"A hero summoned to the polluted soil of Melromarc . . ."

the lion said. "It's repulsive that he was recognized as a hero in the first place. He'll finally meet his end."

"I just wish he had been killed by Melromarc on his way here," another said, "or that we could simply kill him, so we could have avoided this whole scheme. That filthy hero is the worst of them all!"

"Assassins and spies won't do us any good here. Even though we knew their location, our previous attacks were unsuccessful. Regardless, the fruit of our labor is nearly ripe," the lion said.

I was starting to get the vague impression that Siltvelt had in fact been responsible for the previous attacks on us.

"Just be patient—we only need our plan to succeed," the lion continued. "And soon we'll create our ideal world!"

What a contemptible lot! As long as I live, I'll never let Father fall victim to one of your cowardly schemes! I had to tell Father right away.

But before that, I had better decide what to do about these villains. I considered letting them go alive out of my deep compassion, but deeds like this are simply too evil. I had to take care of this immediately or we would regret it later. To betray Father is a grievous sin.

Well, I had better get started.

I began to cast a spell. But I knew I couldn't destroy the whole building, and since it would be annoying if I made too much noise, it would be best to destroy them without anyone else knowing. I opened the door and left the room.

"What?" someone shouted. "The door—it just ... opened!"

A magic spell was the best solution. So I called, "Liberation Firefloor X!"

That's a handy spell because you can specify the range. And the range that I specified was the very room they were all standing in. Instantly, the meeting room was engulfed in the raging flames of hell.

I heard ghastly screams coming from within.

I completely incinerated each and every one of those villainous dastards. The flames devoured their screams and reduced even their bones to ashes.

Perhaps now I had managed to guarantee Father's safety, at least for a little while.

After confirming that the entire room had been burned and that not a trace of evidence remained, I released the magic to make the flames disappear and started making my way back toward my room.

Although I had erased those traitors, on my way back through the castle, I noticed that no one in Siltvelt was even pretending to look flustered. Maybe no one even cared about that group of demi-humans in the first place. Still, if I ignored them, they might've caused trouble, so it was probably better that I did something about it.

"Bath time!" I declared.

It seemed like some Siltvelt attendants had prepared hot water, and I wanted to get right in. I decided to also sneak a look at how much Yuki and Kou had grown. Since hardly any time had passed, there might not be much of a difference. But you can't hide anything from Motoyasu Kitamura, I say! I can recognize even a millimeter of a filolial's growth!

For example, after Filo-tan started living in the village, Father put her in charge of leveling up his slaves. Since she started fighting and training just a little more, she grew stronger. It was proof that repetition is key to training. Through daily training, Filo-tan, who was already beautiful and strong, became considerably mightier! Healthier than ever before, her plumage even started to glitter.

Father was a genius to appoint her to that task, I say!

Filolials truly can grow at a dizzying rate. So I had to take a peek at them every chance I got.

As I thought about such things, I made my way across the castle and back to our rooms. All of a sudden, Father came running out half-naked with Sakura behind him.

"Hey, Motoyasu!" he shouted.

"What's wrong, Father?"

"So they told me that the baths were ready and to come over, right, and they showed me these gorgeous baths. And there were *tons* of women gathered there! Man, if Sakura wasn't there, I have no idea what would've happened."

While Father was catching his breath, I carefully looked around and turned to Sakura.

"Thank you, Sakura," I told her.

"You're welcome!"

Then a large group of pigs came over toward us. My nose nearly fell off my face at the stench. There was one pig in the middle that smelled the worst of them all, almost like something rotten—all of this mere moments after I had told Father to guard his chastity! I, Motoyasu Kitamura, would take care of these pigs!

"Oink!"

"Oink-oink!"

The pigs squealed as they approached, but I couldn't understand what they were saying.

"Sorry, but I don't have time for that right now!" Father told the pigs, who continued to oink around him. "I'm too busy fighting to save the world!"

The sheer stink of the pigs made me violently ill.

In the middle of the pigs, there was also a puppy who was . . . talking? Something besides a pig?

"Oh, Shield Hero, we just want to prove our undying love for a god like you!"

Demons capable of human speech . . . are they saying that they want to worship and devote themselves to Father?

"I know, I know! But none of you know anything about me, right? If we all take a bath together, I'm going to be the one in trouble!" Father said.

Then there was a loud bang. Éclair was coming over, scowling over at us.

"All you noble ladies of Siltvelt!" she said. "Sorry, but Mr. Iwatani—the Shield Hero—is tired. I'd like to ask you to act with a little more decorum." She put her hand on her sword hilt threateningly.

The pigs all at once started to make a racket.

"Can't you all shut up?" I asked. "Or at least control your smell?"

"Hey! Motoyasu, you don't need to say anything," Éclair said. "If you do anything reckless, we might have to escape all over again!"

Just as Éclair was speaking, the shusaku representative Werner appeared.

"What's all the commotion about?" he asked.

"All these women were waiting for me in the bath," Father explained, "and they came out after me."

"Hm, well now, I sincerely apologize for all that," the shusaku said. "We were simply trying to provide the best service by dispatching our most beautiful women, but it seems like they didn't win your favor."

This was the group that the lion therianthrope said they

had substituted, I supposed. Most likely Werner didn't even know what had happened.

"No, it's not that . . ." Father began.

It was absolutely absurd that they sent those pigs to try to fool Father! Well, at least I had already killed the ringleader before the battle even started. It was nice to feel safe.

I would emulate Father's compassion here and, out of mercy, only half-kill Werner for being deceived. Just as I extended my spear, Father grabbed me.

"Motoyasu, calm yourself!"

"I am calm, I say!"

Father's orders are absolute, but he gave them nearly too late! I glanced at Éclair, who was shaking her head.

Just then we heard a knocking sound. I turned around and saw an old genmu with a cane walking toward us.

❘ Old Genmu ❘

This old, plump demi-human was using a cane before he even turned sixty. He is shaped like a tortoise and has a tail like a snake. He is a well-known aristocrat in Siltvelt. Though he's on the decline, he is a sensible character with a remarkable power of observation.

"So this is the great Shield Hero!" the old genmu said. "You've done well to make your way here all the way from Melromarc. It is a true honor to meet you."

"Yes . . ." Werner began.

"Now, what might all this fuss be about?" the genmu asked.

"I can explain," Éclair said. "In order to try to appeal to the Shield Hero, a deluge of women were waiting for him in the bath."

"Hmmm. The Shield Hero doesn't look particularly bothered. Still, I believe that if our girls did anything beyond just stand there, it would be against our country's religious doctrine. What do you think, head shusaku?"

"Y-yeah, that's right," the shusaku mumbled.

"Now then, girls," the genmu said. "Stop this abominable behavior and show the Shield Hero and his friends some courtesy, or you'll all be punished."

They did as he said. All the pigs slowly began to leave. The shusaku started to leave as well, so I called to him as he passed by.

"After this, why don't you confirm the safety of your colleagues?" I suggested. "You'll find that they may have had an interesting experience."

The shusaku looked at me in shock at first but then continued on his way, falling deep into thought. Surely that will help further reduce any villainous plots against Father.

"Thank you very much," Father was saying to the old genmu.

The genmu waved off his apology. "I just did the obvious thing to those lacking basic courtesy toward the Shield Hero of all people."

"Eclair, thank you too," Father added.

"Don't worry about it," she replied. "I don't have any political power in this country, so I quickly reached out to some people who we can trust."

"We can trust him?"

"Well, I don't have that sort of political power anymore," said the genmu.

"What do you mean?" I asked. "It seems like with your help we could certainly have an easier time here."

"Hm . . ." The genmu rubbed his chin. "Shield Hero, what exactly do you want to achieve in Siltvelt?"

"Me?" Father asked. "At the very least we need to fight the wave—that's why we were summoned here, after all. Is there anything else?"

"I think you understand how to best respond in this situation," the genmu said.

"Ah . . ."

Did Father figure out what he meant? What could it be? I, Motoyasu Kitamura, had no idea what was going on.

Yuki looked like she understood, but Kou and Sakura had their heads cocked sideways in confusion.

"I can imagine a few things we'd like to do. We'll be as careful as we can."

"It seems that you're quick on your feet. The Spear Hero should also be careful."

"What are you referring to?" I spoke up.

"We're talking about how we need to be careful about what we say about international crises," Father explained. "For example, we have to be careful and not talk about attacking another country directly."

"Naturally. So that's what you were talking about before."

Father nodded.

"In this country, the Spear Hero doesn't have the influence of the Shield Hero, but I would still like both of you to take special care," the genmu said. "Your enemies may even take action, using another hero to get close to you."

It all seemed pretty annoying. I wonder if Father in the previous run-through made it through all of these challenges.

"It sounds like you'll take good care of me, but I don't feel at ease yet because I'm not strong enough," Father said. "It might be best to go out on a little adventure to level up faster."

"That's no problem at all," the genmu said. "My grand-daughter could also lend you a hand."

"Noble genmu—"

"Oh no, no. My granddaughter is very shy, so don't worry. She won't try anything like that."

"Mr. Iwatani, I'm going to work with this noble genmu to contact the queen of Melromarc," Éclair said. "I want to put a stop to the violence there."

"Sounds good," Father said. "Thanks again, Eclair."

"Don't worry about it. This is all just tidying up. It's the least I can do for you and Mr. Kitamura for forgiving my wrongdoings."

"Yep. Let's keep working together."

"By the way, Mr. Iwatani . . ." Éclair trailed off. "I think you should consider going back to finish your bath."

"What? Oh!" Father blushed and quickly hid himself behind his towel, hurrying back to the bath with Sakura.

"Regardless, I'll stay here in Siltvelt for a while," Éclair said. "But, Mr. Kitamura, please be safe. For some reason or another, it seems like the Church of the Three Heroes is prone to taking extreme action. But plenty of dangerous things can happen in Siltvelt too."

"Understood, I say!"

Éclair gave me a bow and turned to Kou and Sakura and bowed to them as well.

After I finished my bath, it was time for our meal. As part of our reception, they held a banquet. The food was not very sophisticated, mainly uncouth roasts of whole animals. They tried to serve us raw meat as well, but Father and I declined. I would never consume something as vulgar as raw meat, although Yuki and the other filolials loved it. Watching them gobble up their portions with big smiles, I overflowed with joy.

Chapter Two: Poison

It was the morning of our third day in Siltvelt.

Around the clock, pig after pig launched amorous attacks on Father. Even with Éclair on guard, the pigs' attacks didn't slow down. It was a deplorable state of affairs.

Whenever the pigs swarmed en masse, Father cut his way out of them one way or another, sometimes with Sakura's help, other times by simply running away as fast as he could. Of course, I, Motoyasu Kitamura, helped him out whenever I could.

Even at night, from my window I could see and hear plenty of rowdy people out and about in the castle and the town. I could also hear distant howling. This was a city—no, a country—that truly never slept, and it was a mess.

Apparently, Sakura also had to help Father fend off attacks at night from different monstrous demi-humans, vampires, and all sorts of nightmarish beasts. Werner told us that it was because Siltvelt's chain of command was all out of sorts, for which he sincerely apologized.

Well, even if it was, it certainly was not my fault. I simply killed an entire room of traitors.

I can't help but wonder how Father got through this crazy

situation in the first go-around. Maybe he had been powerful enough to create a protective sphere to sleep through the night. Or perhaps Filo-tan's sister protected him.

"Motoyasu," Father said to me, "day and night, they've tried to trap and seduce me in every way you could possibly imagine. But all their efforts have just had the opposite effect. I don't know if I'm even interested in marriage anymore."

"Opposite effect, you say?"

"Yeah . . . Women are scary," Father murmured, trailing off. "I'm finally starting to get what you're always saying, Motoyasu," Father said. "Even I'm starting to see the women coming at me as pigs."

"Naofumi's becoming more like Motoyasu!" Sakura chimed in.

"Well, no, I hope not," Father quickly corrected. "I've just gotten bored of all the marriage proposals. I'm ready to go out and level up a bit."

"If that is what you desire," I declared, "I, Motoyasu Kitamura, shall ensure that you do not befall any danger whatsoever!"

"Yup. I knew you were going to say that, so I was trying to avoid mentioning it," Father said. "Anyways, I heard that the Siltvelt seven star hero is coming to meet us after our lunch meeting today. Once that's over, I think I'll be free to do whatever, so long as we stay in Siltvelt." On our way to our meeting,

Father had figured out our plan for the day.

I forgot to mention that over those few days I had also decided to conduct some research on the life force of special filolials. In a country as diverse as Siltvelt, I wasn't surprised to hear that there were one-of-a-kind filolials in the castle town. One of the Siltvelt ambassadors who had escorted us here introduced me to a number of local ranches that bred filolials.

"That means we'll class up the filolials afterward, I guess," I said to Father.

"That would make sense," he replied. "Since the meeting should end just after noon, at that point we can just do our own thing until you've finished classing up the filolials."

"We can meet up at the portal, I say."

"Sure. Once you set a location, it'll be easy to meet up there," Father said. "And once we head off to fight the wave, I figure there'll be a lot of chances to level up."

"I would think so."

"Thanks, Motoyasu. Again, I'm really grateful for all your help."

The magnanimity! "Don't waste your words on the likes of me!" I cried.

"You don't need to be humble," Father said. "It's only thanks to you that we've been able to get this far."

And with that, we headed up to the terrace provided exclusively for Father's use, where we would have our lunch meeting.

> **Portal Skill**
>
> A movement skill that allows you to travel along with your party members to any registered location. It's pretty handy, but there are a few restrictions: in order to register a location, you have to go to the place yourself first; you have to wait after using it once before you can use it again; and you can only register a certain number of locations. If you boost your Portal Skill, you can reduce some of the limitations.

In the back of my head, I remembered Father's explanation from the first time we were summoned. I really was so grateful for Father. And for Yuki, Kou, and Sakura too, I say!

Meanwhile, our cook had set plenty of food on the table. I noticed that a number of prominent Siltvelt leaders had been assembled.

After Father sat down, one stood up and announced, "Let the meal begin!"

Everyone put their hands together in deep prayer and muttered, "We thank our lord the Shield Hero for all that he has provided us. Thanks to Him we can eat and become strong. May He have the strength to continue to protect us all."

"Protect us all," the room echoed.

What a weird prayer.

Then everyone started eating with the clink and clatter of the silverware.

"Sakura, say 'aaah!'"

"Aaah!"

Father was feeding Sakura. How delightful! It reminded me

a bit of Father and Filo-tan. How strange. As a matter of fact, I felt like I had seen that exact same scene before.

"Sakura, why aren't you eating the food on your own plate?" Father asked her.

"This food? Wellll, it's poisoned!" she chirped, pointing at her plate and cup. "Aaaand I don't feel like it."

"Poison!?"

In an instant, the whole room froze in place.

Father took a spoon to Sakura's plate and examined it closely. Since he had probably learned countless poison-detection techniques on our journey, he must have been able to deduce whether or not the food was in fact poison merely by looking at it!

"It's a fast-working neurogenic killer poison," Father said, "but no, not just that. It can even work on filolials."

My God! Father even researched poisons that could affect filolials. His intellect was unparalleled! Now that he mentioned it, I noticed that neither Yuki nor Kou were eating their food either.

I could never forgive such an act of barbarity!

"Yuki and Kou, did you notice that it was poison?" I asked them.

"We didn't say anything because it was such a nice meal, and everyone else seemed to be enjoying it," Yuki said with a shrug.

So classy! But I had come to expect such impeccably refined behavior from a thoroughbred filolial like Yuki.

"That's right!" Kou agreed.

Is that why Sakura's plate of food had taken so long to arrive? What contemptible fools! My filolials had sniffed out their plot in the blink of an eye!

"Is there anything in your food, Motoyasu?" Sakura asked.

Now that she mentioned it, I had started to notice yesterday that all of my food had been poisoned. But it was so pathetically weak that I could simply ignore it. At my level of strength, that kind of poison wouldn't even make me blink.

I paused in thought. "Now, say, what *exactly* is going on here?"

Father looked around the room with that old piercing glint of discernment in his eyes. The Siltvelt leaders finally started to move, looking back and forth around the room uncertainly.

Father had a look that was as cold and sharp as ice. There was an intensity in his look that I had never seen before. I couldn't bear it anymore!

"This is unforgivable!" I bellowed. "Who prepared this food? Take the chef out right now—and execute him!"

"Execute the chef?" Father cried. "Motoyasu, the chef isn't responsible for this."

The leaders in the room glanced around at each other. It appeared that even after I killed that conniving lot, there were still some troublemakers around.

"I suppose you're right," I said. "But a crime like this—attempting to assassinate filolials, I say! We need a punishment that will make the perpetrator regret having ever been born into this world!"

"I don't disagree," Father said. "If the filolials hadn't noticed, they might have died."

"I got it!" I exclaimed. "While the perpetrator is still alive, I'll remove his skin and wear it as a costume for your enjoyment, I say!"

"My God, Motoyasu, how did you even come up with that? Please calm down!" Father pleaded. "I'll find a proper punishment, don't worry. Please just wait a minute."

The room had erupted into chaos. The Siltvelt leaders were kneeling on the ground in front of Father, profusely apologizing. They promised countless times to investigate where the food had been prepared right away.

Father was sitting on the Siltvelt throne, and he did not look pleased. The other day, Father also had an unhappy look on his face when they made him sit on the throne, but that was nothing compared to his expression now.

Surely that was because they had tried to assassinate the likes of Sakura and myself! Sakura was sitting on Father's lap as he stroked her feathers. It was absolutely adorable.

I renewed my vow to smite all of Father's enemies. From his mighty position on the throne, I was confident that he would uncover the truth of what had happened.

"Naooofumi! Don't stop!" Sakura whined.

"Just a minute," he cooed. "I'll pet you later."

"Just now we are preparing a list of potential suspects," the shusaku leader was telling Father. "Please wait just a little longer."

"That won't do," Father said. "You'll just choose your own political enemies or find some other way to take advantage of us."

"N-n-never!"

Under the piercing power of Father's glorious gaze, the shusaku couldn't even move. That shusaku representative . . . what was his name again? I was very confused by the situation, I say.

"Mighty Shield Hero, please calm your anger and let us find the perpetrator!"

But Father wouldn't be moved by such a pathetic plea.

"I was calm," Father said. "In fact, I was calm this whole time. I was calm until someone tried to kill my friends. Every second of every day you've bombarded me with marriage proposals and all sorts of obscene, disgusting incidents, and I always took care to ask them as politely as possible to leave and not cause any problems for anyone—all because Siltvelt did me the favor of taking me in. But considering that Siltvelt has attempted to kill Sakura here, who just so happens to be the member of the opposite sex that I'm closest to, just to get

closer to me—if this had just been an ordinary mistake, then that would be a different conversation, wouldn't it!?" Father was talking quickly, rattling on and on.

Of course, I agreed with everything that Father said. But we couldn't afford to give our enemy a chance to strike!

"I'm over here," Father railed on, "being polite, doing my best, but does anyone in Siltvelt even care? No! Maybe I should explain myself more clearly. Yes. Everyone who's trying to get near me, who's trying to hurt my friends—whoever you are, it should cost you the price of your life! But no, that's not enough. It's worth the life of everyone involved in the crime! I think that sounds about right. If you give me the lives of every single person involved in this ridiculous assassination attempt, don't you think that might settle things more fairly?"

"P-p-perhaps! Shield Hero! P-please calm down!"

As terrified as all the Siltvelt leaders already looked, Father didn't stop there.

"Before we even think about war with Melromarc, we need to take care of this country. We need to expel the pus of this festering, rotten country first." He paused. "Okay, I have an idea. Go down the street and shout as loudly as possible—tell everyone to get out of the way. I'm going to show you all something."

Chapter Three: Beast Spy

"My Lord Shield Hero! Please! Calm down!"

The Siltveltian representatives had their heads down. As they should.

Father imposing his will—what a magnificent scene!

"Great. Is everyone out of the way now? Motoyasu, can you finish off the person who attempted this careless assassination?"

"Leave it to me, I say!"

I took a proud step forward.

"I, Motoyasu Kitamura, will do whatever Father commands!" I roared.

"Then take aim outside the castle . . . Aim for that mountain over there and do the magic that you did when we were at the Melromarc border. Of course, don't kill anyone."

"Anything for you, Father!"

I looked out the castle window and noted the location of the mountain Father was referring to. I wasn't sure if there would be any people over there or not. Well, even if there were, it would be a good warning for them to not mess with Father.

"Liberation Firestorm X!"

Concentrating, I condensed the magic and blasted it against the mountain with all my might.

I drew the sphere of magic out into a flowing stream and directed it toward the mountain. A river of fire bounded over the castle walls as I pulled and twisted it into a whirlpool of flames sweeping toward the mountain. I adjusted its speed to draw out its power even more, and when it arrived at the heart of the mountain, it grew into an enormous tornado of fire and exploded.

Everything in its path had turned to magma.

"I can destroy the whole mountain, if you like," I told Father.

"That's fine," Father said, turning to the Siltvelt leaders. "Destroying the mountain would be a good next step."

They audibly gulped.

Father hit them with his piercing gaze again, and they all took a step back nervously. Others in the crowd started to bow in reverence to Father.

Father turned to me. "We can't let them keep doing these terrible things to us. I don't intend to let us get thrown off track, and of course, I won't let them kill us either. To that end, Motoyasu—you're incredibly strong, but I also want you to use your head."

"And by that you mean . . . ?"

"Even though you're incredibly powerful, I heard that you lose your life in a future wave."

"W-what in the world!?"

But after a moment of thinking about it, I understood Father's objective. If in the past I ended up dying despite my strength, Father intended not simply to use power to force our way to victory. Rather, he wanted to use our strength to instill a fear in our enemies that will help us win in the long run!

"When I even mention that I'm the Shield Hero, they try to kill me. So I need to find some way to make sure we stay safe," Father told me. "Since it seems like we're going to get caught up in other battles besides the waves, I want you to be ready to use all of your strength to help us get through them. Right, Motoyasu?"

"I got it! If it's your command, I, Motoyasu Kitamura, will completely and thoroughly eradicate our enemies, no matter who, what, where, when, or why!"

Normally this is the part where Father would say something like, "What on earth are you saying, Motoyasu?" But this time, the fun just kept on going.

"A Shield Hero can't defeat anyone on his own," Father called out to the Siltvelt leaders. "So my policy is to avoid war at all costs. If you don't like it, go out and fight on your own. If you all want to fight, then I'm out, because the role of the Shield Hero is to guard—to protect."

There was a pause.

The immense gravity of Father's words—the whole room seemed to grasp it.

"So until we defeat the wave, there won't be any more marriage proposals or interruptions to our life here in any way," Father told the crowd.

"Yes! Yes! Yes!!"

And that was how Father drove out any possibility of further assassination attempts and the like.

"I think everyone understands that it's impossible to assassinate us," Father said.

"Y-yes!" The shusaku representative whispered.

"So is the seven star hero on his way?"

The seven star hero . . . A memory tugged at me. Oh? Father appeared in the back of my mind to explain.

‖ The Seven Star Heroes ‖

Just like the four holy heroes, the seven star heroes are heroes chosen by one of the seven weapons. The seven weapons are the staff, hammer, projectile, gauntlets, claws, axe, and whip.
People not from Japan can be seven star heroes too. But the seven star heroes are people who are chosen only after they've exhibited great effort and struggle.

"We believe it's a possibility that those on the side of the seven star hero are aiming to kill the Shield Hero as well," the shusaku told Father.

"If that's the case . . ." Father trailed off. "Hm, well, let's at least talk to him first. What kind of person is he?"

"He's dedicated to honing his strength," the shusaku said. "Nowadays he rarely leaves the mountains to make public appearances of any kind."

"A martial-artist type," Father said. "He's not too different from us. I think we'll be fine."

The Siltveltian leaders finally left us alone. I still wasn't sure what they were planning in their heart of hearts, but at the least they probably wouldn't do anything rash. Surely they realized they had no chance of killing us with something as rudimentary as poison and that even if they were to attack us by surprise, it would have no effect whatsoever.

Father exhaled deeply and leaned back on the throne, looking exhausted.

"Well, I did it." He sighed.

At that point, Éclair and the old genmu opened the door and came in.

"Hey, Eclair," Father said. "Were you able to get in contact with the Melromarc queen?"

"We're making preparations," Éclair said. "But before that, Mr. Iwatani, are you all right?"

"I'm sorry," Father said. "They tried to poison Sakura and the filolials and I completely lost my cool."

"Poison? I'd probably lose it too," Éclair said. "You had the right to get angry, so don't worry about it. It takes a lot to make someone like you that mad."

"Lord Shield Hero, you mentioned that you don't want there to be war in our country," the old genmu said. "Just saying that might be enough to help your cause. Even the radicals should calm down after that. In the meantime, we ought to seek reconciliation with our neighboring countries."

"Definitely," Father said. "It's not that I want to unify the world into one nation or anything like that . . ." He paused. "So I'm not sure the best way to say this, but if you look around this world—well, I don't think I know enough to achieve my goals. I want to know more about the world. Since being summoned here, it's like a dream come true to travel with friends like you, Motoyasu, Eclair, Sakura, and the filolials."

Father glanced at me and Éclair and stroked Sakura's feathers.

What a glorious dream! I, Motoyasu Kitamura, would work even harder than I already was, I say!

"It's a bit sudden, but if I may, can I explain the preparations we have in place?" the old genmu asked.

"Ah, sorry," Father said.

"No, surely we're the ones at fault," the old genmu said. "Anyway, we have been working to help you face the coming wave unhindered."

"Thank you very much," Father said. "About what just happened though—I feel like I kinda overdid it. Sorry about that."

The old genmu waved Father's apology off as one of the Siltveltian leaders returned to the throne room and explained the schedule for the day.

"So," Father clarified, "is the seven star hero on his way to the throne room?"

They were in the middle of talking about how the seven star hero had just arrived for his official audience with Father.

"What kind of person is he?" Father asked.

"He is a capable citizen of Siltvelt," the leader responded.

Now that they mentioned it . . . had I even *met* this seven star hero? I was trying to remember before, but I couldn't bring him to mind at all. All I had was a bad feeling about the whole thing.

"I was asking before, but you said he's kind of the martial type?"

"That's correct."

"What race is he? Is he from the same world as us?" Father asked. "He's not from this world, at least, right?"

"Actually, he's a citizen of Siltvelt," the leader explained, "specially selected and trained as the seven star hero."

"Oh really? I thought since he was from Japan we'd be able to talk about a lot of things," Father said, glancing over at me.

That's true. If he were from Japan, it would be much easier to bond with him.

"I suppose you can call him a wanderer. As for his race, he's a wolfer—not one of the four holy beasts of this land, but he's a tough, experienced fighter. We think that, together, you'll be able to achieve many military victories."

"A real warrior, huh?" Father said. "I'm excited to meet him."

As they kept on talking on and on, a soldier entered the throne room.

"The Claw Hero has arrived!"

The door burst open with a slam and the man known as the Claw Hero entered.

He looked like a muscular wolf covered in blue fur. Despite his intense, bulging muscles, he had a light, gentle step. He had scars all over his body. But rather than being ugly, they seemed to highlight his experience, to the point where they looked like medals of honor for his achievements on the battlefield. He wore pants but was shirtless. He looked nimble and sure of his movements.

"Claw Hero here," he said, "reporting before the Shield Hero. I'll change my shape."

Keeping one eye on the shusaku representative, he inclined his head deeply and transformed into a demi-human.

I couldn't tell how old he was. But I could tell he knew a thing or two about fighting and that he also had a piercingly sharp gaze. Still, the first thing you'd notice about the guy was definitely his blue fur.

He had a nice face too. Maybe he was in his late twenties or early thirties. Rather than looking young, he was more refined, a silver-fox type. I knew plenty of pigs that would go wild for that kind of guy.

I couldn't stop staring at his massive claws.

This seven star hero . . . my memory was so hazy—I still couldn't remember anything about him, but a voice whispering in my ear told me to be careful. I suddenly realized that my spear was shaking and clacking against the floor of its own accord.

All of a sudden there was a high-pitched shrill. What the . . . ?

I checked my status and I noticed that my weapon book was responding to something. I looked into it and it said that my spear was using a move called "Beast Spy."

Had I ever heard of Beast Spy before? I didn't remember in the slightest.

My weapon book said that Beast Spy automatically identified and attacked enemies. But why was it starting to happen now?

And yet it must be the hands of fate working in my favor once again. I decided to use Beast Spy and see what happened.

I gasped. As soon as my spear activated Beast Spy, it targeted the Claw Hero and flew right at him.

"Spear Hero! What are you doing?" someone shouted.

"Motoyasu!" Father yelled.

They hurried to stop me, but my spear had already launched into Air Strike Javelin.

The Claw Hero roared furiously and burst into a sudden

attack, rushing directly into the full force of my spear. It was a noble effort, but my Spear blew his head straight off.

The spear had activated skill enhancement without even asking for permission, and in its powered-up state, it managed to strike down the Claw Hero in one fell blow. Yikes. One-hit KO!

The attack had been so powerful there had literally been no point in trying to take it on. My spear continued to pulse and vibrate, as if Beast Spy had a heart and mind of its own.

"The Spear Hero's gone insane!" the shusaku announced.

"What do we dooo!!" someone yelled.

"Motoyasu, what the hell is going on!?" Father shouted.

Everyone around me kept prattling on.

"Wait!" the old genmu said.

"Wait—look!" The shusaku—what was his name? Werner?—and the old genmu were shouting at me. Even though we had gotten into quite the pinch, they seemed relatively calm. As they should be. They were representatives, after all. Werner, was it? Man, I really can't remember. Anyways, he kept pointing at the Claw Hero's dead body, which was beginning to transform before our very eyes. The blue fur and a foxlike tail were growing out rapidly.

"Huh?"

"What the . . ."

"Is the Claw Hero transforming into a fox beast?"

"It seems as if the Spear Hero realized that the Claw Hero was an imposter," the old genmu muttered, stroking his chin. "That's why this is all happening. The body is returning to its original state."

"So the Spear Hero ended up saving us?" the shusaku announced.

"And that fox beast, what in the world . . . Where could the actual Claw Hero possibly be?"

"We need to investigate immediately," the genmu said. "But everyone should apologize to the Spear Hero first. He saved us."

Everyone started praising me for some reason. I can't say I disapprove of people recognizing my many good deeds. But it doesn't compare to praise from Father or my beloved Filo-tan!

"What's going on?" I asked.

"I can't believe it! He disguised himself down to the smell!"

"Incredible. Just how did he transform like that?"

Everyone in the room was talking about it, I say.

"Regardless, I'm worried about the real Claw Hero. Could this be because of the wave?" Father asked.

"I couldn't say," the old genmu responded.

"I don't like this at all. What is happening to this world . . ." Father trailed off.

The old genmu and Éclair were poking at the fox beast's dead body with their swords. The fox beast looked to have been completely and utterly annihilated. After all, with the might of Motoyasu Kitamura, such a small fry can be easily disposed of, I say!

But still, I thought, *why?* Looking at the dead fox beast, I started to remember one of the heroic sagas that Filo-tan's older sister told me about. I had this memory of Filo-tan bursting with pride. But wait, wasn't Filo-tan's older sister a tanuki demi-human? How dare I lump her in with a fox beast like this?

Eventually, the meeting was suspended and they decided to investigate the whereabouts of the actual Claw Hero and the origins of the mysterious fox beast.

"We must report this to the diplomatic meetings of nations immediately," the old genmu was saying. "Lady Seaetto, I presume we can beg your assistance?"

"Of course," Eclair said. "I planned to help from the beginning."

The old genmu and Eclair were having a pretty serious discussion, I say.

"We've begun our search for the Claw Hero's whereabouts all across the country, but as to whether we'll find him or not . . ."

"This is pretty disturbing," Eclair said. "I can't believe that someone impersonated the Claw Hero."

"It's almost unthinkable," the old genmu agreed.

You could almost see a shadow fall across the throne room.

I, Motoyasu Kitamura, was assailed by a deep fear that I could not put into words. But that fear was exactly why I needed to keep fighting for Father. The world was on the road to ruin. Just as Father had warned me, my godlike strength alone wouldn't be enough to get us through it.

I had chosen this path—to achieve the world peace I had promised to my beloved Filo-tan. To make a better world for all filolials!

The only thing that kept me going through it all was a shining light in my heart known as Father. And the hope that we could make it through the battles to a better future!

"Regardless, Shield Hero and Spear Hero," the old genmu said. "The wave is coming. I have no choice but to ask for your assistance."

"That's the plan," Father said.

"That's the plan!" I echoed.

"So while we're trying to level up anyways, should we try to find the Claw Hero?" Father asked.

"Before something as dangerous as a wave, I would ordinarily recommend that you prepare in a safer place," the old genmu said. "But given the situation at hand, I would like to formally request your help in searching for the Claw Hero."

"No need to be formal," Father said. "Would it be . . . would it be better to assume that the Claw Hero is already dead?"

"No, we believe that he's still alive. We're able to verify whether or not the heroes are living or dead, and his death has not yet been confirmed."

"Well that's at least one piece of good news," Father said. "Do you think he's being held captive somewhere?"

Father has such a kind heart. So we were going to be searching for the Claw Hero, I supposed. I wondered where he could possibly be. In the previous go-around, did I ever meet him? No, I didn't . . . I think. But I still felt uneasy.

"Most likely," the old genmu said.

"So until the wave comes, we'll make it our mission to level up while searching for the Claw Hero," Father said.

"Got it!" I declared. "I, Motoyasu Kitamura, will embark on the search for the Claw Hero so long as Father commands it, I say!"

"Let's do this," Father said. "We should head out now. I want to figure this out as soon as we can."

We explained our plan to Eclair and set out from the castle.

As we left, Father turned to me. "In order to get stronger, I'd also like to learn some magic if I can."

"To learn elementary magic, first we'll need a crystal ball," I told him.

"Wouldn't it be easier to learn it from a tome or something?"

"That might be true. If we use a tome, it'll be easier to increase the power of the spells, and you can even keep the magic power consumption in check."

"But I also heard that the best place to start is with magic that you can sense on your own, without using a tome."

Hmmm. That very well may be true. I remembered when I, Motoyasu Kitamura, had obtained a crystal ball and launched my first magical attack. I could still feel the magic coursing through my veins, I say!

"In that case, let's have you learn your first spell from a crystal ball, and if we have time after that, we'll use a tome, I say!"

"That works," Naofumi said.

And that's how, while in our pursuit of the Claw Hero, we decided that Father should learn a bit of magic.

Soon after we set out from the castle, we were approached by one of the Siltvelt leaders.

"Spear Hero, if there's anything at all you need, we'll do everything in our power to help. You helped escort the Shield Hero to Siltvelt, after all. Is there anything we can do?"

"As a matter of fact, there is," I declared. "I would like lots of money."

Father had quite the look on his face.

"Motoyasu, rather than asking for money, why don't you tell them what you actually want it for?" Father said.

"Various items, I say. Specifically, to buy more filolials, I say!"

"Uh . . . Then why don't you ask Siltvelt for filolials instead?" Father asked me, that strange look still on his face.

"Of course," the leader said. "If the Spear Hero desires filolials, we'll have ones to your liking sent straight away."

"That won't do."

It wouldn't do, indeed. My original objective was to become the master of my beloved Filo-tan, after all. In the first go-around, before Father started to raise Filo-tan, he had purchased her from a monster trainer. So if I were to go to the same monster trainer, there was absolutely no doubt that I would be able to obtain Filo-tan as well!

To that end, I needed tons of money. And I intended to get it from Siltvelt.

"Even though we're focused on searching for the Claw Hero, you're still stuck on filolials . . ." Father sighed. "You're really quite the character, Motoyasu."

"This search will be a real challenge," I proclaimed. "So if we have a lot of reliable filolials, it will be that much easier!"

"So that's what you're thinking?"

"Therefore, I, Motoyasu Kitamura, want more filolials, I say! I'll send Yuki and the others to go class up with you, Father," I told him.

"That works," Father said. "So today I'll go out with the filolials to level up. Motoyasu, have fun shopping."

"Father, I leave you in the wings of the filolials!"

"Yaaay!" said Kou. "We get to go out with Iwatani! I was so bored, and now we finally get to play!"

"I'm going to try my best and get stronger too!" chirped Sakura.

Filolials, I leave Father to you, I thought. After I got a fat purse of coins from the Siltvelt leaders, I set out as well.

With this much money, I'd have no trouble getting my hands on Filo-tan!

My God, in just a little bit longer, I'd be able to meet my precious Filo-tan. Just the thought of meeting her made my heart swell.

"Well, I'll be back after buying some filolials," I declared.

"Take care," Father said.

"Bye Motoyasu!" the filolials called.

Waving at them from the castle garden, I activated my Portal Spear. Destination: Melromarc castle town!

Chapter Four: In the Back Alley

Using my portal, I arrived at the location I had set near the Melromarc castle town. I set off on foot.

Oho? The village closest to the castle town . . . was it Riyute? I heard Father's voice in the back of my head.

> **Riyute**
>
> Riyute is the village neighboring Melromarc's castle town. Rare items can be found among the minerals of the adjacent ore mine. It's the town where Motoyasu first met Filo.

But now Riyute was a wasteland. The buildings were burned black, and some sort of evil magic had destroyed the fields. The homes were eaten by ruin and the shops a wreck. I could hardly see the remnants of the original town.

I saw some people who had set up tents as temporary provisions, and they all had bleak looks on their faces.

Well, since it wasn't strictly necessary to come to Riyute, I figured I'd just skip it. I wondered if perhaps the wave had come here, since it was so near Melromarc castle. I tried to remember if there had been this sort of damage before. In my memory, it hadn't looked anything like this, but maybe I wasn't remembering correctly.

Even if I worried about it, unfortunately, it wouldn't make any difference whatsoever. So I left that village and its bad vibes and hurried on to the castle town, I say!

Very well then! My objective today was to find the monster trainer and purchase Filo-tan. Let the mission commence!

I had got plenty of money to get it done. I intended to buy every single filolial they had, I say! With pep in my step, I skipped over to the market district in the castle town.

Hmm. Most places seemed to be closed for some reason. The pharmacy and the magic shop were closed too. Well, I didn't need them anyways, so who cares? I continued into the back alley where the monster trainer's tent was.

"Hey, is that you, Motoyasu?"

As I was walking down the alley, I bumped into Ren, who for some reason was calling my name. Should I kill him? But if I killed him, I'd just end up resetting the time loop again.

That settled it. I would silence Ren without killing him, if I could.

"W-wait! I don't want to fight you! I don't want a scene!" Just as I had begun to raise my spear, Ren held his hands out and took a step back.

Hmm. This time around, Ren had a laudable attitude, I say. If Ren wasn't my enemy, perhaps I ought to talk to him, at least a little.

On the other hand, maybe he was just putting on a front.

Perhaps he was just buying time to attack me while my guard was down.

"What kind of foul play is this?" I demanded.

"Nothing. No foul play—I told you I don't want to fight," Ren said. "But, Motoyasu, why are you here? I thought you went to Siltvelt!"

"My beloved Filo-tan is here, so why wouldn't I be here as well?"

"I have no idea what you're talking about, but listen, there's something I need to tell you."

"That's just a trick—you're going to call for help from the castle, I say!"

"No! I just want to talk! I'm not going to do that!" he shouted.

What to do? What to do? I really couldn't bring myself to trust him. When you think about it, it's always best to crush your fears into oblivion before they come back to haunt you later. I had already managed to get Father safely to Siltvelt, after all. But perhaps I should hear him out, at least to get information on the Church of the Three Heroes, who were after Father's life.

"I'll let you choose where you want to talk—wherever— but I just need to tell you something," Ren said.

"Very well," I said. "In that case, here will do just fine. So what is it that you need to tell me?"

"Right in this back alley?" Ren looked around. "Okay, fine. Well, a lot. I want you to also let Naofumi know—it's about what's happened to this country."

Ren, who had stepped closer, began talking about this so-called thing he needed to tell me.

He explained that after Naofumi and I fled, Melromarc treated him and Itsuki well. With funds from Melromarc, Ren bought equipment and started to level up to get stronger. In the meantime, he heard rumors about us, but he kept focusing on getting stronger and familiarizing himself with the world. So all that was smooth sailing.

However, according to Ren, the whole country had been slowly overtaken by a disquieting gloom. One of Itsuki's companions was apparently lynched by a demi-human who fervently believed in the Church of the Shield Hero—and was acting on the Shield Hero's orders. Ren started to look into the evidence, but a lot of it seemed suspicious. It didn't make sense that Father would be after one of the other heroes since he was already on the road to Siltvelt.

Said Ren, and so on and so forth.

"So," he continued, "is Naofumi really trying to kill us? And if so, did you come to kill us too?"

"Not in the slightest," I declared. "The only reason I came to Melromarc is to buy Filo-tan, I say."

Ren stared at me blankly. "Well, I suppose if you wanted to

kill us you would have already done it." It seemed that he was finally satisfied with my response.

And he was right, of course. There was absolutely no reason to kill Ren or Itsuki. And it would be doubly meaningless, because I'd just have to start everything all over again. If I had to kill anybody, it would be Trash and the high priest, I say.

"Okay, so back to what I was saying," Ren said. "There are a lot of strange things about this country. For one, the princess is showing a lot of favoritism to Itsuki and it's really making him a pain in the ass."

"A pain in the ass, you say?"

"Yeah, and the king and the princess are acting really fishy in general. When we pressed them about whether they caught Naofumi in a trap on that first day, all their responses were basically obvious lies and acting, just saying that it was all a big misunderstanding and that Melromarc would help you as soon as they could. But they attacked you at the border, didn't they? They said that they'd help you, but instead they attacked you and our own border. Everything they said was just littered with contradictions."

I got the sense that now Ren would finally believe me.

"In the end, last night, after defeating the wave boss I went to a big celebration at the castle, and what do you think they told me? 'It appears that we can't trust the strength of the heroes. Please train with more discipline.' That's what they said, after I beat the boss!"

For some reason Ren appeared to have accumulated a lot of stress and was grumbling on and on. Since I'd be able to get plenty of useful information, I nodded and kept the conversation going.

"Yeah! And so when I asked them why they told me the training wasn't enough, they said, 'The legendary heroes are far stronger than what you have shown. Please obtain godlike strength.' I heard a crazy rumor that you blew up an entire fortress, so I wonder if they were actually measuring us up against that."

"That actually happened," I declared. "It took a single blow."

"Right," he said. "Not a rumor, just a little embellished."

Ren didn't seem to be able to comprehend the true strength of a hero. When I first came to the world, I was the same as him and Itsuki, not even believing what Father had told me about the false accusation. But even now, Ren simply didn't understand what it took to get stronger.

"The king and princess gave me funds and hinted that Naofumi might actually declare war on Melromarc. I don't want to get caught up in such a pointless war. That can't be true, right?"

Father? War? Surely that's impossible.

"I was thinking about going to Zeltoble and hiding away there. So if you need anything from me, come find me in Zeltoble." Ren nodded. "Okay. See ya."

With Ren having said whatever he had wanted to say, he ran off. I supposed he was headed to Zeltoble.

Zeltoble, huh? That country was the perfect place to hide. It's not the safest place in the world, but it's not terrible, and there's a dragon hourglass there.

But enough with Ren. I had to purchase my precious Filo-tan.

When I entered the tent, the monster trainer came to greet me.

"What do we have here? A customer? Welcome! Yes sir," called the monster trainer.

"Give me Filo-tan."

"Um, excuse me?"

"Filo-tan."

"Yes sir. Um, I'm not sure that I understand . . ."

The monster trainer was staring me up and down. Then he suddenly gasped.

"Um, I see! Y-you are the Spear Hero that I've heard rumors about! Yes sir." For seemingly no reason at all, he started to nervously sweat all over his body.

"That is correct! It is I, Motoyasu Kitamura, the Spear Hero, I say!"

The monster trainer fell over with a clatter and scrambled back up.

"Um, so that means you're the criminal mastermind wanted

for the destruction of the Melromarc fort . . . C-can I help you? Yes sir."

Criminal mastermind?

Oh, was he talking about the time Father asked me to demonstrate my magic? But that was just a little sprinkle of fire, nothing major. And even if I was a wanted criminal, I had just walked around the castle town without anyone saying anything. I supposed people didn't expect to see a wanted criminal walking around in broad daylight. Regardless, the deed had been done.

"I've come to buy Filo-tan, I say!" I repeated.

Since today was the day after the Melromarc wave, if I count backward based on the previous go-around, today was the very same day that Father bought Filo-tan. Therefore, Filo-tan must be here today!

"Um, Filo-tan . . . ?" The monster trainer started whispering to his associate next to him. They conferred back and forth in hushed tones before responding to me.

"By Filo-tan, do you mean a filolial?" he asked me.

"That is exactly what I mean. Or will you not sell me one?" I gripped my spear and raised it a little. A technique I learned from Father.

"U-um, of course, no problem at all! Yes sir. Look over here!"

"I'll buy every single aria-type filolial egg that you have in this tent here," I proclaimed.

"Um, all of them?"

"Precisely. I would like to purchase every single aria-type filolial egg here. I have this much money."

I dropped the purse they gave me back in Siltvelt at the monster trainer's feet with a thud.

"I'd expect to get some change back as well," I told him.

The purse was filled with gold coins, I figured. And if it wasn't enough, I'd go back to Siltvelt, get more money, and come back here again. And if that wasn't enough, I'd go kill some bandits and get enough money that way.

"I see that this is Siltvelt currency. Yes sir. Isn't it?" the monster trainer asked.

"Will that be a problem?"

"Um, no, since I sell between different countries, it's no problem at all. Yes sir. But since we're in Melromarc now, it just means that the currency will be worth a little less, if that's acceptable?"

"That's acceptable, I say."

"In that case, I'll give you all of the aria-type filolial eggs that we have. Yes sir," he said.

The monster trainer's associate counted up all the money and let out an audible gasp. Even the monster trainer was staring at the money and was at a complete loss for words.

After a while, they brought me the pushcart loaded with filolial eggs.

"This here is all of the filolial eggs that we have. Yes sir," the monster trainer said.

"This is it?"

"Yes, this is all of them. Yes sir. We've even included a filolial egg vending machine as a bonus. Yes sir."

Hmmm. But that means . . . that Filo-tan's egg must be one of these!

I was filled with overwhelming gratitude. "Perfect! This is perfect!" I declared.

"How will you handle the registration and hatching them, if I may ask? Yes sir."

"That's no problem." I'd just have some people in Siltvelt do it. "So then, farewell!"

"Thank you very much," the monster trainer said. "Um, so . . . yes, because we arc being suspected of, umm, collusion by the Melromarc, umm, government, we'll be closing our shop for a while, yes, for a while . . . Yes sir."

I skipped merrily out of the tent. It was basically a mountain of filolials! And just like that, I was ready to take them all back to Siltvelt with the portal.

How should I do it? I could go to a safe place, split up the eggs, and transport them via portal in manageable loads that way. I pulled the pushcart through the castle town, my face beaming with joy.

I split up the filolial eggs and put them into pouches and

started to take them back to Siltvelt. Of course, well aware of my past mistakes with the portal, I made sure to prepare it properly. Before, I could only register four different locations to my portal, but with skill power-up and the seven star power-up, I could now register many more locations to my portal. Using the portal had also gotten much easier.

So after transporting all the eggs to Siltvelt, I spent the rest of the day taking care of registering and preparing to hatch the eggs. One of them will definitely be Filo-tan, no doubt about it!

"Well then." I had completed the preparations. Without reporting to Father, I decided it was time to deal with the core problem at hand: crushing Melromarc, the Church of the Three Heroes, and Trash! Since Father had mentioned a grim atmosphere before, I figured I could cheer everyone up by simply steamrolling our enemies into dust.

Soon it was the dead of night. The perfect time to launch a surprise attack, I say.

Way back when, this was also the perfect time to get pigs out of my room. I also used to sneak into school on dares and go to shrines at this hour.

I transported myself back to the Melromarc castle town in front of the Church of the Three Heroes and blasted my way into the church.

"Brionac V!"

I remembered the Church of the Three Heroes from the

previous go-around. Only something in Melromarc castle town would be this ridiculously big! And yet at the same time, it was also pretty small. It was only about half the size of the Church of the Four Heroes in Faubrey and the Church of the Seven Heroes.

> **Faubrey**
>
> A massive country that has modernized into a sort of steampunk era. Faubrey has upheld the Church of the Four Heroes and the Church of the Seven Heroes for generations, and there are a number of descendants of the heroes in the royal family. They have deep faith in the heroes, and the country has a lot of power on the world stage. But I've also heard there's a lot of corruption there.

In fact, this church was even smaller than the Church of the Shield Hero in Siltvelt. I wondered how that could be. I had absolutely no interest in the history of the Church of the Three Heroes or anything, but with a lame church like this, it certainly seemed like it wasn't doing its best to convince its followers to stay put.

Regardless, I planned to destroy it.

I blew open the door with a thunderous roar, went inside, and after a lot of fuss and noise, eventually a monk and a pig of the Church of the Three Heroes came running out. Two sinners guilty of the same crime, I say.

"Who are you?"

"I am the Love Hunter, I say! I have come to teach Father's accusers an important lesson!"

"What in the world!?"

"Aiming Lancer V!"

Using multi-lock, I targeted as many believers in this idiotic church as I possibly could. I activated the skill and exterminated them all.

"Ahhhhh!"

"Noooooooo!"

"Hahahahahah!" I cried with glee. "I'll destroy this seed of evil before it can even sprout!"

Well, you know, I tried not to kill *too* many people. But I had far surpassed the limit of my restraint.

"Now, where is the high priest?"

I pointed my spear at a surviving monk who was begging me for his life. Since Father told me not to kill people, I had decided to kill only enough to instill mortal fear in the living. But depending on where he was, I intended to turn everything surrounding that high priest into ashes.

"I don't answer to demons!" he cried.

"Well, then it looks like this demon is going to tear you apart," I said. I stabbed my spear into his mouth and twisted bit by bit, moving my spear from left to right. My spear—the legendary spear with countless power-ups that had made corpses of monsters. Human flesh was like paper to it.

He screamed in blood-curdling agony.

Finally he told me where the high priest was.

"The h-high priest left the country! He's not here!"

Hmmm. It seemed like a suspicious answer, but since I didn't see the high priest anywhere, I figured he wasn't lying.

What a self-centered religion. He gave me the answer so easily in the hope that I would spare his life. If he really believed in his faith, giving up his life for it should have been his heart's desire. For Father and Filo-tan's sake, it wouldn't be disappointing to lose my life, I say.

I knocked the monk in the head with my spear and left him unconscious.

Next up . . .

"This Spear Demon is headed straight to the castle, I say!" I proclaimed.

"Hurry! Prepare a line of defense!" people were shouting.

After I destroyed the Church of the Three Heroes, I walked across the town with my eyes on the prize: Melromarc castle.

Huge groups of soldiers attacked me in waves, but they were no match for me. I tore them apart and cast them aside in a way to get past without killing them.

"What insane power!"

"Aiming Lance X!"

Screams filled the castle. As I mowed down row after row of soldiers, they began to cast their own spells at me, blasting a sea of fire my way. In order to avoid their flames, I chanted a fire spell of my own. If you can control fire with magic, you can erase it, I say.

I mean, it was a little tricky, but I didn't come here to start a war or anything, so I supposed I had no choice. I just came to defeat the villainous fools who were trying to kill the heroes.

"Well then . . . where might Trash and Witch be?" I asked aloud.

Soldiers had closed the castle gate, so I blasted it open and marched into the castle. Slowly making my way through the halls, I disposed of any soldier that tried to attack me. They ought to know how much of a pain it can be to hold back for so long!

Did no one understand that it would be so easy to destroy a pathetic castle like this with just a sprinkle of strong magic?

"Trash! Witch!" I called. "King! Princess! Where are you? I, Motoyasu Kitamura, have come to punish you without killing you, I say!"

I went past the throne room, into Trash's bedroom, and then into Witch's bedroom, but I didn't see them anywhere.

The cowards had run away! Just what I expected! Fast legs for fleeing.

"Hey!" I shouted. "The king and princess took the troops and got out of here! They're not even here!"

I looked over at the nearest minister-looking type, who was on his knees and begging me to spare his life.

So this had been a giant waste of time. What a pain. Well, at least now they'd understand what the Spear Hero was all about.

"Tell the king and the princess what happened here, I say," I told him. "Tell them it's meaningless to try to defeat me. I can easily mow every last one of you down. I want them to think carefully about that, I say! Think carefully! Hahahahahahaha!"

"Curse you," he moaned. "You—you're an imposter. You're with the Spear Demon! The gods will punish you for this!"

I ignored his agonized groans and returned to Siltvelt via portal.

"Hey, welcome back, Motoyasu. You're pretty late, aren't you?"

Father came to greet me upon my return even though it was so late, I say!

"What were you doing up so late? I saw that carriage full of eggs. Does that mean they are . . ." He trailed off.

Incidentally, in this world there was a slight time difference between Melromarc and Siltvelt. So in Siltvelt it was already early morning. That Father would come to greet me even at this hour demonstrated the profound depths of his compassion, and overwhelmed, I burst into tears.

"They're filolial eggs, I say!" I bawled.

"I should've realized. You bought a lot."

I wiped away my tears. Yuki and the filolials, now woken up by my return, also came out of their room.

"So we're going to get some more underlings?" Yuki asked.

"Awesome! It's gonna be so fun!" Kou said.

"No matter what happens, I'll still protect you, Naofumi!" Sakura chirped.

"Thanks, Sakura. Okay, Motoyasu, explain yourself," Father said. "You bought quite a lot of filolial eggs."

"I have reason to believe that Filo-tan is in one of those eggs," I declared.

"So you bought them all. I guess this is just your crazy way of doing things." While Father was staring at me with sleepy eyes, Sakura was hugging him tightly from behind. What an absolutely delightful sight.

My heart raced at the thought of Father reuniting with my beloved Filo-tan.

"At last, I infiltrated the Church of the Three Heroes in Melromarc," I proclaimed.

"What?" Father exclaimed. "Wait, you did what? Back up, back up. Don't you realize that if you mess that up it could lead to war?"

For the next few hours, Father kept requesting various things from me. That is to say, in a fiercely authoritative tone, he commanded that I not do anything reckless without consulting him first. That is to say, he admonished me.

I, Motoyasu Kitamura, was ashamed to the most remote chambers of my very soul.

"So even though we're supposed to be searching for the Claw Hero, it doesn't seem you have the slightest interest in looking for him," Father was saying angrily.

"Preparation is essential!" I told him.

"I suppose that's just how you do things, Motoyasu." Father sighed. "At the very least, with this many filolials, we'd be able to launch a filolial-wave attack, I guess. In the meantime, a lot of people from Siltvelt are helping in the search for the Claw Hero, reaching out to any connections they have for leads."

Father gently calmed the filolials and told them that it was time to get back to bed.

"It's really late," Father said, "so we all better get back to sleep. The only problem is that tomorrow is already about to start."

"Yes! Bedtime, I say!"

And just like Father told me to, I returned to my room and went back to sleep.

Chapter Five: Shieldfreeden

The next day, without any further delay, I focused on hatching my filolial eggs.

"Yuki, Kou," I called, "I want you to take the filolial chicks out to level up!"

"Leave it to us!"

"Roger that!"

Little filolials of all different colors chirped, bowed, and hopped up on to Yuki's and Kou's backs. They set off.

I had hatched about one-third of the filolial eggs, but not a single one of them was the same color as Filo-tan. I couldn't afford to take any more breaks. One can't quit in the middle of raising filolials, I say.

Father stopped by my room and looked around. "Motoyasu, this is getting a bit out of control," he said. Filolial chicks, chirping merrily, covered every inch of the room.

"There will be even more tomorrow," I informed him.

"No kidding. It's not too many?" Father asked.

"Father, what are you saying?" I cried. "This isn't nearly enough!"

"So many filolials! Awesome!" Sakura said.

"It's an entire army of filolials," Father said. "How are you going to feed them all?"

"They can take care of themselves, I say!"

Father glanced at me. "That's frightening. That many could make whole monster populations go extinct."

Oh, Father, what in the heavens were you saying? Yes—as the number of filolials increases, the number of monsters will naturally decrease. I was creating a paradise!

Regardless, I didn't have nearly enough filolials to cause any serious problems. And so I continued to hatch and raise the filolials.

Still, I didn't see a single filolial with the same coloring as Filo-tan. I fell to the ground and wailed in misery.

How could it be? I had bought every single filolial egg from the monster trainer, but I had yet to hatch Filo-tan. Father had told me he had purchased Filo-tan from that same monster trainer, but had he been wrong? Had I been wrong?

What could I do? At this rate, any criminal off the street could end up buying Filo-tan!

What could I possibly do? I had already reached my borrowing limit from Siltvelt.

I had no choice but to come up with a new plan.

"Okay, now it's my turn to level them up!" chirped Sakura.

Yuki had just gotten back from classing up a group of filolials. They were progressing smoothly.

I had to devise a new strategy. Oh, my beloved Filo-tan, where could you possibly be? My heart cried out in agony!

I, Motoyasu Kitamura, vowed to chase Filo-tan to the ends of the earth if I could only find her there!

But before that, I figured I should go rob some bandits.

"While searching for the Claw Hero, I'll go hunt some thieves to make more money!" I announced to Yuki, Kou, Sakura, and Father.

"Sounds good," said Yuki.

"Are thieves yummy?" asked Kou.

"Motoyasu, please do me a favor and prioritize finding the Claw Hero," Father said and turned to Kou. "And, Kou, you can't eat people. You know that!"

"Aw man!"

Sakura was riding piggyback on Father with a sleepy expression. I watched her for a moment.

Oho? Was it just my imagination, or did Sakura almost smell like Filo-tan?

No, it must have been my imagination.

"All right, I'm out, I say!"

"Take care. I'll also head out with Sakura a bit later," Father said.

That's pretty much how we spent our day-to-day in Siltvelt. Each day, Father rode Sakura to different places around Siltvelt and told me all about what he saw. Father seemed to have an entirely different personality from the first go-around. Sometimes he went out on adventures without Sakura, and he told me about his various battles as he gained practical combat experience.

"This world is so amazing, isn't it?" Father told me. "It's incredible how many different races there are!"

As Father earnestly helped the local population with its problems, he only wanted to see more and more of the world.

"You wouldn't believe this," Father said. "I only saw it for a moment, but there was this therianthrope that looked like a panda! I had no idea there were ones like that. I saw elephant and hippopotamus therianthropes too. They looked like serious heavyweight fighters."

"It means the world to me that you're enjoying yourself, Father," I said.

A panda therianthrope, hm? I couldn't help but feel like I had some sort of memory about a panda therianthrope, but I really had no clue as to what.

"It's so cool seeing so many types of people. I suppose we'll all have to fight the wave of destruction together . . ." Father trailed off.

Father's eyes twinkled with hopes and dreams! He had completely changed since the first go-around. But we had just three more of those peaceful days in Siltvelt before the wave of destruction arrived.

"It sounds wrong, but I'm kind of looking forward to the wave of destruction," Father said.

"I was the same way. My heart was dancing with anticipation before my first wave of destruction," I informed Father.

I could remember it clearly. Applying the knowledge I had gained into action against chimeras, unleashing my skills for the first time—it had been a really fun battle. But if I remember correctly, back then Father had an uncomfortable expression.

After the wave, the crimson swine informed me that Filo-tan's big sister was being held as a slave. Without realizing that Father and big sis were actually happy together, I challenged Father to a duel.

It was the worst mistake of my life. Fortunately, Father mustered the might of his wisdom and used it to utterly defeat me. Only Father could win a war with his wits alone! He had me down for the count when the crimson swine intervened to engineer a worthless, false victory for me.

I was such a fool for challenging Father to a duel. There was no way for me to even land a hit against him! I was the real loser.

I must learn that sort of fighting spirit from Father, I say!

Even if it meant dragging my own dead body through the mud, I vowed to find my beloved Filo-tan.

Motoyasu accused Naofumi of recklessly overworking Raphtalia as a slave and **challenged him to a duel**. Before Raphtalia had a chance to raise any objections, the king decided that a duel would be held and that Raphtalia would be offered as a trophy to the winner.

Many assumed that the winner of a duel between the battle-tested Spear Hero and a Shield Hero who was unable to even launch an attack would be obvious. But Naofumi decided to use the monsters he had collected near the castle and, pulling them out from under his cloak, launched an attack. Combining the strength of the monster's attacks with his shield skills, soon Naofumi had Motoyasu pinned.

But it was too late. Myne used magic to interfere with the fight, and Motoyasu was eventually crowned victor.

After the duel ended, Naofumi realized that he only lost **because of the tricks** of Myne and the king. It was then that a darkness overtook his heart and his shield first activated its curse series.

When Motoyasu turned to Raphtalia after supposedly saving her, Raphtalia slapped Motoyasu in the face and defended herself as Naofumi's slave. No one had been injured in the duel, but only Raphtalia understood that was due to **Naofumi's kindness**.

Naofumi fell to immense depths of despair and wouldn't listen to anyone until Raphtalia reached out to him. When Raphtalia spoke to him, they were the first kind words Naofumi heard from anyone since coming to another world. Naofumi realized that he could keep going if he had friends that believed in and trusted him. That was the moment that Naofumi found a friend who **believed in him from the bottom of her heart**.

Anyways, I went out and earned a bit of money from bandit-hunting. I figured I would go back to Melromarc later and buy some more filolials from a different monster trainer. Those were some dull days, now that I think about it. But what happened the next day changed everything.

"So the seven star hero in charge of Shieldfreeden and Faubrey is being dispatched to help fight the wave of destruction?" Father was asking. That's what the shusaku representative had just told Father and me at the morning meeting. "Shouldn't Siltvelt be fine with Motoyasu and myself?"

"That may be true, but we tend to work in cooperation to protect our neighboring countries. Understandably, Shieldfreeden's seven star hero is concerned about the disappearance of the Claw Hero."

"I see."

"Of course, we believe that with the Shield Hero alone he could safely get us through the wave of destruction," the shusaku added.

"So you're just being careful?" Father asked.

"Exactly."

Father waved me over and whispered into my ear. A secret, I say!

"If I'm remembering correctly, isn't Shieldfreeden a pretty extreme country? I'm sure they'll treat me well since I'm a hero, but I've heard that they have human slaves there."

"That is correct," I told Father.

I, Motoyasu Kitamura, had never been to any slave country besides Melromarc, but I certainly got the sense that they didn't treat people well in Shieldfreeden. The slave hunters targeted demi-humans, but since there were so many demi-humans, I supposed they went for human slaves instead.

"What's the right way to put it?" Father continued. "Based on the standards from my world, Shieldfreeden is kinda like a country of Vikings, right? Really militaristic."

"Perhaps," I said.

Father nodded. "But here in Siltvelt, race is really important, right?"

Now that he mentioned it, the lion therianthrope had talked about this sort of thing before. Father went on to explain the history of Shieldfreeden to me.

Siltvelt was founded by followers of the Shield Hero and the upper class was a famous line that continued for generation after generation. So Siltvelt had a solidified aristocratic class. The four races in the upper class were the shusaku, genmu, aotatsu, and hakuko—the four holy beasts. However, in a great war long ago, the hakuko were forced to take responsibility for the defeat and ever since have remained the lowest among the four ruling races. But overall, those four races had excellent combat strength and continue to be upheld in society and by the government of Siltvelt.

"So," Father continued, "people who couldn't follow the racial hierarchy of Siltvelt went on to found Shieldfreeden."

Shieldfreeden—established just 100 years ago—had a short history in comparison to Siltvelt. It was a country with a frontier mentality.

"I heard that ordinary citizens from common races—not the four top ones—who couldn't bear the hereditary class structure created Shieldfreeden," Father explained.

"I must say, I don't follow," I declared.

"Well, just think of it as low-wage laborers deciding to move elsewhere. Siltvelt doesn't have a system where humans are supreme like Melromarc. But there are so many different races of demi-humans that any system that allows for hereditary rule or wealth will end up discriminating against groups that are less fortunate."

I figured that Siltvelt and Shieldfreeden weren't so different from our own worlds. It appeared that discrimination and inequality existed no matter the world.

"But listen, Motoyasu. It's probably best not to ask anyone how Shieldfreeden claimed the land for its country in the first place or what happened to the people who originally lived there. I think it's an ugly tale," Father said.

"I see. It's a history very similar to the world that I came from."

"Me too. That's the kind of history a country like that will have. Long ago, humans and demi-humans had a war over slavery in Shieldfreeden. So by all appearances, it's supposed to be free of discrimination."

"'By all appearances,' you say?"

"Well, I'm not sure Shieldfreeden is as equal as it claims to be," Father said. "But that's just my impression. One way or another, at the current moment, demi-humans are controlling the country and it seems to be pretty stable, so I could be wrong."

"Would you have wanted to go to Shieldfreeden?" I asked Father.

Father thought about it. If the time loop ended up resetting and we needed a different place to go, we may as well consider Shieldfreeden. Of course, only if Father desired it, I say!

"I'm not sure. Are you talking about if one of us dies and we have to start over?"

"Just so."

If we didn't understand what kind of country we were going to, even if the time loop resets, we could end up failing all over again. If Father, rather than myself, could retain his memories after the time loop, I would have no concerns whatsoever. But if I couldn't start remembering any details about the world around me, we would end up making the same mistakes over and over.

"If possible, I think we should avoid Shieldfreeden. I think it would end up being pretty similar to what we've already gone through. In fact, if the Shield Hero were to go there, the country could get belligerent, as they expect heroes to have a lot of strength on the battlefield," Father concluded.

So that's what Shieldfreeden was like. Not too different from Melromarc, I guessed.

"On top of that, the aotatsu—who are one of the leading races here in Siltvelt—may be starting to gain power in Shieldfreeden."

The aotatsu, huh? I felt like I had seen some around before, but I couldn't recall.

"You don't see a ton of them around here in Siltvelt. They're here, but they have about as much authority as the hakuko. I've heard that at one time in the past, the hakuko drove them out of Siltvelt, but I haven't looked into it enough to be sure."

Which meant that, in essence, Siltvelt was split between the shusaku and genmu. Oho? I suddenly felt like I had heard somebody say once that those two races were the more moderate factions. So it wouldn't be unusual to assume that radicals would rise up eventually.

Father turned back to Wer—Werwer, was it?

"So when will the seven star hero arrive?" he asked.

"We have an official audience with them tomorrow around noon," the shusaku said.

"Got it. We'll try to be in the castle at that time, then."

"That would be greatly appreciated."

And that's how the meeting ended. As we left the conference

room, I noticed that Father's shoulders were sagging and he had a troubled expression as he looked out at Siltvelt.

"The wave of destruction, the Seven Star Hero . . . I suppose it's good that we'll finally get to meet them this time."

"Indeed."

"Thanks to your strength, Motoyasu, we'll be all right, but . . ." Father trailed off.

Father was exactly right. If you befriend other heroes, you could be much stronger together. That's why I gave Father my precious filolials to be his friends! So long as the filolials and I were around, Father had nothing to fear!

Sakura seemed very attached to Father, and the rest of the filolials had a good relationship with him as well.

"All the women attack me and none of the men understand me," Father was muttering to himself.

Now that he mentioned it, Werwer and the old genmu both had sent their female relatives as prospects to be Father's wife.

"Anyways, we can focus on finding new friends after we fight the wave of destruction," Father said.

"Of course!" I declared.

"Eclair also went out, didn't she?" Father paused. "Okay, so in terms of urgent matters, we have to prepare for the wave of destruction and find the missing Claw Hero."

"According to Yuki, they still haven't found him," I said.

"Yep. People are investigating what exactly that beast was

doing disguised as the Claw Hero. Supposedly, it was a beast that was sealed away in another country. But being that it was sealed in another country, they can't confirm what it was."

"Shall I, Motoyasu Kitamura, go help with the investigation, Father?"

"I guess so. You were the one who brought down that beast, after all. Of course, we'll need your help when the wave of destruction hits."

Beast Spy ended up taking out that monster all on its own, I recalled. When I gripped my spear, I could still feel its anger toward the fox beast. Most surely, Beast Spy was designed to take out fiends like that!

While we were talking, we went out to the castle garden.

"We're going to practice our formations, everyone," Yuki called. "Let's do it!" Yuki was leading the other filolials through training drills in preparation for the wave of destruction.

"Yes, ma'am!" they chirped in unison.

"So many . . . filolials . . ." Father whispered.

Father was expressing his wonder at Yuki leading such a mighty, disciplined formation of filolials! Those same filolials that I purchased were well on their way to becoming mighty warriors.

They did make the castle garden pretty crowded though.

"Isn't their training getting in the way of everyone at the castle—" Father began.

"Father, don't say such nonsense! Yuki is a magnificent leader of the filolials, I say!"

A number of demi-human soldiers who had gotten caught up in Yuki's training drill appeared to be confused. Since the drill required beast transformation, the movements were considerably difficult for them.

But now that I thought about it, there were also demi-humans that could transform back in Father's village before. In particular, I remembered a pig that could turn into a dog. I think she was quite attached to Father's cooking.

"Well, if the training drills are going smoothly, hopefully that means we won't have too much trouble with the wave of destruction," Father said.

"I certainly hope so!"

Our preparations continued without interruption. That night, I heard Father organize and prepare our personnel for the coming wave of destruction.

Chapter Six: The Seven Star Whip Hero

The next day, we sighted an airship making its way toward the castle, along with some other flying aircraft.

"Are those ships from Faubrey and Shieldfreeden with the seven star hero on board?" Father asked.

"That's what they informed us," Werwer replied.

"So there are airships in this world? Wow!"

Monitored by a soldier riding a dragon, the airship landed in an open plain near the castle. Droves of people exited the airship and the castle gradually grew crowded and lively. Father and I went to wait in the throne room for the seven star hero.

"The seven star hero from Faubrey—what kind of person is he?" Father was asking Werwer. "You said he was the Whip Hero, right?"

"He's considered to be a genius. He started studying magic at a young age and they even said that he invented new technology for papermaking."

One little drop at a time, memories of the Whip Hero came back to me. But I could only remember general information about his accomplishments.

"In addition, he has put great effort into reviving this long-lost mode of transportation," Werwer said, gesturing to the airship.

"He seems like a pretty amazing person," Father said. "I suppose if people from other worlds are summoned here regularly, it's not surprising that someone brought the ability to create airships and airplanes over once."

"It's not hard to fly if you have a dragon," Werwer grumbled.

"Well, that's true," Father agreed. "If you think about it from a cost standpoint, it's probably best to just use dragons."

So the Whip Hero built that airship, huh? Father continued talking about the Whip Hero's potential motives.

"Does he aspire to help a lot of people move or something like that? Airships could be used to help people that way."

"That's right, Shield Hero," Werwer said. "To that end, we'll begin research on constructing air transport in our country at once!"

"No, I didn't mean that . . . Why doesn't anyone understand the simplest things I say?" Father muttered to himself dejectedly.

"The Whip Hero has built friendly relations with Faubrey as well," Werwer continued.

"He's quite the impressive character."

A soldier called out, "The Whip Hero has arrived!"

Soldiers opened the door to the throne room and in came the seven star hero. I held my breath, but this time Beast Spy didn't exhibit a response.

A man walked briskly toward us. He had a nice face and Filo-tan's blonde hair and blue eyes. He was wearing denim jeans and a jacket—excellent fashion sense, I must say. It was just my intuition, but I had a feeling that this kind of fashion was all the rage in Faubrey.

"I am the Whip Hero, Takt Alsaholn Faubrey. Pleased to make your acquaintance."

He got down on one knee and bent his head toward the ground in a gracious bow while a number of pigs behind him greeted us.

"Oink oink!"

In the back, a pig with fierce horns like a dragon chattered on about something.

"Thank you for coming to Siltvelt," Werwer said. "We'll welcome your party as warmly as we can."

"Thank you kindly for your hospitality," Takt said. "Now . . . it seems sudden, but I was hoping to have an audience with the heroes here." The Whip Hero looked over toward Father and me.

Father read the gesture perfectly and took a step forward. "I'm the Shield Hero, Naofumi Iwatani. It's nice to meet you."

I was supposed to be next, wasn't I? I took a step forward exactly as Father did and bowed.

"It is I, the Love Hunter, Motoyasu Kitamura!"

"Motoyasu, you really struggle with introductions. Uh, he's

the Spear Hero. He's a little weird but he's strong and reliable."

Takt stared at me for a moment and nodded. "Understood. It's a pleasure."

I caught a whiff of something suspicious in that gaze, I say.

"Is that the airship you restored yourself? That's amazing, to have an airship in another world," Father said.

"Oh, that wasn't too hard. It's a pain to make fuel though."

After the introductions finished, the Whip Hero started talking incredibly casually to Father! How dare he! I was sure that Father would respond with fierce admonishment for speaking so rudely. But Father's attitude wasn't quite what I expected.

"So before the wave of destruction comes," Takt continued, "we'd like to take a look at the remains of the fox beast, if that's all right."

"Ah, yes, this way . . ." Werwer said. Werwer also looked greatly displeased at the Whip Hero's arrogant behavior. But since the Whip Hero held such a high position in another land, I supposed he couldn't say anything about it. Werwer reluctantly ordered his subordinates out.

"Should we go along with you?" Father said.

The Whip Hero gave Father a sidelong glance. "Don't worry about it. It's not worth your trouble, Hero."

Father nodded. I noticed that the Whip Hero's pig companions were carrying guns. Something about those armed pigs made me uncertain. Was it a memory that refused to come back? I had an ugly feeling that I couldn't shake.

Was I left with no choice but to launch a preemptive strike? Father would probably scold me later, and there was absolutely no reason to attack in the first place, so I reluctantly decided to hold myself back.

"Oh, and by the way, who was it that defeated that imposter hero?" Takt asked.

"It was I!" I proclaimed. "I, Motoyasu Kitamura, erased that masquerading monster from this universe!"

Even though it was technically my spear and Beast Spy that attacked on their own initiative, it didn't hurt to take credit, I say. The fox beast had been pathetically weak, anyhow.

Takt nodded slowly, watching me even as he left the room. What was up with him?

"Well, he seems like a hard person to please. It was like he wanted to kill that foul beast himself for impersonating a hero," Father mused.

"We'd better keep an eye on him," I said.

"Motoyasu, do you know something about him?"

"I have absolutely no memory of him, but I have a feeling this is not good in the slightest."

"'Not good?'" Father sighed. "Well, we can't really be too careful about it if you don't even remember anything."

Afterward, Takt went to investigate the corpse of the transformed fox beast. Then he went back to his airship to rest. There were whispers around Siltvelt that they could hear strange noises and the sound of weeping coming from his airship.

"Takt didn't say very much, did he?" Father commented.

I kept my eyes on the airship. "He didn't say much at all," I agreed.

"Hmm. Well, this is just my intuition, but I don't think we can trust him," Father said. "He went straight to take a look at the fox beast—it's almost like he was looking for something specific."

"If he's up to no good," I declared, "I'll punish him with all the fury of hell! While leaving him alive, of course."

I suddenly had a vague recollection that the seven star heroes were supposed to be the subordinates of the four holy heroes. It would only be right for us to teach him his place.

"I think it'd be best to just let him do what he wants and keep a close eye on him. There's the welcome reception tonight and all," Father said.

A welcome party, he says? I couldn't wait to see what the Whip Hero would try.

Father and I hurried over to the reception.

"The Whip Hero has traveled a long way to be with us tonight," a Siltvelt representative was saying. "Please give him a warm and gracious welcome."

I noticed that the Whip Hero had a dark expression on his face, but when the food arrived at the table, he noticeably brightened up.

"Even though the wave of destruction is almost here, I really appreciate you all going to so much trouble to welcome me," Takt said.

Father and the Siltvelt leaders were engaging in nonsensical prattle with the Whip Hero. And I couldn't help but notice that the Whip Hero's subordinates kept looking at me.

The gazes of his pigs revolted me to my core. If Father hadn't been on guard as well, I would've decided to destroy all of them.

"There's no poison, so please enjoy the food," Father was telling the Whip Hero.

"I can sense poison, but thanks. No need to worry about me."

"Oh, no kidding?"

It seemed that Father was letting his guard down. At this rate, things could get sticky.

Even more suspicious was the fact that Takt wouldn't make eye contact with Father. Any person born into this world must affix their eyes to glorious Father's at least once, I say. But the Whip Hero failed that test.

"Ugh . . ." Sakura moaned as if sick and snuggled up to Father. I looked over at Yuki and Kou and they were also groaning unpleasantly.

"What's wrong?" I asked them at once.

"The Whip Hero brought dragons and griffins . . . and they keep staring at us," Yuki said.

"Dragons and griffins, you say?" I stood up at once. Those mortal enemies of filolials were no friends of mine.

However, Father did have a dragon once. So although Yuki and the filolials were in bad moods because of them, I shouldn't rush to destroy dragons that weren't necessarily our enemies.

However! The very fact that the Whip Hero was not raising filolials but griffins and dragons was a dangerous sign. When I got the chance, I'd give the Whip Hero a lengthy sermon on the error of his ways!

"So before the wave of destruction comes tomorrow," Takt said, "I'd like to have a strategy meeting in my airship. Shield Hero and Spear Hero, you don't think you'd be able to come, do you?"

"Sure, we can come," Father said. "I don't know much about the waves of destruction, but Motoyasu seems like he does, so he can tell you more then. So should we head over there now?"

"Uh, I meant tomorrow . . . I'm kinda drunk now, actually."

"Oh, okay."

The unpleasant reception continued.

What was this ugly feeling that I had? It had plagued me ever since the Whip Hero arrived. A sense of duty held me captive, insisting that I had to remember something at all costs. Even more vexing was my inability to remember! I spent the whole banquet engulfed in such annoyances, I say.

The next day, Father paced nervously back and forth.

"The wave of destruction is almost here," he said. But before that, we had the strategy meeting with the Whip Hero.

In my opinion, the strength of Yuki and the filolials alone would be enough to take care of the wave of destruction. But I figured cooperation and teamwork and all that were important. Supposedly, the Whip Hero had some tough soldiers in his group, with the Faubrey troops under his command being especially capable.

The Siltvelt leaders called us in and we found a bunch of pigs waiting for us. I had absolutely no idea what they were oinking about.

Fortunately, Father interpreted for me.

"They're saying, 'Shield Hero and Spear Hero, Lord Takt is waiting for you. You'll discuss the wave of destruction in the airship.' They're inviting us in," Father said.

There wasn't much time left until the wave of destruction came, I noticed. Leaving a strategy meeting to the last possible moment was the very height of insolence against Father.

Should I take their lives as punishment?

"Motoyasu, I can tell you're thinking about killing someone right now," Father told me. "Please stop."

"Anything for you, Father!" I declared.

Father, Yuki, Sakura, Kou, a bunch of Siltvelt leaders, and I headed to the strategy meeting.

The airship had been stationed near the castle and stairs led up to the aircraft door. When we boarded, the Siltvelt leaders goggled at the airship's interior. It was the cultural difference, I supposed. The interior was certainly large and built for comfort. They led us through a long hallway to an observation deck. Takt took a seat in the center of the room. It was like he was the king of the world, his legs stretched out and comfortably lying on his back. Armed pigs stood stationed around the corners of the room. How arrogant.

"You finally came," Takt said with a smirk.

"So . . . what about the strategy meeting for the wave of destruction?" Father asked. "Is that going to start now?"

"Huh? Strategy meeting? You're still talking about that?" Takt spat.

It was an unsettling response. Father raised his eyebrows.

"What do you mean?" Father asked.

"I'll show you what I mean!"

The pigs raised their guns and, surrounding us, fired.

"Die!" Takt shouted. "Enemy of Tulina! We'll kill every last one of you!"

Gunshots rang out and the bullets started flying.

But in this country of demi-humans, we also had plenty of elite warriors at our disposal. Of course, they weren't on my level, but they immediately activated beast transformation. Father's skills had also evolved considerably, and he responded with his shield as well.

"Air Strike Phaser Shield V!" Father chanted the skill just as he had in the last go-around and a shield of feathers surrounded us. The filolials! No, not the filolials—I could tell by the smell. Apparently Father's skill summoned filolial feathers.

As I wondered about the glory of Father's majesty and the like, I, Motoyasu Kitamura, knew I had to act as well.

"Windmill!" I called, spinning my spear and striking nearly all the bullets out of the air.

Takt seemed pretty surprised by it. He raised his voice and shouted angrily.

"Impossible! Deflecting bullets shot by soldiers all level 250 or higher? It's not possible!"

I noticed a suspicious light glittering from Takt's hand. He was about to unleash a skill.

"Wahnsinn Claw!" he roared. The trajectory of his attack . . . Something about that skill gave me a very bad feeling. All of a sudden, I fell into a memory.

One of the four benevolent animals spinning through clear skies, a bird . . . the powerful glimmer of light that toppled one of the Phoenixes. Afterward, the remaining Phoenix had launched a self-destruct attack. Even Father hadn't been able to withstand an attack that powerful.

I lost priceless filolials in that explosion. Renji, Grape, Hailo . . . So many had lost their lives that day. Father had taken the man responsible and showed him hell, calming my anger. That man was none other than Takt.

At the time, my spear filled with fury. I went so far as to activate the Spear of Wrath, but Filo-tan managed to hold me back. When I witnessed the sight of my precious Filo-tan filled with sadness for her fallen friends, when I saw the sight of Father mourning the loss of his comrades, I, Motoyasu Kitamura, became enveloped by a fire of rage that consumed every inch of my flesh.

I remembered how Father had risked his life to save us. But it had been a pig that put her life on the line to protect Father. In the end, she was the one that saved me, Filo-tan, and the rest of the filolials, so I had the utmost reverence for her.

I had to become strong like they had been on that fateful day. At last, I remembered everything.

Takt

Seven Star Hero, Whip Hero

Born into a Faubrey noble family loosely related to the royal family, Takt is one of the rare geniuses occasionally born into this world. He has a beautiful face, but he tends to look down on others and hide his true intentions.

He obtained his legendary weapons by killing the other seven star heroes.

THE STORY OF THE BATTLE AGAINST TAKT

n Faubrey, Naofumi and his friends faced Takt, **who was the reason that Atla died in the Phoenix war**. Naofumi, in a state of rage, attempted to battle Takt, but Takt stole his shield. Due to a **grave wound** at the hands of Takt, Naofumi fell unconscious. He woke up in a strange place. There he saw Atla and Ost, who both had already died. They told him that this was the world of the shield spirit. The holy-weapon spirits there told Naofumi they could send him back to the world he was born into. But Naofumi chose instead to continue to fight in the world to which he had been summoned. In exchange for having his shield stolen, Naofumi was allowed to temporarily borrow the **power of all the other legendary weapons**.

When he woke up again, Naofumi prepared for the battle against Takt and stormed back for round two. With the legendary powers of his friends, he had an **overwhelming advantage** over Takt. Naofumi defeated Takt and avenged his fallen friends.

Chapter Seven: Half-Burnt Charcoal

"You—you—!" I gasped.

Like the final piece of a puzzle, my memories all fell into place. He killed the filolials. He injured Father. The man behind it all was standing in front of my very eyes, trying to hurt Father and my friends again.

I, Motoyasu Kitamura, had to act at once.

I matched the direction of my spear with the burst of light from Wahnsinn Claw and redirected it to strike down one of the pigs. It oinked in horror and blood spurted everywhere. Then I carved a hole in the airship floor.

"W-Wahnsinn Claw . . . blocked? M-my weapon, defeated . . . ?"

The pigs, shivering in terror, looked to Takt, who was staring blankly downward.

"I have no idea what you want to achieve here, but if you're trying to betray us—" Father seemed to be talking about something with Takt. But there was no point in even exchanging words with scum like him.

"What exactly was the fox beast pig, hmm?" I interjected loudly. "Even being your ally was enough reason to take its life! But that was its punishment for daring to impersonate a hero!"

"You bastard!" Takt roared. He raised a claw and started to charge at me.

"Motoyasu! Stop!"

"This fiend, this villain—we can't let him live!" I said. After the crimson swine, Takt was the second-most evil creature alive! He had to be punished for his deeds, even if no one could remember them. I felt blood rush to my head.

Father's screams, Filo-tan's sorrow, the corpses of my precious filolials . . . This man standing before me now was the cause of it all.

"Calm down!" Father was yelling at me. "You're facing the seven star hero! If you make the wrong move—"

I knew I shouldn't ignore Father's orders, but this time my anger overpowered his calls for restraint.

"I will end your life no matter what!"

"Motoyasu!"

I broke free from Father's restraint. I raised Brionac to its maximum power and aimed it at Takt. I launched all of my strength at him, full throttle.

A pig in a maid outfit let out a high-pitched squeal and rushed between me and Takt.

"Briiiiooooonac X!"

The high-powered beam of light unleashed from my spear pierced clean through the pig's body and Takt screamed in agony.

I turned him to half-burnt charcoal, I say. You couldn't stop Brionac with a pig like that.

Wind rushed through the hole in the observation deck with a hiss.

I suddenly realized that even though I had killed one of the heroes, the time loop hadn't reset. It seemed like the only conditions for the loop were the lives of Father, Ren, Itsuki, and me.

Which means that it was no problem at all for me to kill villains like Takt.

I almost started to laugh. This time, yes, this time I would send them all to the grave! This time, I would kill all of the enemies of Filo-tan and Father!

"Pigs!" I bellowed. "Your deeds are unforgivable! I'll make you regret having been born into this very world!"

The pigs started squealing frantically. They really needed to calm down. I was going to treat them all the same—and send them to the afterlife to meet their precious Takt.

"Oh, Takt!"

"Takt! Where did Takt go!?"

Two pigs started to show their true forms. One transformed into a dragon and another into a griffin.

"Spear Hero, you've killed Takt and even our father! I'll kill you!"

Even in such a small room, the griffin started to charge at me.

"Your father? I have no idea what you're talking about," I said. "But now that you mention it, I did kill a big griffin in the mountains. His drop items were superior."

"Die!" she shrieked.

What a bunch of grumpy griffins, grumbling on and on about things I knew nothing about. How childlike. But as Takt's subordinates, they were complicit in his crimes, so their lives belong to me, I say!

"Air Strike Javelin X!"

Brionac was in cooldown mode, so I had to use a different skill. The chaos on the deck was getting a bit out of hand, so I had to use Aiming Lancer to make sure I didn't accidentally hit any of the filolials. Eventually I decided to just aim directly at the griffin.

But weak attacks weren't nearly enough to clear up my pent-up rage.

The griffin howled madly as I blasted off her head.

"That's it!" I declared. "I remember that the great filolial Fitoria-tan mentioned how much she wanted to kill you griffins. You all ought to know that the world would be better off without you!"

According to one tale, griffins were the ones who exterminated flying filolials. That was enough reason for me to punish them ten thousand times! Every time I saw a griffin, it was my duty to exterminate it. They might even be worse than the dragons.

Meanwhile, the dragon roared. "This machine just gets in the way!" it shouted. "Enemy of Takt, prepare to die!" I heard crackling bones as the dragon expanded to a monstrous size and, tearing through the airship with its claws, started to breathe fire.

So Takt was hiding a beast like that after all! I was itching to fight it. There was no reason dragons should even be allowed to live in the first place, but the fact that this dragon was Takt's colleague made it even more abominable. Merely killing this dragon would be far from satisfactory!

"Everyone, get out of here!" Werwer cried to the Siltvelt leaders, who started to escape from the hole I had carved in the airship floor.

I heard more ear-piercing squeals.

"Die! I say!"

I chased around after Takt's pigs that were trying to escape and stabbed them all. The airship was falling apart thanks to the dragon's fire, and the whole surrounding area had turned into an ocean of flames. I continued to use Aiming Lancer to target Takt's pigs, but there were so many of them, and Aiming Lancer was too weak to get all of them at once. So even though it was easy to target them, I wasn't killing nearly as many as I would've liked. I was starting to get frustrated.

"Motoyasu! Motoyasu!"

I turned to Father, who had been calling my name.

"What the hell is happening?" Father asked. "This is a disaster—you killed Takt. Well, maybe you needed to kill Takt . . . but to kill people who are begging for their lives . . . What are you doing!?"

"I remember everything!" I proclaimed. "He—Takt—he's not just the Whip Hero. He's gathering the weapons of all the other heroes by killing them all! He's on his way to becoming your mortal enemy, Father!"

"That's exactly . . . Why . . . Motoyasu, dammit, just look around!"

Only because Father told me to, I looked around.

Fires raged everywhere, in the airship, in the field, and fires had even spread to the forest surrounding the castle. A group of Siltveltians were desperately trying to put out the flames, but the massive dragon had started to attack them as well and cause a panic.

"The dragon's attacking!" they cried.

"Get it! Get it!"

"Everyone, save the castle!"

The filolials were just barely managing to protect the castle from the dragon. But the damage could start to drastically increase at any moment.

That meant I had to kill all of Takt's pigs as fast as humanly possible!

"Stop—stop it, Motoyasu!" Father grabbed me. "If you

don't stop, the people you want to protect are going to die!"

Father was grabbing me from behind amidst the flames, I say.

"This is horrible," Father said, turning me to face him. "I understand that you remembered something horrible. That's why I want you to calm down—because if you don't, something even worse than what happened in your memories could happen today!"

"Father . . ." I whispered.

"Motoyasu—you saved my life. I want to be able to help you in return. So please, please, stop."

In the raging cascade of fire, I lowered my spear.

"Thanks to Takt, you shed so many tears, Father," I whispered. "Countless filolials died."

"I get it," Father said. "I get it. And it looks like Takt was the one who killed the Claw Hero and sent the fox beast as well."

Near the castle, Yuki continued to direct the filolials in battle against the dragon.

"Okay," Father said. "Did you calm down?"

"Cool as a cucumber," I said. "It looks like that even though I killed Takt, the time loop didn't reset."

"That's true. That could be good for us. But for now, let's stop the damage from getting worse—we need to finish them off. The wave of destruction is almost here too."

"Whatever you say!" I declared.

Just like Father told me to, I rushed to fight the dragon in a boiling whirlpool of rage.

"Brionac X!"

I aimed for its head and unleashed the skill with all of my might. I heard its furious roar ring out.

But because I was too far away, the dragon managed to dodge the straight-line attack. Curse you! If it could dodge Brionac, then I had to go for a different high-level attack. A certain high-level Aiming Lancer skill, named after the Norse god renowned for its power and accuracy. My spear glittered darkly as it homed in on its target.

I shouted, "Gungnir X!"

I hurled my spear in a black curve and an enormous ray of light blasted right into the dragon's eye.

The dragon bellowed. Gungnir had struck the monstrous beast right between the eyes. After a moment, a high-pitch sound rang out—and then the dragon's head exploded.

With a tremendous thud, the dragon landed dead across the castle gardens.

"You did it! You did it, Motoyasu!" cried Father.

"Of course I did it! Now I just have to kill the rest of Takt's pigs!"

"Wait, wait! They already ran away, and, Motoyasu, we have to prepare for the wave of destruction!"

I took a glance at the clock in my field of vision. We had exactly ten minutes until the wave of destruction hit.

"Well, since we still have a whole ten minutes, should I take care of the pigs until then?"

"No, Motoyasu, no!" yelled Father. "What do you have against those poor women?"

Oho? I stared at Father in shock. I supposed he was right. I shouldn't discriminate against pigs. If I chased after them now, I might end up killing plenty of Siltveltian pigs, too, since I had no idea which pigs were Takt's and which weren't.

"Let's hurry up and do whatever preparation we can," Father said. "If we don't, it could get rough."

"Terribly rough!" I agreed.

The shusaku representative flew down in front of the dragon's corpse, changed from therianthrope to demi-human, and bowed his head to Father.

"What's wrong?" Father asked. "We only have a few minutes left to prepare for the wave of destruction."

"Shield Hero," Werwer began, "I regret to announce that the Melromarc army has invaded Siltvelt!"

Father looked dumbfounded. "Excuse me?"

It seemed as if Melromarc decided to use the chaos to invade. This situation had become quite the emergency, if I must say so myself.

"N-now, of all times?" Father's face had turned pale. "What's happening?"

"At this very moment, we received an official declaration of war from Melromarc! Their army is advancing rapidly. The troops number—"

He said the number. Now *that* was a lot of troops. But I seem to remember the Melromarc army being bigger than that. While I didn't remember the exact number when we fought in the first go-around, I think the Melromarc army had been even larger then.

"How long will it take them to reach the castle?" Father asked.

"It will take at the earliest three days for them to be in the range for a battle," Werwer said.

"Got it. So before that, we need to take care of the wave of destruction—it's just a few minutes away. Once we get that under control, I want to immediately begin preparations for war. The only issue is . . ." Father trailed off, but Werwer looked like he understood what Father meant.

"Of course," Werwer said. "We won't use you or the Spear Hero for our wars."

Father had mentioned he had been concerned about getting involved in unnecessary wars, and Éclair and the old genmu had agreed and decided that we wouldn't deploy in the case of war. But the problem isn't just limited to the battlefield—there are still people out there who might try to hurt Father. And I, Motoyasu Kitamura, will stop them.

It was hard to believe that Melromarc had decided to invade now. It seemed probable that they were cooperating with Takt. But no matter what enemies appeared, I'd blow them out of the water, I say!

"Just one thing—" Father began.

"You're going to say that the only circumstance in which you'll fight is if our enemies send a hero, correct?" Werwer asked. "We understand. After we've conducted an examination of the situation, we'll report to you."

"If you violate this agreement, I'll have no choice but to leave the country," Motoyasu said. "My job here is to save the world by fighting the waves of destruction, not to get involved in wars."

"Noted," Werwer said. "As long as King Aultcray the Staff Hero doesn't attack us directly, we won't call on you."

Werwer, of course, was responding with concern to Father. But he seemed to be ignoring me. Werwer thoroughly misunderstood the magnitude of my power!

"So, Motoyasu," Father said, "let's get the filolials and fight the wave of destruction!"

"Fight we shall!"

"If Melromarc ends up moving alongside the remnants of Takt's forces . . ." Father trailed off. "I just get a really bad feeling about all this."

"As you say, Father."

I saw the countdown to the wave approaching zero. I guessed there'd be no lunch break today. First, we got tricked by that villainous Whip Hero. Now we had to deal with the wave of destruction . . . There was no doubt that Melromarc was using this as the perfect time to invade Siltvelt. If the battle with Takt had dragged out, the wave would've struck and we'd have been flung to it during our fight. I bet they had intended to kill us that way. I do remember griffins and dragons giving us serious troubles in the last go-around.

But compared to back then, now I had infinite power, I say! I killed them all instantly!

The world became quiet.

"All right, Motoyasu, it's up to you," Father told me. "I'm going to do my best to minimize the damage on the area."

"You can leave it to me! It's still one of the early waves of destruction, after all. I don't think it will be particularly dangerous."

"Just be careful," Father said.

The magnificent wisdom of Father! He always made sure to look before he leapt.

The clock in my field of vision hit zero. The Siltvelt wave of destruction was on the way.

"Here we go . . ."

We were flung to the source of the wave. Surveying Siltvelt from our position, I saw that we were in what looked like the mountains. The boss was an enormous, bald-headed humanoid giant, like a Daidarabochi of legend. A huge shadow from the mountains started storming toward us. Just based on appearance alone, intuition told me that it wasn't particularly strong, maybe about level 35. Piece of cake.

But since Father told me to, I'd be careful.

"Yuki! Filolials!" I called.

"Got it!" Yuki announced. "Everyone, simultaneous attack!"

The filolials chirped and cawed, rushing in a unified strike toward the enemy. Siltvelt demi-human soldiers also hurried out to meet the wave of monsters spilling out from the mountains. The Daidarabochi boss was surrounded by lots of Japanese-style demons and monsters.

Since there were a number of nearby towns at risk, Father rode Sakura out to evacuate the villagers. But the Siltvelt demi-human villagers wanted to fight for themselves and looked like they were going to join the battle too.

Anyways, I figured it was about time for me to cut through the monsters' vanguard.

"Aiming Lancer X!"

I locked onto the monsters and launched the attack. Instantly monsters scattered everywhere as I carved a fissure through the earth that sunk the boss along with the rest of the monsters. It worked pretty well, if I had to say so myself.

But still, I had to be careful. Even when you think you've defeated them all, there could be remnants. I waited, but nothing came out of the fissure.

Even though I had put so much effort into being careful, I guess this time it ended without an issue.

"All right!" Father called, riding back toward me on Sakura. "Now let's prepare for the war with Melromarc! Get back to the castle!"

"Yes, sir!"

Siltvelt soldiers shouted in unison, bowed, and went off to prepare for the upcoming battles. It looked like there were very few injured soldiers and that we had minimized the damage. It was all over almost too easily, but I figured there was still plenty of fighting to come.

The shusaku representative came back toward Father and me just outside the castle.

"So? What's the status of the Melromarc forces?" Father asked.

"Suddenly the forces started to retreat, withdrawing from the front," Werwer said. "We're in the middle of deciding whether or not to pursue them."

Father and I went back inside the castle and joined the meeting with the other Siltvelt leaders.

"Deserting in the face of the enemy, huh?" Father asked.

"We suspect that Melromarc thought we'd be distracted by

the wave of destruction and Takt," Werwer said.

Naturally. We couldn't throw out that possibility. It was still suspicious behavior, even if the wave monsters had ended up being fewer in number than the attacking Melromarc army.

"It's that Wisest King of Wisdom. What could he possibly be up to?" one of the leaders asked.

The Wisest King of Wisdom? Oh, that was one name for Trash. But do we really need to worry about someone as powerless as him?

"Motoyasu, you said Ren—you said the Sword Hero—went to a different country, right?" Father asked.

"That's what I've been informed," I told Father.

"So Itsuki—the Bow Hero—must be with the Melromarc army?"

"Thankfully not," Werwer said. "We've received a message that he is not with them."

So Itsuki isn't with the army? I didn't know if I believed that. Something was fishy. But I also figured I didn't really know Itsuki anyways. We didn't talk much in the first go-around. In fact, I hadn't bothered to get to know him in the first place.

Suddenly I remembered something. That pig—there was this pig with an unhealthy romantic obsession that was unjustly discharged for acting improperly and Father was really angry. And then . . . what was it? I remember that Father and the pig went somewhere after that. Where had they gone?

"Where is Itsuki, then?" Father asked.

"Our spies have reported that he's still in Melromarc, carrying out his own activities," Werwer said.

"So we won't need to face him in battle," Father said.

"Yes, but something suspicious may be going on," Werwer stated and stared at the map marked with small pieces for the locations of the troops, lost in thought.

"Okay, so there's the potential war with Melromarc, but how's the damage to the castle from the wave of destruction?" Father asked.

"Due to flames from the airship battle, the surrounding forests caught on fire, but we managed to put them out without too much damage. But there were many casualties—almost all of them subordinates of the Whip Hero."

"Really . . ." Father frowned.

"There were many who were shot in the chaos, as well as victims of the Whip Hero's dragon. However, thanks to the valiant efforts of the Spear Hero, many were saved."

"Motoyasu really saved the day, didn't he?" Father said.

"I say!" I declared, overwhelmed with emotion. But deep down, I, Motoyasu Kitamura, had let Father down. Next time would be different, I swore to myself.

I had let far too many pigs survive. Next time I'd kill every last one of them!

"We're making fixing up the castle the first priority,"

Werwer continued, "as well as preparing our defenses for the next invasion." Werwer was standing tall and proud, almost seeming excited.

"I mentioned it before, but just remember that we won't be getting involved in matters that don't involve the heroes," Father said.

"Oh, we understand!" Werwer said. "Okay, everyone!" He called out to the other Siltvelt leaders. "As the Shield Hero says—we'll never let ourselves be defeated! Remember your strength!"

"Aye!" the crowd called.

I, too, had to do as much as I possibly could to help Father. I couldn't be picky about our methods here.

"Father," I called to him.

"What's up?"

"It's about the dragon corpse," I said. "I hate to suggest doing anything with the likes of a dragon, but with a dragon core you can undergo a ceremony that enables power-ups beyond level 100."

"No kidding? Well, I don't think we have the time to do much with it right away, but let's definitely collect it."

"Understood, Father!"

THE LOVE HUNTER OUTFIT

Hair ornament:
In the first go-around, Motoyasu artfully wore a few of Filo-tan's feathers in his hair. He doesn't have the same colored feathers this time, so he took different filolial feathers and dyed them to be more or less the color of Filo.

That way, I'm always with my precious Filo-tan!

Hooded cloak:
Motoyasu can stuff plenty of filolial feathers into his wide hood, keeping him warm and the hood fluffy. His cloak smells vaguely of filolials.

Motoyasu remade the hood he had in the first go-around. The pattern of Filo's feathers (a queen filolial) is embroidered on the breast of his tunic. He designed the strap across his chest to remind him of Filo's ribbon.

It's proof of the Love Hunter's boundless fidelity!

Sleeveless shirt:
A sleeveless shirt makes it easier for Motoyasu to wield his spear. But even better, when he's riding a filolial, he can also feel their feathers on his arms.

Waist ornament:
A balanced arrangement of colorful filolial feathers. After all, heroes have to show off their style. Incidentally, it's a feather arrangement often used by filolial hunters, but in Motoyasu's case, he gathered feathers that were naturally shed. It doesn't really fit his persona, but he wears it anyways.

Boots:
To help Motoyasu move nimbly, his boots are always firmly buckled on. They are also designed to make it easier for him to ride filolials.

Soft but sturdy and oh-so-warm, these feathers give me courage and strength!

Chapter Eight: Remnants

We spent three days in a state of vigilance. We didn't receive any word from the Melromarc army, and all we could do was wait for Siltvelt scouts to spot their troops. Taking a long glance up at the sky, Father muttered that, of course, if there ended up not being a war at all, that would be better. But still, everyone in Siltvelt was sitting on pins waiting.

In the meantime, Siltvelt communicated to Faubrey that the Whip Hero had been cooperating with the fox beast that impersonated the Claw Hero and that Takt had tried to kill us as payback for defending ourselves against that monster. But that seemed to just put an even further strain on Siltvelt's international relations.

Around noon of that third day, a messenger burst into the throne room with a bang.

"Shieldfreeden has officially declared war on Siltvelt!" the messenger shouted.

"We can't even figure out what's happening with the Melromarc invasion," Father exclaimed, "and now Shieldfreeden is invading?"

"Yes, sir! The Shieldfreeden representative Nelshen gave us a statement that declares that even though the Whip Hero came to Siltvelt with the virtuous intentions of helping fight the wave of destruction, we ensnared him in a trap to kill him!"

The reporting soldier showed us a crystal that projected a picture.

The image of a pig, badly beaten up, let out a series of hideous squeals. Utterly unable to understand, I leaned over to Father, who interpreted for me.

"'The Shield and Spear Hero have betrayed our virtuous intentions. They trapped our sacred Whip Hero Takt, Hammer Hero, and dragon goddess and sent them to violent deaths. They killed their own nation's Claw Hero and our Whip Hero Takt—we won't let this stand! We will fight for justice! We won't allow those perpetrators of evil to live in this world unpunished! We will exterminate the root of evil from Siltvelt! We will have our revenge!' Wow, talk about angry!"

Father had an ugly expression on his face. I, too, was enraged. Of course, I regretted killing as many people as I did that day. For that, I murmured a humble apology.

"They were the ones who launched a preemptive strike!" Father said. "And they're declaring war on us for the sake of so-called revenge? After they plotted to kill both the Claw Hero and the Whip Hero, now they're accusing *us* of killing them!"

"Shieldfreeden has notified all the countries of the world about this matter," Werwer said. "We've submitted a response denying their claims, but I don't think a militaristic country like Shieldfreeden will let go of a motive for war." Werwer frowned. "Truly, this must be the workings of the Wisest King of Wisdom!"

A grim atmosphere fell among the Siltvelt leaders in the throne room.

"So it's a combined invasion by Melromarc and Shield-freeden," Father said. "But Takt's surprise attack already failed, right? There's no way they could've thought a reckless attack like that would actually work."

"It is the Wisest King of Wisdom who tries to make the impossible a reality," Werwer said. "So now we are being put to the test by his schemes. I would've never imagined that the Church of the Three Heroes would join hands with Shield-freeden, of all countries."

"Exactly!" Father said. "I thought maybe I was overthinking it, but—"

Another messenger flung open the doors and cried out, "Shieldfreeden has already launched its airships and is currently on the way to Siltvelt!"

"They're attacking by airship?" Father asked. "They must be planning to drop bombs, then."

The room collectively gasped and many of the Siltvelt leaders' faces went sheet white.

Eventually another messenger came and informed us that the airships weren't coming to the Siltvelt castle but instead planned to drop bombs on the neighboring villages.

"The remnants of the Whip Hero's forces are launching acts of terrorism!" a leader cried.

Father stood up, unable to contain his anger. "That could kill countless innocent people!" he shouted. "Whether this has anything to do with the heroes or not, we have to do something!"

The Siltvelt leaders began to bow down and pray to Father.

"Oh, mighty Shield Hero, please calm your anger! Let us use the might of our country to defeat our enemies!"

"Lately I've been the one telling people to calm down, but this is horrific!"

Up until now, Father had been trying to avoid war at all costs. But now he pledged to protect the people of Siltvelt. Father's heart overflowed with loving kindness, I say.

So Father wanted to help Siltvelt, but we had to come up with some sort of plan.

"Father, I have a suggestion," I informed him.

"What is it?"

"Takt's remnants are after us. Since their objective is revenge against us, I suggest we launch an invasion led by the heroes."

Father nodded. "Since their cause revolves around defeating me and Motoyasu, we'll fight against both Shieldfreeden and Melromarc!"

The Siltvelt leaders started praying again. "We praise the eternal mercy and compassion of the Shield Hero!"

"I'll do everything I can to protect Siltvelt!"

So with that, Father and I went out to face Takt's remnants. My spear was aching to kill a few more pigs.

As was my heart.

We set out with Yuki and the filolials for the Siltvelt towns under attack. Just as we were walking down to what looked like a peaceful street, a group of Takt's remnants rushed out and surrounded us.

That was surprisingly easy. So easy it was a bit of a letdown.

"Motoyasu, do you really think you're strong enough to beat everyone on your own?" Father asked.

"Well, pigs are generally powerless," I informed Father.

"What? I thought maybe you'd say it was easier to take down enemies driven by revenge since they're not as inclined to cooperate or something, but if that's what it is, then go for it."

There were pigs firing their rifles at us from afar, pigs stabbing their swords at us from close range, and pigs casting magic spells at us too. I killed all of those would-be avengers, I say!

"The messengers claim that in west Siltvelt, a Shieldfreeden leader is planning to give a formal address about the war," Father said.

"That means more pigs are probably on the way," I said.

"Yeah, probably," Father agreed. "Takt really had quite the army."

"And they're all pigs!"

We were riding the filolials as we continued to discuss our next steps.

"He basically had a harem. Women are scary." Father sighed. "I suppose you're glad we get to keep fighting, but I wish they had thought more about their crazy strategy."

"Their own foul plot backfired, so they're dressing their deeds up with the name of revenge," I declared.

"I understand how they feel about Takt's death," Father said. "But it's one thing to be upset and another thing to bomb another country. Motoyasu, you mentioned that in the future, Takt was the main ringleader who tried to kill all the heroes, right? But in this world, that's like the cardinal sin. We can't afford to stand by and let it happen."

Yes, he was right. It was the duty of the heroes to save the world from the waves of destruction. To try to kill those heroes—and then pretend like it never happened—was a betrayal to the entire world. It was an act of barbarity that sacrificed innocent lives! Only pigs would be stupid enough to blindly believe and tolerate such horrible crimes simply because they like the perpetrator.

I barely managed to hold in my vomit.

"So it looks like we were able to reduce the number of remnants, but they weren't the brightest bunch," Father said.

"Next up, we need to take care of the scheming pigs and their twisted, underhanded affairs," I proclaimed.

Father glanced at me. "I guess so. But it seems like most of the other remnants fled back to Siltvelt, so it could be tricky. Maybe a diversion . . . We also know there are remnants prepared to commit acts of terrorism in Siltvelt. Did we have trouble taking care of Takt's remnants in the previous timeline?"

"I don't think so," I said.

"Really? Even though he has so many soldiers?"

Father had that ugly look on his face again. I tried to remember how Father had dealt with all of Takt's soldiers. I, Motoyasu Kitamura, was utterly clueless when it came to Father's grand tactics.

But I did have a memory of one of Takt's pigs getting executed.

"In the last go-around," I told Father, "you captured Takt alive, stripped him of the power to use the seven star weapons, and had him publicly executed, I say!"

"Public execution?" Father gasped. His face was contorted into shock, like he couldn't believe the kind of person he used to be.

I could keep talking about the deeds of Father forever. Hmm, yes. What exactly did happen?

"Yes," I continued, "so you took all the remnants and publicly executed them before Takt's very eyes!"

"Execution right in front of him? Did . . . Did I kill them myself?"

"I don't know about that," I said. "But I do remember that you looked pretty bored after the public execution was over."

"What do you mean?" Father asked. "Was it boring for me to watch all the executions? Or was I trying to show off how bored I was to make a point?"

"I have no idea," I said.

Truly, I had no idea. I also got the sense that it had been hard work for him though.

"The public execution of all those women before Takt's very eyes . . ." Father closed his eyes. "What a cruel punishment."

Father let out another sigh of boredom, I say.

Still, a leader can win over people's hearts with that sort of cruelty. It's a move that ensures that even your enemies won't oppose you!

"When you prepared the public execution, you stated the charges, if I remember correctly," I said. "You said something like, 'It is a grievous sin to try to make the world your own. For deceiving the heroes, I appoint to you a fate worse than death!'"

"I can kinda see what I did there," Father said. "I probably did it to make sure that someone was punished for starting a war and to allow the people to vent their anger. I've heard that execution was often used to appease the public."

What a just reason!

"Okay, so getting back on topic, do you remember how we rounded up Takt's remaining soldiers?"

"I had left the battle against Takt to you, so I didn't see any of it," I said.

"Gotcha. Well, did you hear about it? Anything would be helpful."

I focused, trying to unravel my memories.

Hmmmmm.

"That's it!" I proclaimed. "You rounded up the pigs that were with Takt, and then for those elsewhere, you used a fake message from Takt to gather them together!"

"A fake message? Of course! In the last go-around, Takt was trying to take over the world, right? If we announced that he had won, all his supporters would come, and we could round them up that way. That sort of thing."

"I don't know the details," I told Father. I was just a helpful hand, assisting with the essential task of pig-hunting. I didn't know the strategy.

Father frowned. "I don't think that's an option for us anymore, since so many of the remnants have already fled all over the place. That means we have no choice but to defeat the remnants a few at a time and slowly convince them to abandon hope of revenge."

That sounded annoying. With remnant soldiers all over the place, now I understood how effective Father's public executions had been at ending things quickly.

But I got the sense that that wasn't the least of it. Father had said something . . . something about Takt's head exploding. Something vaguely floated in the back of my mind. What had happened?

"So in the end, we have no choice but to win the war and prove our innocence," Father said. "The world doesn't know what Takt did to us."

"Father, if you command it, I, Motoyasu Kitamura, will chase Takt's pigs to the ends of the earth if need be!"

"I appreciate the offer, but we don't want to cause too much of a fuss," Father said. "Although the other heroes may end up having to join the war between Shieldfreeden and Siltvelt, I suppose."

Father fell into deep thought and looked up at me.

"Motoyasu."

"What is it, Father?"

"If the time loop were to end up happening again, please do everything you can to avoid this kind of situation. Remember everything."

"Remember I shall," I declared.

"Again, this is in a worst-case scenario when the time loop resets, but please use all your memories and knowledge to try to avoid war. Help the future me avoid war as much as you possibly can." Father looked straight into my eyes and then lowered his head.

I pledged to remember.

I, Motoyasu Kitamura, would prevent war at all costs in the case of a time loop reset. I would fulfill Father's wishes, I say!

I couldn't even imagine how Father managed to avoid war in the first go-around. I figured I'd just start thinking about it, at least.

"I shall carve your words in my heart, Father," I declared.

"Please do," Father said.

As we talked, we continued on our journey to expose and destroy Takt's remnants. A few pigs popped out while we were discussing Takt, and after we finished them off, we headed back to Siltvelt castle.

We went inside and Father called out to the shusaku representative.

"Hey, we're back. What's the status of the Shieldfreeden invasion?"

"At present, the Shieldfreeden army is advancing from the south. They're launching gunfire and bombs from their airplanes. The damage is accumulating fast."

"In this world, you can use guns depending on your level, right? So the soldiers firing at us from the airplanes must be pretty high level?"

"We believe so."

"Just based on what Motoyasu told me, I'm not sure how we can stop those airships. It sounds like previously we could only stop them thanks to the ingenuity of the Melromarc king."

"It would be a simple matter for the Wisest King of Wisdom to stop the airships," Werwer said. "But alas, the Wisest King of Wisdom is our enemy."

"That's true, but maybe we can figure out how to do what he did," Father suggested. "By the way, did you find the locations of the holy claw and whip weapons?"

When I had defeated Takt, Brionac's beam of light had apparently blown his weapons quite a ways away. According to those watching the airship from below, an orb of light fell out of the sky after the blast of my Brionac.

I remembered that glorious blast of light! But I certainly had no idea where the weapons ended up falling.

"We determined the location," Werwer said. "The weapons have been enshrined in consecrated grounds."

"Consecrated grounds?"

"A deep forest close to our castle. The seven star weapons are kept there."

"So neutral ground," Father said. "Now that there are three of the seven star weapons there, be sure to announce that you don't intend to keep them there forever."

"Yes, we have already done so," Werwer said. "We have announced that we have enshrined three of the seven star weapons in our sacred precincts."

Siltvelt had done well. According to what Siltvelt told us, the four holy heroes were summoned before the claw hero and hammer hero went missing, so Takt must have killed them in the few days that passed since our arrival.

"Faubrey has plans to also dispatch an official investigation of our country," Werwer said.

"It seems unlikely that we'd be able to trust their investigation," Father said.

"To say the least," Werwer agreed. "We believe that Faubrey was also operating under Takt's orders. Even if they claim to be impartial, we can't ignore the fact that Takt's remnants may be pulling the strings."

"So we're pretty much cornered," Father said. "We have no choice but to hope that someone in Faubrey's group will be willing to listen to reason."

"Yes. Because of Takt's attempts to control Faubrey, we believe that their country has also been enveloped in confusion."

"So either way, we have to settle this," Father said. "Let's do our best to prove Siltvelt's innocence!"

"Yes, Lord Shield Hero! I am terribly sorry that we could not fulfill your request to avoid getting you involved," Werwer said.

"Don't worry about it. That's water under the bridge."

"We are thankful for the Shield Hero's mercy," Werwer said.

Father looked like he didn't know how to respond as Werwer gave a deep bow. Since coming here, Father was often muttering to himself, I say.

"This war might have only happened because I came here in the first place," Father said. "Of course, Takt was evil, but if we don't handle this carefully, the situation could get even worse."

I vowed to remember Father's words. Certainly, Takt himself was evil, but all of this only happened because I killed him so easily. If the time loop were to reset again, I would have to think twice before killing him.

"So what we really need to take care of are the Shieldfreeden airships," Father said. He fell into deep thought as we went to the Siltvelt military's headquarters and started to examine the map there.

Looking at the map of the battlefield, Father explained his strategy.

"It might be difficult, but our best option would be to use therianthropes that can fly to fight off the airships," Father said. He glanced over at me. "Like a dragon."

No.

On our journey so far, Father had let me, Yuki, and the filolials lead the way and become courageous members of our army. I was grateful to him for that.

But upon hearing his plan, I couldn't contain my anger.

"Never!" I screamed. "I won't do it!"

The very notion of Father's strategy caused hives to instantly erupt all over my body.

"Motoyasu, please. This is the best choice we have."

"Never!"

I stroked Yuki's feathers to escape cruel reality.

"Ah, Motoyasu, don't stop!" Yuki chirped.

"What about me?" Kou shouted. "Pet me too!"

Yuki took a step forward. "I'll get everyone together, and using our magic, we'll take out those airplanes!" she declared.

"I thought about that," Father said, "but the airplanes are so high up that I don't know if your magic will reach them or not. So we need a method that is guaranteed to work. Motoyasu, that's why I need you to cooperate."

"But—"

"I'm sorry, Yuki, Kou. I hope you can understand. If we can just minimize the damage one way or another . . . Motoyasu, you have no choice."

My head was pounding and my skin crawling. Father was even trying to convince Yuki to do it! I respected and loved Father with all my heart, and I always did my best to follow his every command . . . but just this time I had to make an exception. When I even thought about following his orders, I feared I would break out in hives for days on end.

And yet we had no other option. I had to do it.

"Fine . . ." I muttered. "Fine. Father's orders . . . are absolute."

"We'll be careful, Motoyasu. I promise!" Yuki said.

"I'll do it for Father," I whispered in agony. "I, Motoyasu Kitamura, will succeed at all costs. For Father," I groaned.

"It's not like it's easy for me either," Father said. "I would want to just do it myself, but unfortunately I can't launch an attack by myself. You can hate me if you want."

I could feel Father's anguish. Very well, I thought. I'd do it for Father. No matter how much I suffered, I would bear any burden.

"Let's start the mission," Father said.

"Yes, Father!" I cried.

I bowed deeply to Father and we went to prepare. I could hear the distant roar of airplanes and the echo of explosions. Even from the castle you could see them circling nearby towns and dropping bombs.

It was time to take out the planes.

Chapter Nine: Lingering Fragrance

"Nice to meet you," Father said.

The horrible creature hissed and growled. Father was greeting the dispatched creature—a gruesome, filthy, evil dragon.

The surrounding soldiers bowed and Father grabbed the creature by the reins and leapt onto it. The dragon growled at the filolials and me.

"Hey, Motoyasu, your turn," Father called.

"I know, Father."

My whole body shivering uncontrollably, I took a tentative step forward. I reached out and took Father's hand, and he helped pull me onto the horrible beast. It let out another fierce growl.

"Everyone stay calm," Father said.

The awful creature writhed unpleasantly, but the soldiers were able to calm it down.

"Sakura, you filolials don't get along with dragons, so you can't ride one, right?" Father asked.

"Buuuuut!" Sakura looked at Father. "But I want to protect you, Naofumi!"

"Come up here, then," Father said. "You can protect us!"

"Got it!" Sakura chirped. "I'll protect everyone!" Father's

words seemed to energize Sakura, and she got on the dragon too.

"Let's protect Motoyasu with ritual magic from below," Yuki called out to the other filolials. "Now then, everyone, let's get ready!"

The filolials all cheered and chirped.

As I looked back at the crowd of filolials, the dragon flapped its wings and took to the skies. My thigh started to itch where it was touching the dragon. I had to get off this thing before my whole body broke out in hives from head to toe. I wouldn't be able to think straight from all the itching.

As expected, the dragon didn't fly particularly fast, which takes away the whole advantage of flying in the first place!

How could I possibly survive so much time on a dragon? By resolving to do it for Filo-tan, I say!

I noticed the father of the Filo-tan I loved so much was right in front of me. So I hugged him tightly from behind.

It distracted me from the itching a little bit.

"Uh, Motoyasu?" Father said. "Where are you putting your hands?"

Embracing Father strengthened my very soul!

"Don't smell my neck! What are you doing!?"

"Filo-tan . . ."

I quivered in sweet, sweet agony. I had caught a whiff of the lingering fragrance of Filo-tan on Father's neck.

Filo-tan?

Filo-tan.

"Ew, ew! Stop sniffing my neck, Motoyasu! Stop it! I'm begging you, please act normal!"

Filo-tan.

Filo-tan. Filo-tan. Filo-tan. Filo-tan.

Fiiiiiloooooootaaaaaaaaan.

Filo-tan Filo-tan

Filo-tan Filo-tan Filo-tan Filo-tan Filo-tan Filo-tan Filo-tan Filo-tan Filo-tan Filo-tan Filo-tan Filo-tan Filo-tan.

"Somebody! Help me! Somebody fix Motoyasu!"

The dragon let out a terrible roar and I suddenly returned to my senses.

"Motoyasu, are you back?"

"Father, I detected the lingering scent of Filo-tan on you, I say."

"Motoyasu, I beg you, please don't get distracted," Father said. "The only scent you're noticing on me is Sakura! I was just riding her a few minutes ago."

Huh? Well, that was true, I supposed.

Yuki and the rest of the filolials looked so small from above.

"Motoyasu! It's time!"

Father called to me and I focused on the task ahead. There were five planes. They stayed in a tight formation as they fired down at the villages below. I had managed to forget the fact that we were riding a dragon just a little.

Takt's pig subordinates were in those planes.

When I remembered that, it was all the motivation I needed.

The airplane guns fired on, raining bullets down below.

"Air Strike Phaser Shield V!" Father called, summoning a shield.

One of the planes aimed at us and started to shoot.

Since there were Takt's subordinates in the plane, they

were likely high-level enemies. Aiming Lancer might not have enough power to kill them, and Gungnir would probably only take out one at a time. I wasn't sure what to do.

I, Motoyasu Kitamura, would never fail!

One of the planes was shooting directly at us, keeping an even distance. I grabbed my spear and locked onto the enemy.

When I thought about it, I realized that I did have an attack that came in handy precisely for times like this. After I learned Brionac, there was an attack that had reduced frequency but still summoned devastating power.

"Shooting Star Spear X!"

Shooting Star Spear, true to its name, is a skill that launches a glittering light like a comet in the night sky, similar to Ren's Shooting Star Sword skill. Certainly, it's an attack that I used against Father in the first go-around. Immediately after the initial attack, even more stars fired at the foe. Still, Father was ultimately able to stop them all.

Shooting Star Spear's attack just grazed the first plane, ricocheting outward and striking two planes further back with stars. How about an attack that packs even more punch than Aiming Lancer, you vile pigs!

The airplane grazed by the attack started to flash red lights before it abruptly exploded. An effective strike! The other two planes suffered direct hits and, emitting giant plumes of smoke, plummeted out of the sky. I guessed that the attack had set the fuel on fire.

"Just two more, Motoyasu! Keep at it!" Father called.

"Leave it to me!"

With two left, I only needed a single attack. I readied my spear and set the target lock. A high-powered skill that guaranteed direct hits would do the trick!

"Gungnir X!"

The spear blasted a ray of light at the airplanes, and it pierced straight through the first one.

"Yes!" Father punched the air.

The last plane swerved back toward us and kept firing.

Did they want to die?

Father summoned another shield. "Air One-Way Shield!"

His shield sprouted a sort of gentle wind around us, and the dragon adjusted its position, hurtling forward to meet the plane. The airplane started to spin as it hurtled toward us, whirling like a tornado.

"Looks like the airplane is using a skill that creates a blast of wind," Father said. "Motoyasu! Stop it!"

"I shall, Father!"

If I used Brionac, it might miss the mark. This time I went for a magic spell. I focused intensely and, raising my spear to the sky, chanted a spell.

"Liberation Firestorm X!"

A whirlwind of fire erupted from the tip of the spear. Sucked through Father's air shield, the tornado of fire grew massive and took down the airplane in a fierce inferno. The fire blazed up the surrounding clouds in a flash of heat, and the weather suddenly cleared into a sunny day.

"Whoa," Father said. "Wouldn't it have been faster to just use that magic from the start?"

"I don't think it would've gotten them all at once," I said. With them flying all around us, it would have been difficult to get a good aim.

"Fair enough," Father said. "Great, so this should put a stop to their bombings." Then to the dragon he called, "Let's hurry back down before Motoyasu goes crazy again!"

At Father's direction, the dragon started to swoop back down toward the ground.

"Ouch!" I yelped. "It itches!"

As soon as the dragon landed, I leapt off to find my skin covered in furiously itching hives! But the feeling started to fade pretty quickly.

We returned to the command center and met back up with the Siltvelt leaders.

"So did Takt's remaining soldiers meet up with the Shield-freeden army yet?" Father was asking.

"At the moment, we don't believe any of them have joined Shieldfreeden's vanguard unit," Werwer said.

"Got it. Does it look like they may retreat?"

"They seem to be relentless," Werwer said with a pained expression.

Even though we took care of the airplanes, we were still in a difficult position.

"They refuse to withdraw on the orders of Shieldfreeden's aotatsu chief," Werwer continued. "They're still furious that the Whip Hero, Hammer Hero, and goddess dragon have been killed."

"Hm . . ." Father trailed off.

"However, since we do have an advantage in hand-to-hand combat, we're confident that they won't start a battle that they don't think they can win."

"Got it. Let me know if anything happens. If any more of Takt's remnants show up, we'll take care of them."

At that moment, a soldier came rushing in.

"It's an emergency!"

"What is it?" Father asked.

"Melromarc's army has suddenly reappeared and is joining the war against us!"

"Again? Now of all times?" Father shook his head. "No, of course—now is the perfect time for them to move against us."

"We've confirmed a sighting of their battle formation!" the soldier continued. "The Wisest King of Wisdom commands from the rear, and the high priest, wielding the Legendary Replica Weapon, is leading the charge!"

"The Legendary Replica Weapon?" Father exclaimed. "What is that?"

"We believe that it is a reproduction of each of the Four Holy Weapons of legend!"

Now that he mentioned it, the high priest did have something like that. It had been quite a powerful weapon. Had Father's cursed shield not managed to stop it, it might have been powerful enough to defeat us. Well, back then, before I had my current strength, that is.

"Motoyasu, what do you think we should do?" Father asked. "My guess is that we could leave the Shieldfreeden army to Siltvelt and handle Melromarc ourselves."

Hmmm. What should we do, indeed?

Like Father said, we couldn't afford to ignore Trash and the high priest. Most likely, they were devising some way to cooperate with Shieldfreeden and take us out. But at least we managed to take out Shieldfreeden's trump card—their airships. I assumed that Melromarc had already started their march by the time they were notified that we took out the planes.

"I think that's right, Father. Let's go face the Melromarc army!" I declared.

"Sounds good." Father nodded. "It's going to be different from last time. I won't let any harm come to any of my friends!"

"Yes, Father!" I said. "If it's been decided, let's go quickly!"

"Faster is better," Father agreed. "Let's do it."

But the messenger had something else to say. "There's one more important piece of information."

"What?"

"We've sighted additional airplanes near the Melromarc army."

They had airplanes circling near Melromarc as well? That made it even more necessary for us to take care of things. It also proved that Melromarc and Shieldfreeden were cooperating.

I resolved to kill every last one of Takt's remnants. We had no choice but to fight.

"Let's get 'em, everyone!" Father called. "To the next fight!"

The whole room roared with applause and agreement as everyone began preparations for the next battle.

Father, Yuki and the filolials, some Siltvelt soldiers, and I were headed to the battlefield where Melromarc's army was waiting.

"They've shown themselves at last," one soldier said. "That evil king that deceived the Shield and Spear heroes."

The battlefield was a wide plain in Siltvelt that looked out on Melromarc territory. A surprise attack was out of the question. Father gave his orders to us as we approached the enemy.

The two armies faced each other in the field and Father marched out to the front.

"All of you," Father called out to Melromarc. "You've been cooperating with Shieldfreeden, haven't you?"

The high priest and the crimson swine stepped forward and responded.

"Cooperating?" the high priest shouted. "We would never cooperate with the filthy likes of demi-humans! This is a holy war!"

"Oink, oink!"

The crimson swine was squealing about something. What a revolting sight.

Should I shake free from Father's restraint and kill her on the spot?

"Father, what is the swine blathering on about?"

"She's saying that they shouldn't have expected the whip hero to win against the evil magic of the Shield Hero. If he had killed the Shield and Spear Heroes, her father had promised that she'd get engaged to Takt, but now that's impossible thanks to us," Father explained.

Then he addressed the crimson swine directly. "What a selfish thing to say. It's your fault that . . . we all know what you really intended!"

The crimson swine kept oinking.

"Cut the nonsense!" Father shouted. "How can you possibly enjoy watching so many innocent people suffer?"

Father and the crimson swine were really going at it, I say.

"This is a holy war," the high priest said. "We'll prove to the world that we are in the right! We'll defeat Siltvelt in this holy war and make your wretched nation vanish from existence! We'll exterminate the filthy demi-humans and witness the birth of the perfect world!"

"Unimaginable," Father said. "We're trying our best to help everyone survive and make it through the waves, but you . . ." Father stared down the high priest and the crimson swine with an ice-cold gaze.

At that moment, Trash suddenly screamed from far behind.

"What are you going on about up there!? Kill them already! Kill all the Siltvelt demi-humans!"

That Trash was no end of trouble. If I killed him now . . . I saw no reason why it would be an issue. Trash had already cast his lot. It was unnecessary to worry about the consequences anymore.

"Motoyasu," Father said, "I thought if we talked things through with them, they might understand our position. But there's no point. They won't listen to us no matter what we say."

Father held his shield forward as if ready to begin a duel.

Father was right. From the beginning there was no point in talking with this despicable lot.

"Very well then!" said the high priest. "In that case, I shall introduce the hero that will be the one to kill the Shield Demon!"

Father turned his head in confusion. The ranks of Melromarc soldiers broke, making room for none other than . . .

"Itsuki," Father whispered.

"Itsuki, I say," I announced.

"I'd prefer if you didn't say my name so casually," Itsuki

seethed, approaching and watching us with an ugly expression.

What was this rebellious attitude of his? Even though he used to do whatever Father asked, like a slave! However, I suppose that hadn't happened yet this go-around. Itsuki had pretty much faded to the background, so I hadn't bothered to remember.

If I had to rank them strongest to weakest, it would go Takt, Takt's remnants, the high priest, Trash, and then Itsuki. So why did they choose Itsuki, the weakest of them all, to fight here? We were essentially guaranteed a victory.

Well, it does cause us a problem since we couldn't just go ahead and kill Itsuki.

"Itsuki! What are you doing here?" shouted Father.

"What am I doing here? Isn't it obvious?" Itsuki sneered. "I've come here of my own will, to defeat you for abusing your powers for evil."

"W-what? I thought you were in Melromarc, preparing for the wave of destruction . . ." Father trailed off. He glanced over at me and then looked out at the Melromarc forces.

"That's true, but the aotatsu chief of Shieldfreeden came to Melromarc to request my assistance," Itsuki said. "He told me about how you caught the Whip Hero Takt in a contemptible trap and asked me to achieve vengeance for his people. I've heard about your evil deeds. You can't hide them!"

"Itsuki," Father said, "listen to me, please. Takt tricked us, not the other way around. We just were protecting ourselves! Shieldfreeden is the evil one, along with Takt's remnant soldiers—and the Melromarc army here right now."

But Itsuki was shaking his head, prepared to ignore every last one of our pleas.

"While there are certainly ideals within the Church of the Three Heroes that are difficult to accept, my eyes, ears, and heart have told me that you are the evil ones," Itsuki said. "You claim that Melromarc is evil? You really think I would believe that? I've lost friends because of your assassins!"

"What are you talking about?" Father said. "Just listen to me for a second! We didn't send any assassins!"

"Of course, I can't believe a word that you say. I am devoted to justice, and for justice's sake—Naofumi, Motoyasu—I will take your lives! And I'll tell everyone patiently awaiting our victory in Shieldfreeden the good news!"

Father took a step closer, his eyes flashing with anger. "Itsuki, are you telling me you agree with exterminating all demi-humans?"

"There's something called hierarchy in this world," Itsuki said. "We're simply on top. There's no way we would actually do something as cruel as exterminate them."

"Hierarchy? That's insane, Itsuki!"

"You're the ones with crimes on your conscience! Don't you dare accuse the innocent!"

Apparently Itsuki really believed that the crimson swine and the fanatical followers of the Church of the Three Heroes were acting out of goodwill.

What a clown. It was almost like watching myself in the previous go-around. Hah! He didn't realize he was being used like a pawn in a chessboard!

Well, to be used as a pawn in Father's chessboard is the greatest of honors, I say.

"I will eliminate evil!" Itsuki yelled. "Mald, Rojeel, everybody! Get them!"

Itsuki and his followers pulled out their various weapons and prepared to attack us.

What a pain. If I wasn't careful, I'd kill Itsuki by accident. And then the loop would just start all over again.

"Itsuki, do you really want to fight us?" Father shouted.

"I can't trust a word you say!" Itsuki replied. "You're my enemy—and I'll end you here!"

"I've tried to tell you over and over again that we didn't do any of it," Father said. "I'm telling you, it's the truth!"

"So you're playing the victim card out of sheer cowardice, now?"

"The victim card? That's not it! We *were* the victims! But Itsuki, if you really intend to kill my friends, I'll fight to protect them. I'll protect them."

Father gripped his shield. He looked as determined as ever.

His words echoed in my heart. If Father would protect our friends, then I would kill every last one of our enemies.

"Itsuki, you seem like you want to kill us, but we absolutely will not kill you," Father said. "To protect the world—to not put anyone else's life at risk—we can't afford to lose you."

"What the hell are you talking about?"

"I'm not saying this because I think you would understand," Father said. "I'm saying it because it's what we have to do!"

Father was right. We couldn't kill Itsuki. If we did, everything we did up until now would go to waste.

Even if we agreed that this go-around had been a failure and we allowed the time loop to reset, everything up until now might just keep on repeating itself. No matter what happened, I swore to never give up.

As I thought about such important matters, Itsuki called to his companions.

"All right, everybody! In the name of justice, eliminate the evil that stands before us!"

"JUSTICE!" they shouted.

From the far back, a military unit waving the Melromarc flag hurried toward us.

"There are that many of them!?" Father exclaimed.

Trash was leading the charge. "Our nation has gathered together to help us defeat our enemy!" he called. "Everybody! No further delay! Begin the battle!"

On Trash's orders, the Melromarc soldiers let out a roar and started racing toward us.

The gates of war had been opened.

Mirellia Q. Melromarc

Queen of Melromarc

The highest authority in Melromarc. Although she believes in the Church of the Three Heroes, she looks upon the Shield Hero kindly and reasonably. She studies mythology and lore as a hobby and is very familiar with the heroes. She is also rumored to have visited the land of legend.

She directly oversees Melromarc's special agent corps and for some reason helps Naofumi and his friends from time to time.

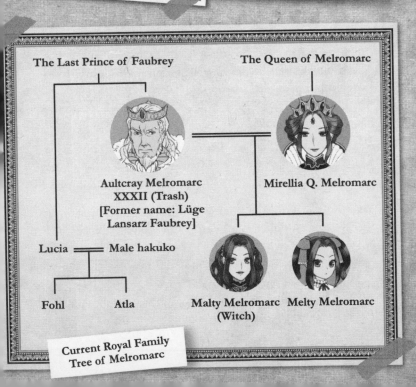

The Last Prince of Faubrey

The Queen of Melromarc

Aultcray Melromarc XXXII (Trash) [Former name: Lüge Lansarz Faubrey]

Mirellia Q. Melromarc

Lucia === Male hakuko

Fohl   Atla

Malty Melromarc (Witch)   Melty Melromarc

Current Royal Family Tree of Melromarc

Chapter Ten: Carved into the Heart

"Eagle Piercing Shot!"

Itsuki locked onto Father with pinpoint accuracy and unleashed his attack. It was an attack with considerable piercing might—powerful enough that I worried it might shatter Father's defensive capabilities. But Father, implementing the power-up method I had taught him, did his best to block the attack.

"Air One-Way Shield!" Father cried, creating a shield that managed to deflect Itsuki's arrow. "Itsuki! Please listen! We can't afford to be fighting now!"

"Shut up already!"

I had to figure out some way to silence Itsuki without killing him. He wouldn't listen to us as long as he didn't know who was really stronger. So if we gave him a little taste of failure, perhaps he'd be willing to hear Father out. He needed to understand just how vast a difference there was between us.

The only problem was that if I launched a high-powered attack, I'd end up killing him.

"That's right! This is a holy war!" cried the high priest. He struck the ground with the Legendary Replica Weapon, creating a massive chasm in the earth.

It wasn't too difficult for our troops to simply run away

from the chasm, but soon magma came bursting out of the ground.

"Yikes!" Father quickly created a shield underfoot as the magma rushed across the plain.

They couldn't even scratch us.

Incidentally, that skill the high priest had used to make the chasm was called Fissure Strike. It's a skill that creates a chasm randomly in the nearby area. If you focus to control the direction, you can also ensure that it only attacks your enemies.

"At long last, the time to exterminate the demonic Shield Hero has come!" cried the high priest maniacally. "Begin the Judgment aria!"

"Don't lose now!" called Father. "Everyone, start the collective ritual magic!"

I turned around and saw the shusaku representative and the filolials racing up from behind, beginning to chant a protective spell. Sakura rushed up to Father and hugged him tight.

"Naofumi, are you okay?"

"We're fine," Father said. "Just be careful, Sakura!"

"Don't be so reckless, Naofumi!" Filo-tan always used to be concerned about Father too, I say.

"Take that! And that!"

Meanwhile, Kou was mowing down Melromarc soldiers with a series of vicious kicks.

"Haikuikku Strike!" cried Sakura, racing into an attack of her own.

Oho? Her attack reminded me a bit of Filo-tan's.

Sakura launched off at a high speed, knocking down count-less soldiers between the high priest and us. It was like Sakura was picking dust out of her feathers.

"We opened a clear path, Motoyasu!" called Sakura. The soldiers that had been standing in the way vomited blood and keeled over. She had wiped out all the soldiers in a straight-line attack.

"Thanks, Sakura!" I declared.

The most troublesome opponent of all remained—the high priest. I was determined to stop him now and took a step forward.

Just then a large group of Melromarc reinforcements arrived.

"Ha!" The high priest laughed. "My reinforcements are here. Eliminate the Shield and Spear Demons where they stand!"

But the new Melromarc reinforcements were attacking their own troops.

"W-what's happening?" the high priest cried. "Why are they betraying their own countrymen!?"

"*Oiyoink!?*" The crimson swine was squawking as if she couldn't believe what was happening.

"That's because you're not the real Melromarc army!" a knight shouted.

A knight on horseback cut through the enemy on the way over toward Father, with none other than the old genmu at her side.

Could that be?

"E-Eclair!" Father gasped.

"Sorry we took so long," Éclair said.

"What are you doing here?" Father asked. "I thought you went to Faubrey!"

"Luckily for us, we ran into the queen of Melromarc on our way over there," Éclair said. "She explained everything to us—the situation in Melromarc, the details of the heroes' summoning, and what barbaric acts the king had planned too."

When Trash saw that Éclair and the old genmu were with us, he called out with a furious expression.

"Eclair! You traitor! You've turned the Melromarc army against us!"

"That's right, I did. But you're not the true Melromarc army in the first place—just an annoying band of misfits, because now, by proxy, I will announce the will of the queen!"

Eclair unfurled a parchment and withdrew a crystal. An image of the queen floated to the surface of the crystal and began to speak.

"I declare that the group claiming to be the Melromarc army is no longer a part of our country. From now on, all these traitors to the Melromarc army—sparing no effort and cooperating alongside the Siltvelt military—will fight Shield-freeden instead!" With that, the projection vanished.

"What . . . What the . . . My wife, betraying me? It can't be! Impossible!"

"The queen of Melromarc has told us the truth—that you're a lying imposter masquerading as the Wisest King of Wisdom," Eclair shouted. "The real Wisest King of Wisdom is still in the castle, opposing this war! Melromarc soldiers! Capture the imposter, bring him back to Melromarc, and we will take his life! Tie him up! The imposter Wisest King of Wisdom!"

Trash couldn't believe his ears. He screamed back at Eclair.

"The one in the castle is the real imposter! Listen, Melromarc forces, the Church of the Three Heroes, annihilate the fraud Melromarc army! I command you!"

The army bellowed its agreement.

"Well, they're not listening, so we don't have much of a choice," Eclair said. She turned to me and whispered into my ear. "Mr. Kitamura, can you do me a favor? Do something insanely powerful and show them all that we can't afford to be fighting each other here."

But as she said that, I noticed that there seemed to be a change in Itsuki's expression.

"Itsuki, who do you think is right here?" Father was saying to him.

Itsuki took a step back, looking flustered.

"N-no way! Just like King Aultcray says, you're the evil ones! Say your prayers!"

How stupid could he possibly be?

Meanwhile, it looked like the high priest had started to cast some magic. I hurried across the path of fallen soldiers that Sakura had opened up for us.

"So you're the Spear Fraud, I see," sneered the high priest. "Your sins are heavy! In the name of God, exterminate him!"

The high priest proclaimed his victory and fired a Brionac in my direction.

But his replica weapon wasn't much of a replica. He wasn't much stronger than any other small fry, as it turned out.

I blocked the attack with my spear and flung it right back at the rows of Church of the Three Heroes priests who were busy chanting that magic aria. Their agonized screams were like music to my ears.

The high priest stared at me in disbelieving horror.

"Maybe you understand now?" I said. "You never stood a chance."

I grabbed him by the collar and lifted him off the ground— and raised my fully charged-up spear to his throat.

"Brionac X!"

"Oh God—" the high priest screamed.

With that, I turned him and his fraudulent replica weapon to dust.

The surrounding priests were at a loss for words.

"He killed the high priest so easily . . ."

"N-no! The high priest is just pretending to be dead! He'll fly back down any moment now! Pray, everyone, pray with all your might!"

They were doing everything they could to escape reality, I say.

"If by some miracle he comes back, I'll just kill him again," I informed them, but for some reason they didn't seem to hear me.

Oho? In the background, I noticed that Father and Itsuki were fighting.

Looking around the battlefield, now I could clearly tell apart the real Melromarc army and the enemy—the imposter army and the Church of the Three Heroes. I could finish off our enemies easily.

"Mr. Kitamura, we've been ordered to apprehend the culprit pretending to be Aultcray alive," Eclair said. "You might not like it, but can you catch him without killing him?"

"Leave it to me, I say!" I declared. "Aiming Lancer X!"

I focused intensely and launched the skill. I activated multilock functionality and sent a flash of light over the enemy army, targeting a wide radius, including the imposter army and the Church of the Three Heroes. I fired.

My spear shot out a burst of light that glimmered through

the sky and, landing in the battlefield like a blinding comet, annihilated hundreds of soldiers and priests in a scourge of flame. Screams scattered to the sky like flocks of birds.

"Air Strike Javelin!" I shouted, cutting down the surviving soldiers.

"Ritual Magic Typhoon!"

By that time, the magic that Yuki and the filolials had been chanting had finally taken shape, and it thoroughly eliminated the remaining soldiers in a violent storm of thunder and lightning.

The Siltvelt army was able to return to the fight against Shieldfreeden in good spirits, leaving the remaining Melromarc imposter soldiers to the real Melromarc soldiers.

All that was left was the imposter Trash. I could see him at a complete loss for words, guarded by a group of soldiers.

"This isn't over yet!" Itsuki said. "We haven't lost yet!"

Itsuki still hadn't learned his lesson. He was preparing to use a skill.

"Shooting Star Bow!"

Shooting Star Bow is a long-range attack that launches an arrow with stars trailing it. Itsuki faced Father and fired.

Cool and composed, Father blocked the arrow with his shield.

"Aiming Lancer!" I shouted.

After my cooldown time had elapsed, I struck Itsuki with Aiming Lancer set to its bare minimum power.

Itsuki and his comrades were knocked off their feet and groaned with pain.

Last but not least . . .

"Paralyze Lance!"

All of his writhing around was a nuisance, so I used Paralyze Lance on Itsuki to freeze him in place. His face had a strange expression. As if he wanted to say, 'This is just a game, right?'

Unfortunately for Itsuki, this was not a game, but very much a real-life defeat.

With the rest of the soldiers finally disposed of, Eclair rode up to Trash on her horse.

"All right then, imposter Wisest King of Wisdom. By order of the queen, I'll be escorting you back to Melromarc."

The imposter moaned. "I haven't lost! I haven't lost!"

"Certainly, the real Wisest King of Wisdom wouldn't have been defeated so easily," Werwer muttered, watching the scene.

Where did the crimson swine go? I figured as soon as she sensed they were at a disadvantage, she abandoned Trash and Itsuki and ran off. But just where did she flee to?

Then I spotted her hiding across the field.

"You'll never escape me!" I proclaimed.

Sprinting after her and leaping forward, I stabbed her with my spear from behind!

Éclair did say that we only had to capture Trash, right? Which meant that disposing of the crimson swine was perfectly acceptable!

"Oink oink!"

The crimson swine was squealing madly after I stabbed her.

"Your despicable deeds have come back to bite you, I say!"

Father and Éclair watched in shocked silence. Finally, Éclair spoke up.

"So you're that scheming princess, Myne. I've received a message from the queen for you too. She says you've gone too far."

"Oink! Oink, oooiink!"

She wasn't dead yet, I observed. Unexpectedly tough.

But her vile pig squeals were making my ears ring. I had to put a stop to them, I say.

"Burst Lance X!"

The crimson swine let out one of the most blood-curdling oinks I had ever heard in my life.

Burst Lance X is a skill that causes the object you stab to explode. I ran my spear right through the crimson swine's gut and thrust her up into the air. She exploded with such a vicious force that not a single trace of her existence remained.

There was a bit of an awkward silence.

Éclair stared blankly at me and the place where the crimson swine had been standing. I had no idea what she was thinking.

Trash, although still restrained by Éclair, flung out his hands toward me in wild agony.

"Malty!" he screamed. "Malty!!!"

I had eliminated one more repugnant piece of trash from this world, I say. I felt refreshed and invigorated.

"Sorry, but it's a pain if you're going to make a fuss like that," Éclair said and gave Trash a heavy blow on the back of the head, knocking him unconscious. He toppled over.

The Siltvelt forces and Éclair's Melromarc troops let out a bellowing roar at our victory.

"Well, I doubt the fight is over, but we can at least take a breather now, right?" Father asked.

"We just need Shieldfreeden to give up the fight as well," Éclair said.

"They'll never give up," I declared. "This won't be over until we defeat the remnant aotatsu."

"Yeah, I guess so," Father said. "But we've probably at least bought some time, as they should realize that they're now at a disadvantage in the war."

"And fortunately, none of the nations have exhausted too much of their fighting power. We still stand a chance against the waves of destruction," Éclair said.

"Yeah—and Eclair, how did you possibly get Melromarc on our side in the first place?"

Father's question was the most important one. Like Éclair had mentioned before, the queen must have been the reason.

"The queen was opposed to this war from the start," Éclair said. "I also explained to her what Mr. Kitamura told us about the future of the country. And so she evaluated that and a variety of other factors and decided that it would be best to end the war here so long as we didn't lose too many soldiers to fight the waves of destruction."

"Of course," Father said, "Siltvelt and Melromarc . . . if either country's forces were to be wiped out, fighting against the waves would be pretty much impossible."

"That's right. Also, at around the same time of the death of the Whip Hero, Takt, in Faubrey it was confirmed that the other owners of the seven star weapons had been killed. So Faubrey abandoned plans of joining forces with Shieldfreeden and decided to focus on clarifying exactly what had happened."

"It sounds like we might just be able to stop all this war and focus on preparing for the waves after all," Father said.

Father was right. We destroyed all of Takt's planes and airships and easily stopped Itsuki, Melromarc's so-called trump card. Now we just needed to prepare for the waves.

Hm?

"I'm not so sure about all that!" called a voice.

One of Itsuki's comrades, wearing a shining suit of armor, stood up on the battlefield. I remember in the first go-around he had been a friend of Ren's. He started walking toward us. It was only hearsay, but in the first go-around he caused Father a lot of trouble, if I remembered correctly. Well, I'd simply destroy him.

Regardless, he certainly was a waste of splendid armor
. . . Wait, now I started to remember. His name was "Smoked
Human," right? I recalled something about the Bull of Phalaris,
so we called him Smoked Human for whatever reason.

"Ugh . . . agh . . ." Itsuki still was completely unable to
move.

"Who's on the side of justice now?"

"You lying Bow Hero! You were wrong all along!"

Smoked Human and his fellow soldiers were standing up
and moving toward Itsuki. My instincts told me to be on guard.
I started to run closer to restrain them.

It seemed to be just quarreling among friends, so Father
and Éclair's response was not quite fast enough.

"Pathetic, lying Bow Hero! Talk to me again about justice!"

Smoked Human and his comrades grabbed their fallen
weapons and lunged at Itsuki, who was still unable to move.

They moved so quickly that even I couldn't get there fast
enough. Only because I had gone quite a distance chasing down
the crimson swine, that is. And if I were to use Aiming Lancer,
I wouldn't be able to lock on in time. Could I use Brionac?
Gungnir? Air Strike Javelin would be fast enough, but it would
only knock out one or two of the soldiers.

"Air Strike Javelin! Gungnir!" I shouted, attacking as fast
as I could.

"Itsuki!" shouted Father. "Air Strike—" Father started to
call for a shield as well.

"Die!"

"Stop—" Itsuki cried.

I managed to take out all but two of the enemies in a furious explosion. But Smoked Human had made it all the way to Itsuki and, raising his axe high, brought it down.

Even though Itsuki couldn't move, he could certainly scream.

"Hahahaha!" cried Smoked Human. "I'll kill you, you false Bow Hero! You lied to us all! Shield and Spear Hero—he deceived us, I tell you!"

Blood squirted from Itsuki as Smoked Human called out to us. He seemed to be trying to help us, so I figured I would hear him out before I killed him.

"No!" cried Father. "We were so close to getting past all this war . . ."

"What have you done?" Éclair cried, charging toward Smoked Human on her horse. She raised her sword, prepared to cut him down.

Things had escalated quickly, I say.

Father turned to me quickly. "Motoyasu—it looks like the time loop reset condition will be activated."

Father, brilliant as always! He had figured out exactly what was going on. And he was right. We had only until Itsuki drew his last breath before we'd be sent tumbling back in time all over again.

"I'm sorry, Father," I cried. "I, Motoyasu Kitamura, was not strong enough!"

"Really, I have a lot I want to say, but since we don't have time, I'm going to be quick," Father said.

"Tell me anything, Father!"

"First, I'm sorry that you're the only one who's going to suffer from the memory of all this. Know that I'm here for you."

"You bestow an honor on my very soul with your words," I wailed.

Father chuckled. "Somewhere along the way, I've gotten used to your weird expressions. I wish we could've met your 'beloved' Filo . . ." Father sighed.

I nodded. I, too, desired to meet my beloved Filo-tan.

"Okay, so let's get serious. Motoyasu, please recognize that you have an extreme side, so you need to think before you act. Check your own actions. Don't assume that if even you make a mistake, things will be okay. That will only backfire. If you just crush the leader of our enemies, it will create hordes of remnant soldiers bent on revenge, like what happened with Takt. Or they'll just get a new leader."

I nodded, teary-eyed. "I have carved your words into my heart!"

A half-smile fluttered on Father's lips, a bittersweet expression that told me he knew exactly how I felt.

"You saved me so many times," Father said. "I'm really grateful we did this together. Thank you, Motoyasu. It was short, but it was fun. If we get sent back again, let's make sure that we don't make the same mistakes—"

Suddenly, Father was cut off.

The bow icon in the corner of my field of vision started to flash. The world was fading to gray and everyone stopped moving. My spear trembled as a clock appeared and started to wind backward.

"I understand, Father," I proclaimed, teary-eyed. "This time, I, Motoyasu Kitamura, will fulfill your every wish, I swear it! Armed with my knowledge and memories of the future, we'll stop war at all costs!"

It seemed as if bringing Father to Siltvelt—even though I had done so for his own safety—only ended up causing war after war. If I were to bring him to Shieldfreeden, I doubted that the result would change. I needed to think more about how to prevent things from becoming this way.

That was what Father had asked me to do, after all.

A world without war. How could I create a world without war?

Now that I thought about it, although there had been a civil war in the first go-around, there was barely any large-scale war like this. If I could analyze what had happened then and move forward based on that, I would naturally be able to fulfill Father's wishes.

Violence is power, but so is knowledge, I say.

I vowed to use the knowledge I gained in this go-around to keep my promise to Father.

And as I thought and thought, I went soaring, spinning, into the past.

Chapter Eleven: A Guarantee of Safety

I groaned. When I opened my eyes, I saw a group of men wearing robes and staring at me in amazement.

"What's all this?"

"Huh?"

How many times had I seen this before? Father, Ren, and Itsuki started to have the same conversation that they did every time. So while they talked, I figured I'd sort out the situation. That's what Father asked me to do, after all.

First and foremost, I knew that Melromarc was going to try to destroy any relationship between the four holy heroes—the four of us summoned here. I knew that they wanted to get rid of Father, so they planned to send a false accusation his way before the four of us grew close enough to believe him. The first time that the time loop reset, I had kept that in mind, so I trusted Father and rescued him from the accusation.

I sent Father off to Siltvelt because I figured it would be safer there. But Melromarc forces were lying in wait at a fortress at the Siltvelt-Melromarc border, and they killed Father with ceremonial magic.

In the next go-around, I made a fuss about the false accusation Melromarc was planning for Father in our first meeting with Trash and the crimson swine, before they were able to execute it. Having ruined his devious plot, Trash wanted to have us eliminated as soon as possible. Thanks to Éclair's help, we were able to stop his scheme and we fled to Siltvelt as wanted criminals.

After that, we arrived safely in Siltvelt. But Takt had been cooperating with the crimson swine, and the crimson swine started a new war in order to get revenge on us. Smoked Human ended up killing Itsuki, and the time loop reset for a third time.

Those were pretty much the main points I remembered from everything up until now.

All that being the case, what would be the best course of action?

What did Father tell me before? Something about using my knowledge of future events to decide what to do?

I had to do as Father said. I thought extremely hard about it.

Q: What are the conditions of the time loop?
A: If any of the four holy heroes die, they will be brought back to the time and place of their initial summoning.

Q: Why did the time loop reset this time?
A: I, Motoyasu Kitamura, changed the series of events with my actions, but as a result, one of the four holy heroes died.

Q: Why aren't you explaining everything to the other heroes in the throne room right now?
A: If I say the entire truth here and now, I might cause the others to mistrust Father. That would put Father in a dangerous situation.

Q: Why are you avoiding your typical flashy behavior?
A: I, the Spear Hero, will be judged as a dangerous character and simply end up pulling Father into danger. Trash and the Church of the Three Heroes could decide to attack Father.

Q: Why do you need to be careful about going to another country?
A: We could end up causing a war involving several different countries. That, too, would put Father in grave danger.

My conclusion: This time, I'll wait until Father is properly leveled up and provide him with a bona fide guarantee of safety!

In order to achieve this goal, I won't try to rescue Father as quickly as possible—rather, to a certain extent, I have to let the series of events play out as they did the very first time we were summoned. In this go-around, we won't just try to run away to another country. Instead, we'll stick around in Melromarc and get stronger.

This sure is a pain, but I'll never give up, I say!

"Hey," Father said and tapped me on the elbow.

"What is it?"

"Are you going to introduce yourself or what?"

While I had been lost in thought, it appeared that everyone had already started introductions.

"It is I, Motoyasu Kitamura!" I proclaimed.

While it would probably be fine to explain some of the truth of the situation to everyone, I had to be careful to not be nearly as dramatic as last time. Unfortunately, I doubted my own ability to stay calm, so I decided to remain silent altogether.

"So Ren, Motoyasu, and Itsuki, is it?" Trash said.

"My lord, and me as well," said Father.

"Ah, yes," Trash added. "Naofumi."

If I let this play out, I would have a chance to talk to Father and the other heroes eventually. In the meantime, Ren explained status magic, to Father's shock.

If I could just stay quiet for now, I would be able to find the perfect time to rescue Father, I say. If I tried to argue with everyone about future events like I did before, Ren and Itsuki wouldn't believe Father about the false accusation. The events of the previous go-around had proved that.

But if not now, when would they believe me?

Trash and the crimson swine's past interference prevented me from knowing the first thing about what happened to Father during these first few days. I didn't even know where he would be staying.

I didn't have enough information. Even if I kept in mind what Father had told me last time, there was still a strong possibility that the time loop would end up resetting yet again.

So in order to gather some information, I figured it would be best to figure out where Father was staying, for one, but also what Ren and Itsuki were up to on the first day of the time loop. The first day or two had an outsized influence on the course of events, I say.

I returned to the core problem at hand—namely, when exactly would Father believe everything I had to tell him?

The answer, of course, is when Father is falsely accused but no one else believes his side of the story.

The mere notion of allowing Father to be falsely accused almost caused me to immediately vomit all over the place, but in order to gain Father's trust and use my knowledge of future events . . . this was the best and only way!

The only problem was that it hadn't happened yet. So even if I let things play out and Father believed me, what would we do after that?

I, Motoyasu Kitamura, would do all that I could to prevent needless war!

There were plenty of options. There was Zeltoble, the mercenary country that Ren fled to in the last go-around. Zeltoble was full of secrets—the ideal country for a fugitive. I could also visit the Coliseum and make plenty of money there.

But would hiding away in Zeltoble actually solve any of the problems at hand?

Of course, Melromarc wouldn't just sit and watch us escape to Zeltoble. Since we couldn't take a portal there, Trash and the crimson swine would undoubtedly cause us all sorts of trouble.

We could take the portal halfway to Siltvelt and move from there. But there was still the strong possibility that Melromarc would eventually declare war on Zeltoble.

On the other hand, even if they knew that Father was in Zeltoble, it could take Melromarc some time to act.

But on the other *other* hand, Zeltoble might offer up Father as a sacrifice to Melromarc in order to avoid war.

But at the same time, it was also valid to wonder if Melromarc would really declare war on a country of mercenaries and traders like Zeltoble.

Father told me to avoid war at all costs, after all.

I couldn't forget about Takt either. He might take action.

However, I knew from the events up until now that it was unlikely that Takt would come directly to us.

There was no doubt that I needed to eliminate him as soon as possible.

Nevertheless, I had to be careful with the timing there. Not only could killing him cause a new war, but we'd also have to worry about his hordes of remnants.

I was starting to get the feeling that Father's advice about using my knowledge of the future to our advantage was not actually very useful.

Don't get me wrong—Father's words are absolute! I would never think that Father was wrong about something.

The ultimate conclusion was therefore . . .

That we would not go to Zeltoble.

The next candidate for analysis was Faubrey. There was always the chance that we'd have to deal with Takt, but since Faubrey is such a large country, we likely wouldn't have to worry about an invasion from Melromarc.

I remembered that back when I was chasing around pigs, the Church of the Four Heroes from Faubrey also played a role in proving Father's innocence, in addition to the queen of Melromarc.

But in the case of Faubrey, my knowledge of future events didn't come in handy either. In the best-case scenario, we could take care of Takt quickly, but what would the ripple effects of killing him be?

I willed my brain to think even harder!

Father asked me to avoid war. When had there not been a war?

When I reflected on past events, I seemed to recall that whenever the queen of Melromarc showed up, she always stopped whatever Trash and the crimson swine had been scheming.

Which means that she can guarantee Father's safety, I say!

For the time being, I could expect the Church of the Three Heroes to take immediate action against Father.

I remembered that in the first go-around, after we defeated Takt after the Phoenix battle, it had pretty much been the end of full-scale wars.

Yes, that was it, I say—fleeing to another country wasn't our best option. And although it would be a bit dangerous, it was in fact the ideal strategy to stay in Melromarc to make our move!

In the first go-around, Father focused on earning money and prepared for the waves of destruction. After that, everything started to go south, but up until then, he had been relatively safe.

This was my best bet!

If I could guarantee Father's physical safety in the interim, things just might work out. We'd act as peddlers, moving quickly from place to place so that the Church of the Three Heroes wouldn't know our exact whereabouts.

There was just one problem with that plan.

Namely, what about my own objective? Last time I hadn't been able to find Filo-tan, even though I bought every last filolial from the monster trainer, I say!

How was that even possible?

I pushed my brain to think even harder, but it was already running at max capacity.

What if Father hadn't bought Filo-tan from a monster trainer, and someone else had ended up buying Filo-tan before I did? It would be far too difficult to gather up enough money to buy all of the filolials from the monster trainer in time.

"I'll make arrangements to find companions for you," Trash was saying. "The day is almost over, heroes. Please take your time and rest, and we'll set out tomorrow. In the meantime, I'll find top-notch talent to assist you."

"Thank you very much," Father said. Father, Ren, and Itsuki bowed. We were to be taken to relax in a guest room together.

Of course. They had only decided to separate us to launch their trap because I had accused them of betraying Father in the throne room.

I suddenly remembered Éclair. What should I do about her? I figured I should probably rescue her from the castle prison, right?

But if we rescued her, we'd just be inviting suspicion from Melromarc. In the previous go-around, it was also because we rescued Éclair that we had decided to flee for safety's sake to another country. And that's how there ended up being a war.

I decided to not rescue Éclair.

I also remembered that in the first go-around, one way or another, big sis ended up with Father. Where had she come from, anyway?

"Hey, this is just like a game, don't you think?" Ren was saying,

"It does seem like a game, but it's not quite—" Father began.

"This world is from a console game," Itsuki said.

"No, it's a VRMMO."

"Huh? VRMMO as in virtual reality MMO? That sounds like something out of the future."

"Huh!? What are you talking about!?"

"Wait a second!" I called out to stop them from arguing.

"What's your problem, Motoyasu? Asides from introducing yourself, you haven't said a word."

Father was already talking to me so intimately, I say! Last time, I always sensed a bit of hesitation when he called my name, but now he was talking to me with his guard completely down!

When I saw a glint of suspicion in Father's eyes, waves of nostalgia swelled in my heart, I say.

Based on previous experience, they wouldn't believe me if I told them the whole truth now. Which meant that even Father wouldn't believe me—yet.

"Ren, Itsuki," I said. "And Father. I want you to listen to me carefully."

"What's up?"

"You just called me Father as if that was really my name,"

Father said with a bemused expression. "Is that some sort of weird joke?"

It was a totally different reaction from the previous and first go-arounds. This was Father's naked, unadorned character, I say!

It looked like he was the kind of guy who got swept up in the excitement!

"Yes, Father, you are in fact Father," I informed him. "This is no joke. To I, Motoyasu Kitamura, you are Father!"

"Uh . . ."

I let Father's confused expression stand for a quick moment and then began to explain.

"All of us came from different worlds," I said. "We're all from Japan, but they're completely different. You should all do your best to remember that."

"Huh? Really?"

"First of all, Ren is coming from a Japan that has VRMMO. And Itsuki was summoned from a Japan where people have psychic abilities."

"What?"

Father was squinting at me like he didn't believe me. Well, in this case there was nothing I could do about it. If you weren't from a world that has VRMMO and psychic abilities, of course you wouldn't believe that they were real. But I knew from past experience that Ren and Itsuki would back me up here.

"But why would someone from a science-fiction Japan with VRMMOs come to yet another fantasy world? Sounds like a bunch of nonsense—"

"Why are you stating the obvious?" Ren said. "Everyone knows that there are VRMMOs."

"What!?"

"Huh!?"

Father's and Itsuki's voices cracked when they yelped in surprise. Ren and I exchanged glances.

"We definitely don't have those!" Father shouted.

"Yeah, there's no such thing," Itsuki agreed.

"Okay then. So what about psychic abilities, Itsuki?" Father asked.

"Is that supposed to mean supernatural powers? Of course there are people with those."

"No there aren't!"

"No way!"

We were repeating the exact same conversation about the differences between our worlds all over again.

It seemed like they had finally calmed down a bit, and they turned back to me to ask more.

"Motoyasu, how do you know about all this?"

"The truth is that this world is caught in a time loop," I informed them.

"A time loop?" Father asked. "You mean the same span of

time just repeats over and over again? So are you originally from this world, then?"

"No, I'm from Japan as well. I was stabbed by a pig in my world and died before being summoned here, I say."

"A pig? So you're from a version of Japan that has intelligent pigs . . ." Father shook his head in amazement.

Father wasn't wrong, but he wasn't right either.

"Father, are you asking me if the world I come from is like a gal game?"

"So that's what your world is like?"

"Unfortunately, since it's my own world, I have no idea what's different about it," I told him.

Father had an amused expression on his face, I say. I, Motoyasu Kitamura, was beginning to have a bit of fun myself!

I continued. "And Ren and Itsuki make the mistake of thinking that this world is that of a game that they know, I say."

"Really?" Itsuki asked. "I mean, this is a lot like a world from a game that I know. That's what I thought, at least, when Ren was explaining about status magic."

"Yeah," Ren said, "this world is the one from Brave Star Online."

"Thinking that is a critical error!" I declared. "The power-up method that you two are familiar with will eventually reach its limit."

"Which means what?"

"There is some overlap with power-up methods that you two know about," I explained.

"Really?"

"I guess we'll see."

At this rate, it was evident that it would be difficult to get them to believe anything I told them.

Getting Ren and Itsuki to trust me was the current biggest problem at hand. Even though I had proven to them my knowledge of their worlds, it seemed like they were just getting even more confident in their limited understandings. Father was the only one listening seriously.

"Based on the game that they know, they call the hero wielding the shield a loser, but, Father, you shouldn't listen to them, I say!"

Ren and Itsuki were staring at me with cold eyes. They were completely blowing me off!

"The hero wielding the shield is a loser?" Father said.

"That is exactly what you shouldn't believe!" I proclaimed.

"Hmm . . ." Father fell into thought. "So there are different kinds of power-ups. And? Why do you keep calling me Father?"

"Because you are Father, Father," I declared.

"That doesn't make any sense." Father raised an eyebrow and began to watch me unpleasantly. Did I say something rude?

Meanwhile, Ren and Itsuki raised their shoulders and

206 THE REPRISE OF THE SPEAR HERO 2

glanced at one another. I was quickly losing control of the situation.

Well, Ren and Itsuki hadn't believed me or Father in the past no matter what we said, so I figured it was out of my control at this point.

"Father, in a previous time loop, you became the father of the object of my devotion, which is why I refer to you as Father."

"Really? But even if that's true, then you're saying we continued fighting in this world so long that I eventually have a daughter. Does the loop last for ten years?"

Why was Father's intuition so off this time around, I say? My explanation must not have been very good.

"That's not the case," I said. "Your daughter, Filo-tan . . . She will be born in about one month, if I'm not mistaken."

Father burst into laughter.

What in the world was happening?

But soon Father calmed down. "Well, I suppose that if this is another world, a lot of things could be different." There was the Father I know! Unparalleled deduction capabilities! "So if that's the case, what kind of person is my wife?"

"After going through many painful experiences with women, you eventually develop a hatred of the female kind," I explained. "That's when you try to sleep with a man."

"What!? You're telling me that men can give birth in this world?"

It seemed like quite a leap of logic to me, but I greatly admired Father's imagination.

Father's tone abruptly changed. "Sorry, but nothing you're saying seems to have much credibility, Kitamura," Father said.

Now he was speaking so coldly to me! After he had been so warm and open . . . I had been demoted several positions in Father's heart, I say!

Ultimately, this meant that I wouldn't be able to talk to him about the false accusation, I supposed.

"No, please listen!" I declared. "You obtained a filolial egg—"

"Heroes, dinner is ready!" called a voice.

That was bad timing. But it was my fault for handling the situation so poorly.

Oh well. I'd try to speak to him the next chance I got.

"After dinner, I'll tell you all about the power-up methods," I told Father.

"No, don't worry about it," Father said. "I think I've heard enough."

Father rejected me so politely, I say.

I didn't understand it at all. What had I done wrong?

As various discussions happened around the dinner table, I passed the meal in intense contemplation. I recalled the dinner from the first go-around. My heart had been racing with excitement, I say.

It's not that I had gotten entirely used to it, but I had accepted the fact that this world was different from the Japan that I grew up in.

After dinner, it was time to go to bed. I thought about following my nightly custom of visiting the filolials in the castle. After I confirmed that Father and the others were fast asleep, I hopped out of bed and went walking through the castle.

Should I get my hands on some money and buy filolials from the monster trainer?

Hmm . . . rather than buying from the monster trainer, maybe it would be cheaper to visit a filolial breeder instead. In order to help protect Father, I had to make sure I spent my money wisely.

But finding Filo-tan was all or nothing. I was vexed beyond words, I say!

Just as I was walking out of the castle to go to the garden, I heard a voice.

"What time do you think we can meet the heroes tomorrow?"

I followed the sound of voices and noticed that they were coming from a guest room in the castle. When I peered inside, I saw a group of soldiers who, if I remembered correctly, were the group that would eventually become Ren's companions. So Trash was in the middle of gathering together companions for the heroes.

Well, it wasn't worth paying any mind to, I decided and continued making my way to the filolial stables. It was my favorite place, after all.

"Hey, this bed is hard! Get me a better bed!"

Wait a second!

That was the voice of the guy who killed Itsuki in the previous go-around! Smoked Human was giving orders all high and mighty about something or other, I say.

I decided to investigate further.

Chapter Twelve: Assassination

"Me, sleep in this piece of trash bed? Have you lost your mind?"

Smoked Human seemed to be dissatisfied with his bed and was shouting at the servants. Even before meeting Itsuki, he seemed like a real piece of work.

Should I do something about it? If I killed him now, would it have a big influence on future events?

Even when I reflected on my past mistakes, I doubted it would cause too much of an issue. Just like with Takt, perhaps getting rid of Smoked Human could even turn things to my advantage.

But if there was a witness, things could get sticky.

Just as I was thinking about it, after delivering his order for a new feather bed to the soldiers, Smoked Human walked out of the room. Where could he be going?

"As the source of your power, I, the Love Hunter, command you! Let the true way be revealed once more! Hide my form in the shimmering heat! Drifa Fire Mirage X!"

I chanted the spell and used Cloaking Lance X to activate a stealth condition as I approached Smoked Human from behind. It worked just as well as it had back in Siltvelt, I say.

I didn't see any witnesses in the garden.

"Pathetic! Not a single good wine in sight!" Smoked Human grumbled to himself as he set out for the castle wine cellars.

I remembered someone saying once that Smoked Human was from an aristocratic family of Melromarc. He seemed to be using his lineage as an excuse to strut around the castle as he pleased and get drunk, I say.

As he came outside and approached the garden on his way to the cellars, I hurried ahead of him. It would be easier to dispose of him outside. Even if I simply gave him a strong blow to the face, I might accidentally damage the castle building.

Smoked Human swaggered about with broad steps, raising a serious racket as he went. I double-checked to make sure there were no witnesses nearby.

Now was the time to strike!

I leapt out and gripped his collar.

"W-what in the—"

I yanked him closer, lifted him up in the air, and ran my spear right through him.

As he screamed maniacally, I checked to make sure that my spear had completely skewered through his body. I prepared to unleash a skill.

Brionac's flash of light might've caused a scene, so that was out of the question. So was Shooting Star Spear.

Hmmmm . . . I wasn't expecting it to be so difficult to decide how to kill him, I say.

Ah, of course.

"Burst Lance X!"

It was the same skill I had used to kill the crimson swine in the last go-around. Smoked Human screeched and an explosion resounded throughout the garden.

"What's going on?"

Soldiers came running out into the garden at all the noise, but I instantly scampered off into hiding, I say.

Without so much as a corpse remaining, it would be impossible for anyone to figure out what, if anything, had happened besides a loud bang. In fact, the soldiers probably didn't suspect that anything had happened at all.

I strutted off, leaving them in the dust, chuckling pleasantly to myself. One more piece of trash eliminated from the world! It was best to destroy those repugnant pieces of trash so thoroughly that no traces remain, I say.

I had no idea I'd be able to get rid of him so quickly. It was a pleasant surprise.

Next up was the crimson swine, I supposed. But she had some work to do before I could take care of her.

At this rate, I'd be able to kill the crimson swine and completely change the course of the future.

Oh, my beloved filolials! I had taken a brief detour to throw out some trash, but now I was on my way!

"Gweh. Gweh."

When I entered the filolial stables, I saw their sweet, sleeping faces. They were chirping gently in their filolial dreams, I say. I planned to feed the filolials and befriend them that way, just like I had done in the first go-around.

I fell asleep right there and then in the filolial cottage. When I woke up the next morning, I went to meet Father and the others.

"Where did you head off to in the middle of the night?" Father asked. "What's that weird smell?"

Father, I regret to inform you that you are incorrect. The scent of Filolials is nothing short of heavenly.

"I went to meet my beloved filolials, I say," I told him. "Your daughter, Filo-tan, is a filolial as well."

"Filolials?"

"None other than the bird-like monsters that pull carriages in this world," I declared.

I was giving them plenty of essential background information to work with, I say.

"Wait. So you're telling me I get married to a bird monster!?"

My heart skipped a beat. Father believed what I had told him before! But the wrong reply here could finish me off. Just like I had finished off Smoked Human!

"Your jokes are a bit much, Kitamura," Father said. "Getting married to a carriage-pulling bird . . . You may want to consider a hospital visit."

Why was Father calling me by my last name? It's like he was trying to distance himself from me.

Ugh. I was acting based on my carefully chosen strategy, but it just didn't seem to be working.

"There's something wrong with that guy," Itsuki said to Father. "I think you'd be better off just ignoring him."

"Yeah, maybe you're right," Ren agreed with Itsuki.

"Well, since we're supposed to work together as heroes, I figure I should at least hear him out," Father said. "Otherwise he'd be pretty pathetic."

Father stepped in to defend my honor, I say. My eyes welled with tears at his boundless kindness!

"He's crying a literal fountain!" Ren exclaimed. "What's wrong?"

"I'm telling you, he's a weirdo!" Itsuki said.

"He looks like a normal, handsome guy when he's not saying anything," Father said, "but there's got to be something wrong with him."

In the meantime, we made it to the throne room where some men and pigs were waiting for us, eleven of them in total. "The heroes have arrived!" came an announcement.

That was new. It was the fruit of my labors, I say. Smoked Human wasn't there, so they hadn't found a replacement for him in time. This was a small difference but at the same time a tremendous one, I say.

"Yesterday, we requested companions for each of the heroes," Trash said. "It seems that they have all gathered here today."

"There are only eleven," Father cupped his hand and whispered to Itsuki, Ren, and me. "So even if they do three per hero, one hero would be a companion short."

Ren and Itsuki nodded. But I knew the truth! Even if they had gathered twelve, they didn't plan for any of them to accompany Father!

So there was no need for me to be concerned. Did any of the original companions they gave us even last until the end of the first go-around? Unfortunately, I didn't remember in the slightest.

Now that I thought about it, shouldn't we be choosing our own companions? The heroes were summoned to this world to be its saviors, after all. Shouldn't the country we were summoned to be showing us some good faith? This was all Trash's devious scheme, I say.

"Well then, future heroes," Trash called to the eleven gathered. "Go stand by the hero you want to work alongside!"

He was playing such a shameless game. Father and the others were watching with great anticipation. The eleven companions came up to us one at a time and stood by our sides.

Four for Ren. Three for Itsuki. Four for me.

And for Father, zero.

"Wait a second, my lord!" Father shouted out.

Very similar to what had happened the first go-around, I say. Father's disappointment was entirely logical. While it probably would have been fine for me to express my outrage here, I remembered what Father had told me in the last go-around and I managed to hold myself back.

That Trash bastard had this all playacting planned from the start. With an exaggerated gesture, he wiped the sweat from his brow. If it's so hot in here, I could make you break out in a cold sweat, you dastardly fiend!

"Of course, I wasn't expecting this to happen either," Trash began.

"You don't seem to be very popular," a Melromarc minister mumbled.

"Enough with the charade, here!" I declared. "Such blatant favoritism! I don't like it at all!"

Saying that much surely wouldn't cause things to go too haywire.

"No, of course, I'm terribly sorry," Trash said.

A minister standing next to Trash, who appeared to be a magician, was whispering to himself. "I did hear a rumor . . ."

In the first go-around, I had asked politely why Father didn't get any companions, but expressing my displeasure seemed to make an impact. Ren and Itsuki stepped forward.

"What did you hear?" Itsuki asked the magician.

Meanwhile, Father was just shaking his head, like he couldn't even believe what was happening.

"Hmm, yes, yes, well, there has been a rumor circulating that the Shield Hero is the weakest of the heroes," he said.

"What!?"

"According to legend, all the heroes should be strong, but there aren't very many people who want to accompany the weakest one," Trash said.

Oho? So in the first go-around he drove the heroes apart by using our lack of knowledge about the world. But this time would be different!

I was reaching the limit of my tolerance for this pathetic charade.

If Father was so weak, he wouldn't have been able to defeat the high priest or the Spirit Tortoise, I say. In truth, Father was incredibly strong. The more I thought about it, the more Trash's lies were riddled with inconsistencies.

"No way. That rumor . . . You're saying that everyone heard it last night?" Father asked.

"We did hear something about how the Shield Hero was the weakest . . ." Itsuki started to say.

Father turned to me. "Kitamura, didn't you hear something different?" he pleaded.

Very well then. I, Motoyasu Kitamura, would help my beloved Father.

"The Shield Hero is not weak!" I loudly proclaimed.

"Yes, that's right!" Father agreed.

"Including scavenging good hunting grounds for plenty of experience, I can teach Father the power-up method for his shield, making him the most powerful hero of us all!" I stepped forward. "Even if the heroes' weapons repel one another, if I show him—"

Trash suddenly clapped his hands.

"This is a marvelous exchange of information among the heroes," he sneered. "However, what about making your companions stronger? And that no companions want to work with the weakling Shield Hero is simply a matter of fact!"

Trash never listens to anyone. Father isn't weak, I'd have him know.

I saw Father's hand curl into a fist. I, too, was filled with frustration. The overwhelming urge to just end Trash here and now hit me hard.

But if I killed him, I wouldn't be safeguarding my promise to Father. I had to restrain myself.

"Ren . . . and Motoyasu, since you both have four people, why don't you let me have one of your companions?" Father asked.

The reserved group that had chosen Ren as their hero quickly hid behind him. Their faces told me that they were worried about what kind of sin it would be to make the Shield Hero their ally in this country.

"I don't really care about companions," Ren said. "You can have anyone who can't keep up with me."

Ren clearly wasn't thinking properly about the situation.

"Itsuki, what about you? Isn't this unfair?" Father pleaded.

What now? I figured Father would ask me first, but instead, he turned to Itsuki.

"Well, it is unfair . . ." Itsuki looked like he was having trouble refusing Father too.

I looked at the people who had been gathered to be my own companions. One of them was the crimson swine! I decided to kill her as soon as I got the chance.

I didn't remember the other three at all. I must've left them in the dust pretty fast.

"It would be bad for morale if we just split up the group," Itsuki said.

"So that means I have to go out by myself?" Father exclaimed.

This wouldn't be a bad place to let things be, I supposed.

"All of my companions are at your service, Father," I declared.

"Huh? Is that really okay? 'At your service' is a little creepy but . . ." Father trailed off.

"Oink!?"

One of the pigs started to oink noisily. Unfortunately, I couldn't understand it in the slightest.

At any rate, I would be able to use the crimson swine's despicable plans to get Father to trust me. The fact that the crimson swine planned to use all of the heroes here would be my godsend. In this case, the pros and cons of sending the crimson swine to Father were one and the same, I say.

"Listen already! Join Father, you pig!"

I kicked the pig over toward Father.

"What's your problem, Kitamura!?" Father was anxiously making sure that the pig was okay and scowled over at me.

Father tried to help the pig, but as if Father had done nothing for it at all, the pig broke away from Father and rushed back to me. It wrapped its slimy arms around me.

"What the . . ."

Father stared at me, dumbfounded. I caught a glimpse of anger in his eyes. Before Father's eyes had been opened to love, I remember that he used to have this look on his face in the first go-around, I say.

I've seen this look from men before. They call it envy.

I begged with all my heart for Father not to feel that way. I was trying to protect him from the pain of being separated from his companions.

"Heroes, I must ask you to stop arbitrarily exchanging your companions," Trash said calmly.

I started thinking in the back of my mind about how to kill him.

The crimson swine raised her hands and started to squeal about something or other.

"Really? Are you sure?" Father glanced over at the crimson swine.

The trap had been set off, I say.

Father had said the same thing the first go-around, I remembered. I restrained myself from telling Father to be careful as my teeth started unconsciously grinding with rage.

"Is there anyone else who would like to go with the Shield Hero?" Trash asked, but the room was silent. It appeared that the game had been fixed from the start. If things hadn't gone as planned, I would've been in trouble.

Trash let out an exaggerated sigh and glanced over at Father.

"There's nothing else we can do," Trash said. "Maybe the Shield Hero can find more companions willing to join him by scouting them himself. We planned to provide all of the heroes with a monthly income allowance, but since the Shield Hero doesn't have as many companions, let's give him a larger allowance than the others, shall we?"

"Yes, my lord!" A soldier came out bearing the money.

"Here is the allowance we have prepared for you. Please use it wisely."

Maybe I should buy something with the money. But no, if things went as they had in the first go-around, Father's allowance would be revoked, so I had to save money for him as well.

Well, it is possible to earn plenty of money by getting a guild job or something like that. But if my actions were too obvious, I'd end up putting Father in danger, I say.

Above all else, I had to teach Father about power-up methods. I really was reflecting on everything that happened in the previous go-around, I say.

By the way, I noticed that rather than calling Father by his name, Trash was only calling him Shield Hero.

"We will provide the Shield Hero with 800 silver coins, and 600 silver coins each to the rest of the heroes," Trash said. "Now that we've finished preparations, it would be best to set out on your journeys."

"Yes, my lord!"

All the oinking was giving me a headache! I truly despised the squealing of pigs.

Once the meeting ended, I thought about approaching Father. In the first go-around, if I recall correctly, when I tried to talk to Father, my pig companions had gotten in the way. Even after I dismissed my companions, they had kept trying to follow me all day. What a pain.

Should I start off by monitoring Father and the other heroes' actions from afar?

That pig was squealing in my face again. Speak human language, you vile swine! Pigs are truly the lowest of the low. There was no point in even speaking to them.

I'm not Ren, but I could take a page out of his book and pretend to be too cool for them. I decided to do that.

Without saying a word, I glanced back at my companions as if they were meaningless specks of dust and set out from the castle.

The pigs followed me silently. It seemed that they wouldn't bother me unless I started acting friendly toward Father.

But that made the situation particularly dangerous. Their role seemed to be to keep watch and make sure that Father stayed isolated from the other heroes. Orders from the crimson swine, I supposed.

It didn't matter. Even if I didn't get rid of them, simply ignoring them didn't seem to cause much of a problem.

Now, what to do?

I knew I had to protect Father. But I had to be careful about the timing. They would probably—no, definitely—summon us tomorrow. The crimson swine planned to make her move and come rushing to the pub tonight, if I recalled correctly.

Which meant that I had some time to visit a monster trainer! Yes! The perfect plan!

I hurried back to the filolial cottage. Several filolials chirped upon my arrival.

"Hey, you're the Spear Hero, right?" the manager of the stables, a refined-looking soldier, called out to me. "What are you planning to do with the castle filolials?"

"I love filolials," I proclaimed, petting as many filolials as I could. "Therefore, I would like to take care of them, I say!"

Since I ended up sleeping here last night, the filolials were already plenty familiar with me.

"Umm . . ."

"Gweh! Gweh!"

Yes, the filolials were letting me take care of them, I say!

I started to relax. I knew that tomorrow Father would be driven out by Melromarc, essentially penniless. All I had to do was resist doing anything reckless. If I made a mistake, who knows what obstacles would appear?

I heard some annoying squealing from one of my pig companions. I couldn't even shake them off for a moment. It's no fun to pet filolials with a hand that reeks of pigs.

It'd be easy to give them the slip. I could just turn the corner ahead of them and use my portal skill. But they'd surely make a fuss if I escaped, causing all sorts of problems. Hmm . . . Maybe there was some other way I could trick them and escape.

Regardless, if these pigs wanted to stop me from telling Father the truth, I'd let them—for now.

Or I could just kill them all.

Either way, tomorrow would determine my victory or defeat. My top priority was holding on to my money so I would be able to protect Father starting tomorrow.

I couldn't decide what to do. I thought about killing some monsters to get drop items like armor for Father, but I remembered that in the previous go-around it took Father some time to put on the armor properly.

On top of that, I had a feeling that I needed to think more about what Trash intended to do.

In the previous go-arounds, I didn't bother to think about Melromarc's plans until after rescuing Father. Of course, we had been safe at first, but then they started sending assassins. Which means that it was highly possible that this time they might try to assassinate Father as well.

But why hadn't they tried to assassinate Father in the first go-around? He had shabby, poor-quality equipment. He had been operating in a narrow radius as well, fighting low-level monsters near Melromarc castle town. Killing him would have been a piece of cake. Even assuming the heroes would level up quickly, and that they had level 20 companions guarding them, that was still 15 levels below that of any ordinary person here. Assassinating Father, who at the time was far weaker than any of the other heroes . . . Perhaps Melromarc had thought it wasn't even necessary?

When Father had tried to save big sis, the crimson swine had played us off one another, resulting in our duel. Maybe they thought that I would end up killing Father in our duel. It wasn't impossible.

A shiver ran up my spine as I thought about it all.

My reasoning was impeccable, I say! Assuming all my assumptions were correct . . . that left me with one course of action.

I had to move carefully, for Father's sake. If we took on a dangerous commission from the adventurers guild to make money, they might suspect that Father had become too strong and send an assassin his way. However, I could always rescue Father from a situation like that to gain his trust.

Because Father had no friends he could trust in the first go-around, his personality had completely changed. I wouldn't let any painful experiences like that happen to Father this time around, no matter what!

Which meant that it was essential that Father became strong enough to withstand any potential assassination attempts as quickly as possible.

My brain was practically overflowing with thoughts! I had never brought a plan like this to fruition before.

While I kept playing with the filolials, I pulled up my Portal Spear to confirm my registered locations. If I could obtain another Portal Spear power-up, I would be able to register even more places. That way, even if the time loop were to reset again, I'd have more options at my disposal.

The last go-around wasn't for nothing, after all! I had registered Siltvelt, a country that worshipped Father. Melromarc was afraid of Father getting there for that exact reason.

But since Father had been kind enough to trust me in the last go-around, we had a whole world of possibilities at our disposal!

And yet a few things were evident. First, I had to avoid helping out Father publicly at all costs, or Melromarc would simply put more effort into driving us apart. Second, in order to avoid war, we had to stay in Melromarc for the foreseeable future.

So any plans involving helping Father or going to Siltvelt were actually pointless to even think about right now.

If only we could secretly collude with Siltvelt. I was so close to the answer!

It was easy for me to imagine what would happen next if I just let things play out. Father would do just as he had done in the first go-around—that is to say, get stronger. So perhaps I should simply do nothing at all.

Then all I had to do was find my beloved Filo-tan, I say!

How could I become her groom? The truth of how Father had acquired her was steeped in mystery.

Based purely on past events, supposedly I should be able to buy her from the monster trainer . . . but I wasn't going to rely on blind faith this time around.

Above all, there was no way I was going to let anything else painful befall Father!

The only problem was that breathing under the same roof as the detestable crimson swine might cause me to go insane before I could achieve anything at all.

I had to search for Filo-tan like a gemstone dropped in a vast desert! Even if someone else ended up buying Filo-tan, I would still be able to find her *somewhere*. Her color was extremely particular, after all. Having just a single color was evidence of her high status and suggested that she might become a filolial king or queen. Yuki and Kou, Sakura, and then even Crim and Marine from before—they all had a base green color that covered more than half of their bodies. Then they had different colors mixed in.

Now that I thought about it, the filolial with the closest coloring to Filo-tan's was Sakura.

Sakura was an underlying pink, with white mixed in. But Filo-tan had been an underlying white with some pink mixed in. Completely different, I say.

The color of their eyes was also different. It's typical for filolial eyes to be the same color as the rest of the body, but Filo-tan had blue eyes. Which means that even if Filo-tan didn't become a filolial queen, I'd still be able to tell her apart based on those two crucial characteristics.

I, Motoyasu Kitamura, would never give up on finding Filo-tan as long as I lived. Even if it took me weeks, months, lifetimes . . . I would find her, I say!

I finally settled on my plan.

"Gweh!"

I leapt up, startling the filolials. I went outside, greeted the filolial caretaker, and hurried off toward the shadows of the main castle buildings.

"Oink!!"

Still following me, eh? Let's see just how far you chase me.

As soon as I entered the shadows of the castle, I used Portal Spear, and off I went.

Flipping through the options in my field of vision, I selected and teleported directly to the giant filolial ranch, I say!

"Excuuuuse me!" I called out to the farmer.

This time he was sitting in the pen.

"Who are you?"

"A customer!"

"And? What is it you're after, Mr. Customer?"

"I'd like you to give me a filolial egg, I say!"

The farmer glanced up at me, looking annoyed. He put a hand on his hip and stared at me. "Why do you want a filolial?" His responses were exactly the same as last time. He was wearing the same clothes too.

"Stop making that weird expression," he added.

"I like your clothes," I said.

"I didn't choose them for you!"

Oho? This part of the conversation was different. But I knew how to convince this farmer to sell me eggs! I knew how much he really cared for filolials, so I had to prove myself to him.

"Anyways, I would like you to sell me a filolial egg," I informed him.

"That's what I'm trying to tell you. I can't split up the filolials here. They're selling filolials other places," he said.

"I cannot accept no for an answer," I said. "Please sell them to me already."

"Why do you want filolials so badly?"

I wondered if this was some sort of strange test that the farmer always administered. But I wouldn't change my answer to his question—there was no particular reason. Filolials exist, so I raised them. You didn't need any thesis or theory about it.

Rather, to love and raise filolials is simply one of the rules of life.

If I had to say it straight, filolials raised by the power of love are the closest beings to gods that we have. That's why I cherish and raise filolials. They're like my sons and daughters.

Of course, the one exception being Filo-tan, my love and devotion.

"A world without filolials is not worth living in," I declared. "Yes! Filolials are the world's greatest treasure. They're like the air that I breathe. Without them, I'd simply choke and die."

"What are you even—" The farmer cut himself off. "You

think I'd let you buy one just by saying something so ridiculous?"

"I love all filolials," I continued. "They're like my children. Whether they're fast or slow, strong or weak, smart or stupid . . . they're the . . . the meaning of my life!" I burst into tears.

"So you like filolials that much?"

"Of course I do!" I wailed.

He watched me with narrowed eyes.

"Okay then. If you answer my questions correctly, I'll sell to you."

He stood up and walked over to me. I easily aced his quiz about identifying types of filolials. *Identifying filolials is easier than taking candy from a baby for me!*

"Wow. I've never met anyone who knows as much about filolials as you."

"I've felt this way each time I've visited your farm, but I must say that it lacks key security components," I told him. "I'm afraid your filolials might get hurt if you're not careful."

"Don't start thinking that I'll listen to any of your crazy ideas," he said. "Okay then, you, just prove to me how well you raised them one day."

"Most definitely!"

Unfortunately, I couldn't show him how well I had raised Yuki and the others last time. But I, Motoyasu Kitamura, had every intention of keeping my promise.

"So?" the farmer asked. "How many filolials do you want, and what's your budget?"

Since I had the funds Melromarc provided me, I had considerably more money than last time I had visited his farm. However, I did have to save money to give to Father.

I held up three fingers.

"Three? Okay then. How about one good one and two cheap ones?"

"That's fine with me."

I don't discriminate between filolials, I say. But I did have the parental love for those that I already raised—so I would love to meet them again!

The farmer took me back to the shed where he kept the filolial eggs. Just like last time, he chose one egg from the back as if it were special and then two from a pile near the entrance.

"That's no good," I declared.

"What?"

According to my memory, he had chosen different filolial eggs than last time. That wouldn't do!

"For the egg from the back, can you choose the one over to the right? And for the other ones, how about these two?" I pointed to the eggs that I recalled were those of Yuki, Sakura, and Kou.

"So does this combination work?"

"That's perfect. I love any and all filolials, but this time, those eggs are the ones calling out to me, I say."

The farmer handed me the filolial eggs. I stroked them

gently and confirmed that they had the same texture as last time. There was no doubt that these eggs were Yuki, Kou, and Sakura!

"Thank you very much!" I proclaimed.

"Come back and show me them some time," the farmer said.

"No doubt! I'll show you the legendary filolials that I raise!"

Yes, I would show him the power of love! Even better, once I established myself, I'd come back to buy more.

"All right then. Your so-called legendary filolials . . . I'm looking forward to seeing them."

"See you!"

And that's how I got Yuki and the others back into my hands, I say. With that, I returned to Melromarc.

Chapter Thirteen: False Proof

I returned to the castle via portal and set up the filolial egg incubator. I registered the monster seal.

"And for Kou too . . ." I registered Yuki's and Kou's eggs and took a long look at Sakura's egg.

Hmmm.

Sakura had been really attached to Father. She had protected him too. Something about their intimate relationship had been etched into my mind.

That's it!

Because all three filolials had helped Father level up, he ended up being considerate and humble. But if we grew the filolials here, and if I had Sakura protect Father from the beginning, perhaps we'd see their true feelings take the stage a little more clearly. Yes, that's it! She would end up a little behind Yuki and Kou, but I would make Sakura Father's exclusive filolial!

And so I registered Sakura's egg to Father.

I heard some vile oinking behind me. I turned around to see a pig pointing and coming my way.

All my happiness vanished in an instant. *Don't approach, you filthy animal!*

As I begged the creature to come no closer, I realized that

the sun was going down. It was time to settle down for the night.

Completely ignoring the pig and concealing the eggs under my clothes, I set out for the room that I had slept in during the first night with all the other filolials.

After that, I went to my usual favorite pub. Soon enough, the crimson swine came rushing in, crying. I figured she was making her vile accusation of Father.

"Oink-oink! Oiiiiiiink!"

The loathsome grinding of her voice nearly caused me to spit chunks on the spot, I say. Should I kill her here and now?

If I did, who knows what sort of strange effects it could have on the future?

I felt pity for Father, not knowing where his companion, the crimson swine, had gone, only to find out she and Trash were plotting his downfall.

I swore to fulfill my promise to Father no matter what. I managed to swallow my pride and not kill the crimson swine on the spot.

"Oink! Oink!"

The crimson swine kept trying to speak.

"Leave me alone already," I declared. "No matter how much you snort and squeal, I won't be deceived, you filthy swine!"

That pig ought to know that the only reason it was still alive is the boundless mercy of Father, I say!

At my merciful disparagement, the crimson swine started whining and squealing even more and started to run away. She would go on to Itsuki next, I supposed.

My God. Was there no way to just eliminate her without messing up the course of future events? I was starting to get impatient.

But I had to fulfill my promises to Father. Killing the crimson swine would cause all sorts of problems.

As we went further and further along, surely we would eventually reach a point where it didn't matter if I killed her, right?

When I thought back to our battle in the first go-around, it was still a bitter memory.

We launched an attack on the Spirit Tortoise thinking that we could win, but the crimson swine fled and we lost. I lost consciousness for some time, and after I was cured to full health, I spent the rest of my time still chasing after her.

There's no point in pursuing a pig that thinks of nothing but herself, I say.

After my heart had been worn out by the chase, it was Filo-tan who finally saved my soul.

That's when my eyes were finally opened to true love!

I supposed to that end, the crimson swine had actually been useful. I decided to be merciful and send her to a painless death.

I had to figure out how to kill the crimson swine as soon as possible without messing up the future. In case the time loop got reset another time, at least I knew where Father, Ren, and Itsuki were during the first few days.

I could clearly see how Trash and the crimson swine were trying to drive the heroes apart with the false accusation against Father. When the time loop reset the first time and I tried to get close to Father, they tried to eliminate us immediately. But now that I was keeping it cool and letting the situation play out, things were moving forward without incident.

Trash had even prepared separate rooms for us. There was no doubt they were trying to prevent us heroes from linking up. And one way to do that was to ensure we all hated Father—the one hero actually capable of bringing us together.

I was slowly but surely accumulating knowledge in order to create a future where the four of us got along, I say.

Of course, I wasn't just going to give up on this go-around so easily.

And I especially haven't given up on my dream of becoming my beloved Filo-tan's husband.

There were plenty of ways for me to acquire more income without causing a fuss. It was just a bit longer before I would be able to take action, I say!

At the very least, I, Motoyasu Kitamura, had once more acquired my precious Yuki, Sakura, and Kou! I could tell it was them by the smell and texture of the eggs!

Well, in the last go-around, I hadn't been able to get Crim and the others, so to a certain extent it depended on the timing, I supposed. Which meant that I simply had to acquire as many filolial eggs as I could from all over. The fact that I hadn't hatched Kuro in the last go-around either was further proof that the timing was essential.

"All right, time to sleep, I say!"

I went back to my room and fell asleep while cuddling my filolial eggs tight.

The next morning came.

As I suspected, because I had insulted the crimson swine the previous night, they didn't come to summon me. So I went over to the castle a little before the time I had been summoned in the first go-around.

As I reached the castle, a few soldiers hurried over to greet me.

"What could you need at such an early hour, if I may ask?" one of them asked me.

"Am I not allowed to go to the castle?" I said.

"Ah . . . at the moment the castle is quite crowded. Would you mind coming back after sunrise?"

At that moment, a carriage with Ren and his companions arrived.

"Hey, Motoyasu. Did they also summon you?" Ren asked.

"They did, I say," I proclaimed.

Ren's group had arrived at the perfect time.

But when I stepped forward to move past the soldiers, they ignored me and signaled for only Ren's carriage to enter.

"What's going on?" Ren asked.

"Please enter, Sword Hero," the soldier said.

"What about Motoyasu? He was also summoned, wasn't he?"

"That's right," I said. "Will you not let me in?"

The soldiers glanced around at each other in confusion. Would Ren be suspicious of their behavior?

"What's the problem?" Ren asked. "And if you only summoned me and not Motoyasu, why?"

"No, that's not it . . ." The soldier faltered. "Please go ahead, Spear Hero."

"Thank you very much."

Hah! That was a big win, I say. I was able to bulldoze my way through with Ren's group.

"Motoyasu, where are your companions?"

"Still asleep," I said. "I didn't want to wake them up, so I came alone."

"Gotcha."

"Where did you stay, Ren?"

"Me? We were resting two villages out from the castle when they called me back here."

"Interesting. If I may ask, which village?"

I pulled up the map of Melromarc in my head. There were two or three villages we could get to in a day's travel.

"It's called—"

For some reason, Ren had gone south from the castle town.

Now that I thought about it, we weren't supposed to overlap in our hunting grounds. I decided to keep that information in mind.

We advanced through the castle and found Itsuki, Trash, and the crimson swine waiting in the throne room.

"Calling us so suddenly back to the castle the very day after we left . . . what's the matter?" Ren asked.

Trash and Itsuki looked displeased at seeing me standing next to Ren. The crimson swine let out a hideous stream of filthy noises from her mouth.

What a painful memory. Every time I think about that first go-around, it still hurts.

The crimson swine had come to my room in tears, saying that Father had been about to rape her. Then she went to the castle to inform Trash. They put on quite the show in front of Itsuki and Ren. She cried about how terrified she was and begged us to help her. It was good acting, and Ren and Itsuki agreed with me that Father's actions were unforgivable.

This time around, the crimson swine, excessively close to Itsuki and Ren, if I might say, was squealing on and on.

And then she pointed at me and squealed some more.

"Motoyasu, is it true that you called her a pig?" Ren asked.

"She is a pig," I informed him. "She's laid careful traps to hide her evil deeds. If that's not a pig, show me what is!"

"Hide evil deeds?"

"Oink oink!"

Ren raised his eyebrows and frowned. The crimson swine rushed between Ren and me and tried to shove me away.

I didn't even blink. She didn't comprehend my true strength, I say. And how about you finally use human words, you disgusting swine?

I was sure that she was spewing some lie or another. If I could understand her, my ears would probably shrivel and rot.

She kept carrying on and on next to Ren. Meanwhile, Itsuki had been glaring at me this entire time.

"Itsuki, is there something that you want to say?" I asked him.

"I wanted to tell you yesterday, but it's seriously messed up to keep calling women pigs!" he shouted. "They're human, Motoyasu!"

I burst into hysterical laughter.

"What's so funny?" he shouted.

Oh, Itsuki, you silly little boy, I thought, wiping tears from my eyes. He was even wearing a suit of armor stolen from Father. He looked so official and serious in his shining suit of armor that it was totally absurd.

"If that's what you think, you ought to look into where you got that suit of armor from," I told him.

"Myne gave it to me!"

"That's what I'm trying to tell you! It's stolen goods, I say!"

"Oh yeah? Show me proof!"

"In this land, they inscribe the maker and manufacturer's name and number into armaments, I say!"

That was an indisputable fact. Of course, the fact that artisans would inscribe their name into a weapon or suit of armor that they make is obvious. But in Melromarc there was also a rule to inscribe the information of the manufacturer as well. It was a rule that came in handy when valuable items were stolen.

There were some items that didn't have this information inscribed. But that suit of armor did.

"Who bought that suit of armor?" Ren asked. "And where—"

"Oiiiiink! Oiiiiink!"

Just as I brought some evidence to the table, the pig started whining in a horrible grating shrill in attempt to stall the matter.

"Cut the nonsense, crimson swine!" I shouted.

I pushed her out of the way and told Itsuki the truth.

"Do you understand now?"

"Is this true?" Itsuki asked, looking up at Trash and the crimson swine.

Trash stroked his chin.

"Mr. Kawasumi, would you mind showing me that suit of armor? I'd like to make a comparison."

A soldier brought a lantern up to Itsuki to illuminate the armor. Itsuki reluctantly took off the armor and held it in front of the lantern. The soldier talked with Trash quietly and then began the analysis.

"According to our documents, this suit of armor is from this very castle!" Trash declared.

That scheming Trash! He even had documents forged! The fact that he had the foresight to think of that meant trouble.

"That doesn't change the fact that it was stolen from the castle!" I shouted.

"Oiiiiink! Oink!"

The crimson swine leapt up proudly and, putting on a show of grace, strutted around the room, squealing the whole time.

"I see," Itsuki said. "So if Myne is the princess, that means that anything in this castle technically belongs to her."

I was beginning to lose my cool. First forged documents, now the assertion that her thievery was justified.

But . . . at the very least, I noticed that Ren was starting to look dubious about the whole exchange.

"I don't care about any of that," Ren said.

But he still wouldn't take Father's side, I supposed.

"So, Motoyasu, listen to me! She's not a pig and she's not evil. Didn't she just give you so many of her own resources from this very castle? Your behavior is offensive!"

"A lying pig is still a pig," I told him. "We couldn't trust them from the moment that the pig's father checked his 'documents,' I say."

"What are you even trying to say!?" Itsuki yelled.

"Claiming that everything belongs to her because she's the princess is just further evidence of what she's trying to pull here! As a princess, forging evidence is a simple matter for her!"

Was this not a statement of fact? The children of the rich make false proof all the time, relying on the authority of their parents to get what they want. This was no different. Verbal evidence is hardly enough to prove anything in modern society! But I supposed that may not apply to this world.

"There is some truth to what Motoyasu is saying," Ren said.

"Ren! Whose side are you on here?" Itsuki began.

"I'm not on anyone's side," he said. "But there's logic to what Motoyasu is saying. If she was just a regular adventurer, then I think we could trust the king here, but she's his daughter. So if they really were trying to take out Naofumi, then they obviously would forge evidence that proves otherwise."

Trash quickly spoke up. "Hm, Mr. Spear Hero, the official audience has ended. Would you kindly take your leave?"

"I will not do so," I announced.

It seemed like Trash was getting nervous, I say, trying to get rid of me immediately after Ren took my side. I had no intention of leaving that room!

Especially because I knew what would happen next.

"Please leave at once!" the king shouted.

All at once, soldiers surrounded me.

"Don't touch me, scum," I warned them.

I scattered them everywhere with a gentle shake of my spear.

"Motoyasu! If you don't calm down—"

Meanwhile, out of the corner of my eye, I saw Father in custody, being led into the room by soldiers. I realized that this was all the result of me not speaking up sooner.

I had to save Father!

"Myne!" Father cried.

Trash and Itsuki glared at him.

Ren broke the long silence.

"Hey, somebody tell me what's going on here."

I could finally rescue Father! I just had to make sure I didn't screw up the timing.

"Well, we haven't finished with Motoyasu, but we may as well get started with you," Itsuki said. "So you're telling us you really don't remember anything that happened?"

"Don't remember?" Father asked. "I rem—hey!"

Father pointed at Itsuki's suit of armor. Of course, Father would display his genius-level intellect!

Every time I saw this scene, I was afraid that my heart might burst.

But if I tried to do something, the soldiers would almost certainly interfere. Should I kill them, just like that cursed Smoked Human?

"I've been robbed!" Father shouted.

"What are you talking about?" exclaimed Itsuki. "Naofumi—I never imagined you would do something so sinful, but—"

"Sinful? What are you talking about?"

"Get out of the way," I informed the soldiers, easily mowing them down and hurrying over toward Ren and Itsuki. I saw how pale Father was.

"So what are the charges?" Ren asked.

The soldiers had realized that I was going to take Father's side, and even more appeared as I hurried back toward the throne room. Didn't they see that I was trying to hold back from killing every last one of them?

"Charges? What are you talking about?" Father asked.

"Oink oink!"

"Huh?"

The crimson swine let out a series of unintelligible squeals.

This time I'd stop those villains from anything and everything they intended to do to hurt Father, I say.

I knew the truth.

I knew how Father was so wise . . . so kind.

I knew how even after he had gone through horrific, traumatic experiences, he never lost his kindness.

I knew the truth, I say!

Even before I discovered the truth, when Father fell into this evil trap the first time, he lovingly accepted even me—the very person who demanded that he be locked up in the first place!

I knew everything. That he would use every last bit of my strength to protect the people he loved. That he would lend his strength to anyone in need. I would do anything I could—not to save the world—but to save Father, for his sake alone. I was going to return his kindness. Even if the time loop reset again and again, I vowed to never forsake my duty.

"Oiiiiiiiiiiiiiiink!"

"What?" Ren looked confused.

"What are you talking about? After we ate dinner, I just went to sleep!" Father said.

"You're lying!" Itsuki exclaimed. "Why was Myne crying, then?"

Wasn't it obvious?

That pig was showacting, you fool!

"She's a pig," I explained to Itsuki. "Fake tears."

"Won't you shut up?" he shouted.

Yikes. Now he was all pissed off. My words weren't even making it to his ears, I say.

But Itsuki's righteous outrage was insignificant compared to Father, who actually had the right to be angry here.

"Why are you trying to defend Myne?" Father asked Itsuki. "How did you get that suit of armor?"

"Well, when everyone was out drinking yesterday, Myne showed up at the pub. We drank for a while and then she gave me this suit of armor as a present. The king checked the records—it came from the castle," Itsuki explained.

"What the . . ." Father trailed off. He looked like he didn't know what to say. I realized that certainly it would be confusing if you were told that the exact same set of armor had also come from the castle.

"Of course!" Father continued. "King! I—someone robbed me while I was asleep! They took my wallet and all of my equipment, everything besides my shield! Can't we please do something to catch the perpetrator?"

"Silence, sinner!" Trash roared. "Attempted rape is an unforgivable crime in this country! If you weren't a hero, it would be a death sentence!"

Ren glanced around the room and closed his eyes as if he understood what was going on.

"That's why I'm telling you it's a misunderstanding! I didn't do it!"

Father's eyes flashed with anger and he turned to Itsuki.

"You! You're accusing me just to get my equipment and my money, aren't you!?"

"Wait, what? You're a sex criminal. What are you trying—"

"Cut the bullshit!" cried Father. "You were after my money from the start, weren't you? You were conspiring from the very beginning!"

It was almost time for me to step in, wasn't it?

It was painful to delay this whole time, to wait and wait for Father's downfall. But I was ready to step in and save the day.

I put my hands on my spear and started to charge it.

"This is obviously a charade," Ren muttered as I knocked some soldiers out of the way.

"Move it! Brionac!"

It would leave a bad impression to turn them into half-burnt charcoal, but in this case, I didn't have much choice. I tried to adjust the power of the attack.

The soldiers let out hideous wails as their bodies disintegrated. I sent the soldiers who were trying to hold back Father flying, I say!

"Huh?" Father gasped.

"I believe you, Father," I said. "I know that you didn't do it. It's a conspiracy, I say."

I gave my spear a twirl and turned to face Trash and Itsuki.

"You wanted to keep me out of this so you could do as you pleased, but there won't be much of that anymore, I say!"

"How dare you!" Trash scowled at me, furious that I had upended his scheme.

"So they were trying to take out Naofumi, huh?"

I turned and saw that the suspicious words were uttered by none other than Ren.

Hmm. I wanted to remain on guard, but this time around, for some reason it appeared that Ren had actually taken my side. So perhaps he would believe Father after all!

But right now, my top priority is to protect Father. I turned to Father.

"This is the second time I've come to protect you," I declared. "So I'll tell you now what I told you then."

Father tilted his head in confusion as I leaned close to him to proclaim the glorious truth:

"I've come from the future to repay your kindness, Father!"

Chapter Fourteen: Avoiding War

Trash, the crimson swine, Itsuki, and the rest of the Melromarc soldiers were glaring at us.

So now what?

I had exposed their outrageous scheme, but if I didn't act carefully, this situation could lead to a war.

I supposed we were right back where we started.

"Father, there's no need to sigh anymore!" I declared. "You're no longer alone! Even if the whole world turns against you, I, Motoyasu Kitamura, will stand by your side!"

"K-Kitamura?"

I helped Father up and turned back to Trash with a furious stare.

"You vile scum!"

Meanwhile, in the background Ren was trying to slip out of the room.

"Ren! Whose side are you on?" Itsuki called.

"I just said that there is some truth to Motoyasu's reasoning, that's all," Ren said evasively. "Even though Myne is the princess, we can't believe her based on verbal testimony alone. Because of what happened yesterday with the companions, it's also easy to believe that they had the cards stacked against Naofumi from the start."

Father stared at both of us, dumbfounded.

"Don't get the wrong idea," Ren said. "I'm not saying that Naofumi's innocent either. But still, there's been the rumor circulating that the Shield Hero is weak, and every time Motoyasu tries to do something nice for Naofumi, a bunch of soldiers try to stop him. That's definitely suspicious."

Trash growled and the crimson swine spat a stream of squeals and oinks, pointing at Father all the while. She was talking to Ren and Itsuki. She seemed to be making some sort of entreaty. Itsuki continued to glare furiously at Father, while Ren watched the scene from a cool distance.

"I didn't do any of it!" Father cried.

"Whoever's telling the truth, there's not enough proof to punish Naofumi," Ren said. "If you want attention, look for it elsewhere. This is a waste of my time." Ren turned around and started to exit. "And don't even think about calling me back here for anything else like this."

Ren's companions hurried out after him.

While Ren hadn't passed judgment one way or the other, I suspected he knew who was truly guilty here. It was a good sign, but I also suspected there could be danger. Perhaps Ren was at risk of an assassination attempt now.

Well, I figured Ren would turn out fine.

"Oink oink oink oink!"

The crimson swine was screaming at the top of her lungs.

Now that things hadn't gone her way, she was showing her true character!

An ugly character indeed.

I couldn't bear to let Father gaze upon such a loathsome sight for much longer.

"Wait!" shouted Trash. Should I just kill him? "The Shield Hero is not yet cleared of these charges!"

"Don't listen to me—why don't you just listen to Ren, I say!" I proclaimed. "There's not enough evidence to punish Father, and that's the end of it. And if you don't let it be . . . I'll spread the word about Melromarc's unjust behavior to other lands."

Trash made a fist and ground his teeth. That finally shut him up.

"Father, let's leave here at once. There's no point in saying anything else."

I took Father's hand and we left the throne room.

All the way through the castle, soldiers watched us unpleasantly, but when I returned their gaze, they quickly broke eye contact. I exhaled as we finally made it outside the castle.

"Um . . . Thanks for saving me, Kitamura," Father said. "No, Motoyasu."

"It's nothing at all," I declared. "I believe you, Father."

"Yeah." Father sighed. "I didn't do it. I didn't even have anything to drink yesterday. I just went to sleep in our room."

I was talking with Father in a wide field in the castle town. He was still in his long underwear since all his equipment had been stolen. Hadn't that happened before as well?

Simply holding a shield made your life more dangerous in Melromarc, I say!

"Motoyasu?"

"I'd like to speak with you alone," I informed Father.

"Huh? Well, that's fine, but this fight isn't just about me."

"You're right, Father. You have me as well!" I proclaimed. "Next up, clothes." In order to make him appear weak, I thought it would be best for Father to wear cheap clothes for the time being.

"Where are we going?" Father asked.

"We're going to buy clothes! Oh, and don't worry about paying, because I have the money for it!"

"No, I'm fine with money," Father said.

Oho? Did Father still have some money this time?

Father showed me the backside of his shield and withdrew silver coins from a small compartment.

I recalled that in the first go-around Father had hidden some coins in the back of his shield too. Father's peerless genius brought tears to my very eyes!

"Uh, Motoyasu. Why are you crying?"

"It's hard to explain," I sobbed. "Well then, let's go! Let's buy you some armor!"

"Let's do it."

We went to the weapon shop that Father had visited in a previous go-around. It was open early in the morning. Once we had gone inside, the conversation went pretty much the same way it did before. The old weapon shop owner believed Father when he explained how he hadn't done anything wrong.

"All right, kid, so what do you want?"

"Before that," I said, "do you mind if I have a word with Father in the back of the shop?"

"Huh? Yeah, sure."

The old guy led us to the back room, where a chair was prepared.

"When you're done talking, come back to the shop and buy something," he said and tactfully closed the door behind him as he left.

"What is it, Motoyasu?"

"There are several things I'd like to tell you about," I announced. "Things like weapon power-ups in addition to our current situation and how to move forward."

"Uh, sure."

"First, I have something very important to tell you."

"What is it? All that talk about the time loop . . . I mean, it was just hard to believe so suddenly."

"It's true, I say!"

"Well, in that case, explain to me why they made such a

ridiculous false accusation against me!?" Father raised his voice practically to the point of shouting! What a righteous rage! Very well, I'd calm him down.

"I'm so sorry about everything that happened to you, Father," I said. "In the previous time loop, I explained it to you right after we were summoned—this country would try to spring a trap for you and drive you out, penniless. Melromarc believes that the Shield Hero is the enemy of the state."

"What?"

Father looked taken aback. Now that I thought about it, Father didn't know yet about how Melromarc discriminated against demi-humans. So he also didn't know about how demi-humans worship the Shield Hero.

"Why didn't you tell me this earlier!"

"In the first go-around, I believed the crimson swine," I informed him. "They punished you and drove you out of the castle. The soldiers were on the brink of killing you."

"I see." Father nodded. "So you were looking out for me this time. Even when I didn't have any companions, you tried to give me one of yours. You tried to tell me about the weapon power-ups and how to get stronger too. So there was a reason why you reacted so strongly to the women trying to talk to you."

Father continued to put his genius on display. He had guessed the entire truth from what I had told him! But what did he mean by "women"?

"Are you talking about the pigs?"

"You keep calling them pigs."

"Because they're pigs, I say! They're creatures that think of nothing but themselves and how to use other people to their own advantage."

"Uh . . . right. So you call women pigs. I think I get it. And so?"

"In the previous go-around, they sent assassins after you. For that reason, we went to a country of demi-humans called Siltvelt, where they worship the Shield Hero, and they welcomed us in."

I went on to explain in detail everything that happened to us in the last go-around—about how we got past the fortress at the border, defeated Melromarc's assassins, and were attacked again at the town on the way.

"So what happened to me after we made it to Siltvelt? Did I try to get revenge on Melromarc?"

"Of course not, Father. Since we were safe there and people believed us, you let it be."

Father nodded. "That's crazy. Well, I guess even now I don't really want anything to do with that royal family. It might be better to just let it be."

"The very first time the time loop reset, I also tried to protect you. That time I sent you off to Siltvelt by yourself, but . . ." I explained how most likely Father had been killed at the

Melromarc border. Father understood what had happened at once.

"That makes sense. This is a tough situation." He paused. "So we made it all the way to Siltvelt last time, right?"

"That's right."

"So why didn't you tell—actually, why *did* you tell me all those weird things?"

"What do you mean by weird things, Father?"

"About my husband and the bird child and all that."

I bowed my head in shame. "Before the time loop reset, I did terrible things," I whispered. Yes, no matter how many times I apologized, my sins would never be erased.

"Uh, Motoyasu?"

"When they successfully launched their false accusation against you in the first go-around . . . I was there alongside the crimson swine, where Itsuki stood today."

Father looked taken aback.

"After that, you were penniless, without a single friend, driven out of the castle. But with your tireless will, you managed to prove your innocence and destroy Trash and this country's foul religion!"

"Whoa, slow down a second!" Father said. "You're not even answering my question!"

"In your broken-hearted state, you tried to sleep with a man, but he ran away from you," I gasped.

"And my daughter?"

"You purchased her from a monster trainer and raised a glorious filolial, none other than Filo-tan, I say!" My voice quaked as I spoke and glistening tears dripped from my cheeks.

Father's shock was visible. "Not even a real child!? A monster trainer—that means she's just a pet! You gave me the complete wrong idea about all this!"

A pet? Filo-tan, a pet?

The image of Filo-tan with a collar around her neck floated into my mind. I started shivering violently at the very thought!

"All right, I understand. In that case . . . Motoyasu, I want you to remember something if the time loop resets again."

"What is it, Father?"

"When I'm first summoned here, I'm still a normal person, so don't tell me all that weird stuff. I won't believe you even if I want to. Part of me won't trust you."

"Of course!" I declared. "I understand, Father!"

So what he meant was that if I told him the part about sleeping with a man, then he wouldn't believe me. Naturally!

Of course, in the case of filolials, I should still tell him everything.

"You'd be better off telling me that I adopted someone that was important to you, or something like that. I'd believe you, then," he said.

What impeccable advice! If I explained that Filo-tan was

adopted, then he would believe me! Since Filo-tan is *not* a pet.

I, Motoyasu Kitamura, seared Father's words into my soul!

"So? Did I miss your explanation about why Melromarc set up this whole false accusation against me?" Father asked.

"That's what you told me in the future!" I proclaimed. "You told me to make my knowledge of the future useful!"

"Uh . . ." Father blinked. "You're still not—okay, so why did I tell you that?"

"Because you went to Siltvelt, there ended up being a lot of wars, and so we weren't able to properly focus on defeating the waves of destruction," I told him.

"I thought I didn't care about getting revenge."

"Yes! But . . ." I explained to Father about all the problems that happened to us in Siltvelt: Takt, the Claw Hero, and the fox beast that impersonated him, then the war with Shieldfreeden and Melromarc.

"So that sort of large-scale war ended up happening all because I went to Siltvelt." Father shook his head, seemingly at a loss for words at the size of the problem.

"Well, shall we get going?" I asked him. "This time we'll make things go smoothly, I promise, Father!"

This time I'd eliminate Takt and all of his remnants in one fell swoop, I say.

Then there would be no war!

It was a bullet-proof plan that used my knowledge of the past, like Father asked me to. Right?

"Well, I agree that because we have your knowledge, things might go more smoothly than last time, but . . ." Father trailed off and he frowned. "No, I think you're right. If we can avoid causing any problems for the first three months or so, it will make a big difference. We just need to avoid any slipups. I wasn't summoned here to fight in wars, after all."

"Yes, Father!"

"We'll do our best to avoid any war," Father said. "I have no doubt that you did actually come from the future, Motoyasu."

"I, Motoyasu Kitamura, will do anything that you ask of me, Father!"

"So what do we do now? You want to stay with me in Melromarc and prevent the loop from resetting again, right?" he asked.

"That's exactly right!"

Father sat down in the chair and stretched his legs. "So in about three months, I'll finally get a chance to see that king and Myne, who put me through all that. No choice but to wait for our chance, I suppose."

"Yes, Father. You told me in the future to not try to solve problems with my strength alone."

"Got it. So until then, I have to do my best to get stronger," Father said.

"It would be best to train unnoticed," I informed him. "Ah, of course, let me teach you about the power-up methods!"

And that's when I heard a crackling sound coming from inside my shirt. I pulled out the filolial egg. Yuki and Kou were about to hatch!

"Uh, Motoyasu, did you buy filolials with your provisions?"

"Of course I did!"

The eggs cracked and Yuki and Kou peeped their faces out of the eggshells.

"Chirp!"

"Wow, they're adorable!"

The filolials jumped into the palm of my hand and scrambled up my arm as Father watched them.

"So you're raising those monsters that pull the carriages here," Father said. He looked at the filolials with an expression of wonder. I supposed he didn't know anything about filolials, so there was nothing I could do about it. Filolials are wondrous creatures, after all.

Which is why I won't ever stop raising them!

"Did you already decide on their names?" Father asked.

"I did. You named them in the last go-around."

"Really? What are their names?"

"Do you want to try to guess? By the way, their names aren't 'White,' 'Yellow,' or 'Chick.' The white one is female and the yellow one is male."

Father watched Yuki and Kou chirp and jump around.

"Well, the white one is as white as snow, so let's use the

Japanese word for snow and name her 'Yuki.' And the Japanese character for yellow can be read as 'Kou,' so let's go with that."

"Amazing! You guessed right!"

"Really? I wasn't sure about it, but that's good to hear. Even something like this must have to do with the way the time loop works, I suppose," he pondered.

"Chirp!"

Yuki and Kou continued to hop around cheerfully.

"All right then. So now I should give you the filolial guardian that I registered to you, Father." I took out the filolial egg that had not yet been incubated and showed it to Father.

"This is Sakura. I haven't imprinted her egg with a monster seal yet."

"You're giving it to me?"

"Sakura was very attached to you, Father. I wanted to make you her master so you could become stronger together!"

I gave Father the egg.

"Do you know how to register the egg?" I asked him.

"I mark the imprinted seal with my blood, right?"

"That is correct. Even if you have no other companions, she will be a perfect partner for you."

Father borrowed one of the knives in the back room, made a small cut on his finger, and completed the monster seal.

"So what should we do next?" Father asked.

"Well, in the first go-around, you . . ." I trailed off. What *had* Father been up to in the first go-around?

I knew that he purchased big sis and leveled up little by little, but had there been something else?

"Motoyasu?"

I remembered that he brought slaves with him and started peddling goods and medicine, if I wasn't mistaken.

"Before the first time loop, you made money by peddling goods," I informed him.

"Peddling goods? Like, going around and selling stuff?"

"Exactly. I remember that you took Filo-tan with you and went from place to place selling. That was back when I was always chasing around pigs."

Even now I could still remember my stupidity. As soon as Filo-tan saw my face, she raised her voice into a furious rage and sent me flying with a mighty kick.

But that pain was what had connected me with Filo-tan, I say! I explained what happened to Father.

"Uh, isn't that crazy? She sent you flying? You seem happy about it," he said.

"That was Filo-tan's rebuke of love," I moaned.

"Hey, Motoyasu! Wake up!" Father shouted.

"Chirp!"

"It's no good. He's totally lost in thought." Father sighed.

Filo-tan.

Where could you possibly be?

I vowed to find Filo-tan and bring her back to me. With all my heart!

"So peddling, huh? I have no idea what we would be selling, but since I was penniless, I probably needed some way to get money. How did I do it?" Father wondered aloud.

Father appeared to be thinking about it.

"You sold prescription medicine, I say!" I proclaimed.

"Ah!" Father yelped. "Don't disappear and come back all of a sudden like that!" Father had been playing with Yuki and Kou, letting them climb onto his shoulder.

"So medicine? Did I know all about that back then?"

"I know that for a fact," I declared. "You made medicine and sold it."

"If this were a game, I might be able to make some medicine. But right now I don't think I'd be able to do it properly."

"With your weapon's mixing skill, it's highly possible," I said. "But I think you were making it even without using that skill."

When you really think about it, Father had so many talents. Of course, there was his excellent cooking, the fact that he was beloved by everyone he met, and his knowledge of medicine too!

"Hmm. Okay. If I can make it with my shield skill, I'll try that. But I don't know what medicine they have here, so we need to go visit a pharmacy. If I don't know what to mix, I can't use the mixing ability, after all."

Now that he mentioned it, Father's shield would have reset

with the time loop, unlike my spear. So in order for Father to remember the mixing skill, we would need to defeat some monsters first.

I looked up the recipe for the mixing skill in my weapon book.

Found it! It looked like we'd be able to gather it from monsters nearby.

"Okay, so once we get my equipment," Father said, "we'll go to get the mixing skill and then start peddling. Sounds like we have a plan."

"We'll also need to get someone to help us sell when we actually start peddling."

"Yeah, I guess so," Father said. "If the Shield Hero is the enemy of the state, then people won't want to buy medicine from him. Now that I think about it, Motoyasu . . ."

"What is it, Father?"

Father glanced at me cautiously. Did I do something strange?

"This seems like a big problem. How do we get someone to help us sell? We can't afford to be betrayed again, for one. And it seems dangerous to get anyone from Siltvelt to help us. And if we leave it to someone we don't know, they might steal from us."

I nodded. Father was right.

"In that case," I said, "we'll just use a slave!"

Chapter Fifteen: A Better World

Father's jaw dropped. He sure looked awfully surprised every time he heard about slaves.

"And slaves can never betray their masters because of slave seals," I explained. "Slave seals are patterns engraved into the slave that cause them pain whenever they disobey their master." No different from a monster seal, now that I thought about it.

However, even without a seal, filolials would never betray their masters. That was definitely a step up from pigs.

"That's terrible! There's no way I could do something like that!" Father said.

"You said the exact same thing before," I told him. "But in the first go-around, without any companions to rely on, you had no choice but to rely on slaves instead."

Big sis was one of Father's slaves, after all. The crimson swine had tried to drive me and Father apart, as I hadn't understood the bonds Father had nurtured with Raphtalia back then.

"With your slaves, you were able to earn plenty of money," I continued. "And in battle, you would defend everyone while your slaves attacked."

"Since I can't attack without your help, and if I had to be on my own . . ." Father nodded in thought. "I suppose slaves would be the only way to do it."

Father was squeezing Sakura's egg tight, I say!

"So will we ask this filolial to help us sell medicine?" Father asked.

"Well, filolials all have very different personalities," I informed him. "Sakura was best at protecting you, Father, but maybe she can be a peddler too."

If I was remembering correctly, I didn't think any of the filolials had helped out with the peddling. Filolials liked having fun, so I think selling medicine to humans could be a bit difficult for them.

"Hmm . . . this is tricky," Father said.

"There's no need to worry, I say!"

"What?"

"Since you were the one who taught your slaves to defeat monsters—and with a smile on your face—I'm sure you'll have no problem with slaves this time around either. You had a whole horde of them, after all."

"That makes it even worse!" Father stood up and raised his voice again. "Just how evil do I become in the future? Making slaves fight and kill monsters, and even worse, brainwashing them to think that it's fun—this is all so messed up!"

Oho? I got the sense that Father did not quite understand the reality here. I had to tell him the truth.

"That's wrong, Father."

"What do you mean *wrong*?"

"All of your slaves knew that it was your job to fight the waves of destruction. They just wanted to help you in your duty! You charmed them with your fabulous cooking. You awakened their stomachs to the light, I say!"

"That doesn't change what I did." Father watched me with a suspicious gaze.

Had I said something strange? It is true that Father cooked whatever the slaves and the filolials wanted. Filo-tan loved Father's cooking more than anything in the world.

Food is energy, I say. Father's delicious food had created an environment where everyone wanted to work together.

"Well, it seems like no one is going to join me out of their own free will, and it's too dangerous to head to the demi-human country where they would actually support me." Father frowned. "There may be nothing we can do about it." He nodded. "So we might get along well enough by having a high level and strong equipment, but is it also our goal to improve our reputation here in Melromarc?"

"I suppose so," I said. "Back when you were a wanted criminal, it was difficult for them to catch you because you went about your business all over."

I thought about the time after he'd been betrayed by the crimson swine and driven out on his own. Back then, finding out where Father had run off to was almost impossible. At first, people who saw the Shield Hero caused him all sorts of trouble. But eventually Father became the saint of the bird god and they began to praise him. I recalled how the crimson swine had kept spreading foul rumors about Father. Trash, the high priest, and the crimson swine declared that Father was controlling the people through brainwashing, but I knew the truth! I explained what had happened to Father.

"I see. We were able to foil the princess's plot because I won the trust of the people."

"Exactly!"

"All right, I get it now. I hate the idea of buying slaves, and peddling too, to be honest, but I'll do it. I'm still a bit worried about getting into trouble though."

"You shouldn't be, Father!"

Was there anything else I needed to tell Father?

Father spoke up while I was lost in thought.

"Okay, so in that case, what do you think I should do first? If there are any tricks to getting stronger, can you teach me them?"

"Yes, that's it! I haven't taught you the power-up methods yet."

"Shouldn't I just carefully read the help screen?" he asked.

"The help screen doesn't include all of the power-up methods. There are more power-up methods in the heroes' weapons. It depends on how much you and your weapon trust each other, and it results in composite power-ups."

"Really? That seems pretty complicated."

I went on to explain the power-up methods in detail to Father. Of course, it would take too long to explain everything to him, so I started with an explanation of the general methods available. We didn't have nearly enough time or materials to test all of them to begin with.

"Well, I'll try my best," Father said.

"There's one thing I'd like you to remember," I declared.

"What is it?"

"I've tried to set a course very close to how things went in the first go-around, but I wasn't your ally back then, so there could be a number of differences. You weren't attacked by many assassins back then, but that could change this time around."

Father closed his eyes. "Even if that's true, this is infinitely better than a cursed world, one where I don't have any allies or friends at all." He looked back at me. "I can bear it."

The most pressing matter at hand was raising Father's level. But in order to do that, we needed the filolials. And in order to start peddling, we needed a seller.

Father could probably handle the selling himself, but if a rumor were to spread about the Shield Hero selling, it could damage our business. I pretty much remembered how Father had handled peddling in the first go-around, but I couldn't help but sense that there had been some other problem at the time. Continuing to investigate would be my best bet.

"So let's get your clothing—that is to say your armor, Father."

"Yep."

"Chirp!"

Yuki and Kou agreed.

We had to do our very best from here on, I say. We left the back room.

"Did you finally finish your talk, kids?" the old weapon shop owner asked.

"Yes, thanks for letting us borrow the room."

"Don't worry about it. By the way, you can't go out looking like that," the old guy remarked, pointing to Father's underwear. "So they stripped you of everything, even your chainmail. You want me to lend you some? No charge."

I knew that the old guy was inclined to help Father. He had offered to help Father in the same way even in the first go-around.

"No thanks. I'll pass."

"But you need something. You can't go around like that," the old guy said.

"In the past, you bought leather armor," I told Father. "So I'd like you to use this money to buy some." I showed Father the money that I had set aside for him. He needed to buy what he needed. He needed to fight, after all.

"No way! I can make do with something cheap."

"Please, take it. Your equipment is important."

Father sighed. "Okay then."

"Did you decide, kid? You've got a good friend here. By the way, Spear Kid, do you need some armor?"

"I'm fine."

"Huh? Motoyasu, aren't you buying armor?"

"You are the priority, Father," I told him. "I'll buy what I can with whatever money is left over."

"I feel like I'm such a burden," Father said. "I'm sorry."

"Don't even think of worrying about it!"

Did I see tears gleaming in Father's eyes? Father rubbed his eyes to wipe them away!

"Thank you. I'll make it up to both of you, I promise," Father said.

The old guy bellowed with laughter. "Not much of a promise, but I'll take it!"

With that, Father selected his leather armor. It looked a bit on the cheap side.

I turned to the old guy. "If you don't mind, I have one more request of you."

"Another?"

"Actually, legendary heroes' weapons have a weapon copy—"

While Father looked uncomfortable for taking up more of the old guy's time, I went on to explain how the weapon copy skill works. I suppose it did sound a bit like I intended to commit robbery or something like that. It wasn't much of a conversation to have with a weapon shop owner.

"No kidding," the old guy said. "The sword and bow heroes came here and were touching the weapons, and it seemed like they were up to something. So that's what it was." He shook his head.

I did the same thing the first time around. I remember when I entered with my pig companions, feeling all high and mighty. I knew Zeltoble's lineup of products from my knowledge of an online game. I had looked down on this store and had no problem making and taking weapon copies with me. An excess of them, at that.

If I thought about it, it was obviously robbery.

"I get it," the old guy said. "It must've been rough for you kids too. Feel all the shields you want. It doesn't reduce my weapon stock, so there's no harm done."

"Thank you so much—"

"Hang on, wait a second," the old guy said and set out to the back of the store. He seemed to be looking for something on the second floor.

Looking around, I couldn't help but notice that there weren't very many shields in the store. But given that the Shield Hero was an enemy in this country, it made sense that they didn't sell a lot of shields. Besides this store, I doubted many sold shields in the first place.

"Found it!" The old guy came back toward us. "Thanks for waiting. This is a rare shield in this country."

He took us into a back room and showed us a shield that I felt like I had seen before—a Zeltoble siderite shield.

They had siderite here, of all places?

"What do you think, Spear Kid?"

"I say there's no problem. He's used a weapon of that type before."

"No kidding?"

It's hard to see something when it's under your very nose, I say. Back when I was chasing around pigs, I thought that this was just an ordinary store. I realized that the old guy had doted on Father and helped him even when he had painful experiences, but he also had amazing equipment like siderite!

I remembered that Father had kept this shield under guard in the village warehouse. He polished it regularly and kept it as bright as a jewel. Back then, I think he used the copy, but it still was a considerably powerful shield.

I think that the sword Ren had used was a copy from this store too, but I wasn't sure.

I also had this memory about a person that Father always used to call Motoyasu II. Who had it been? But if they weren't around now, thinking too much about it wouldn't be any help.

And what had I been using as a weapon in the first go-around, anyway? Eventually I had copied that spear that big sis's older sister had. I learned Brionac by borrowing that spear, if I'm not mistaken.

"Go ahead and copy this," the old guy said. "It was made from a meteorite that fell from the sky. It's a rare siderite series item purchased from a special exhibition in Zeltoble."

"Siderite, huh?" Father examined it. "Motoyasu, is this really that rare?"

"You couldn't copy something like this unless you went all the way to Zeltoble," I said. "And even then you'd need a considerably powerful skill to do so."

"Wow." Father nodded and turned to the old guy. "I really don't know how to thank you."

"Don't worry about it, kid," he said. "Come do me a favor someday."

"Yes," Father said. "I'll come back. No doubt about it."

"Don't be shy about it, kid," the old guy said. "At least be a little more excited!"

Father held the shield and passed it back to the old guy.

"You're right." Father closed his eyes and took a deep breath. All of a sudden, he looked livelier than he had ever been. "I'm coming back, so you better look forward to it! I'll have you make me some first-rate armor with the money that I'm going to earn!"

The old guy was right. Father was, in truth, an excitable character. But in the previous time loops he had held back too often. Kudos to this old guy, who was able to pull that side out of him with his interpersonal skills, I say.

I also wanted Father to let loose more around me!

"That's the attitude, kid!" The old guy smiled. "I'll see you soon, then!"

"See you next time!"

"Farewell!"

And with that, we left the weapon shop.

Meanwhile, Yuki and Kou were chirping and playing, trying to fit into the holes in Father's armor.

"So are we going to buy a slave now? Or are we going to level up Yuki and Kou first?" Father asked.

"Good question." It's not that it would be impossible to level up while staying under the radar. But as we thought about it, it wouldn't hurt to go find a slave. "A slave it is!"

Father nodded with a gulp and followed after me.

What was he so nervous about?

If I had to say, he looked like someone attempting to muster up all of his courage to speak to a crush.

We attracted a lot of unpleasant glances as we walked through the castle town. This happened every time we went outside. Should I dispose of them all?

We left the main road and went to the monster trainer's tent. In front of the tent, Father tapped my shoulder.

"I-is this where they sell slaves?"

"It is. They also sell monsters."

"M-monsters! If we just needed to get stronger, using monsters would be enough, I suppose."

But our objective was to acquire a salesperson. For leveling up quickly, you simply can't beat filolials. It must have been Father's hesitation about buying a slave acting up.

"All right, we're going in," I told Father.

"Okay."

As we walked into the tent, I saw the monster trainer, the same as ever. But he had a strange expression. It looked like he was also running a circus.

Huh!?

A filolial circus!

Lovely sounds massaged my ears. I fell into a dream. It was the perfect evolution of a filolial farm, I say.

"You are a new customer, I see. Yes sir."

"Filo-tan," I whispered.

"Yes . . . sir?"

"Motoyasu, what are you going on about? Filo-tan is my future adopted child, right?"

Oho? Suddenly we were talking about Filo-tan. Hadn't I decided to find Filo-tan later?

"That is incorrect," I declared.

The monster trainer spoke up. "By your appearance and the weapons you're holding, I'm assuming that you are the Shield and Spear Heroes?"

Father hesitated and cast a suspicious glance at the monster trainer. Perhaps he was thinking that the monster trainer would try to pull something if he realized who we were.

"But rest assured, I won't change my prices on you just because of that. Yes sir."

Father nodded and took a tentative step forward.

"So the Shield Hero, right? Yes sir. By the way you look, you might be thinking you have no business being in a place like this, right?"

"Sorry, but I can't stand being treated like a fool," Father mumbled under his breath. He took a deep breath.

Yes, because Father is the greatest peddler of them all! I could let him handle the negotiations with no worries at all.

"It sounds like you think we're fools," Father said.

"No, not at all! People just have a response to you. Yes sir. The Shield Hero . . . Ah! Sorry, that's rude of me to talk about. Okay, heroes, what can I do for you?"

"Coming to a place like this, shouldn't you already know what we want?"

"Ahh, very well. So you would like a slave. Yes sir."

"Show us what you have. We can negotiate later. Don't even think about trying anything with us."

The monster trainer smiled suggestively at Father's words. "Please come this way. Yes sir."

He took us into the back of the tent and showed us the slaves he had.

"A lot of demi-humans, huh?" Father said.

"In Melromarc, they follow a rule of human supremacy," the trainer said, "so it's quite difficult to get your hands on a human. Yes sir."

"I figured. I'll have to go to a different store to get one of those," he remarked.

I saw that Father was gripping his own wrist to prevent his hands from shaking.

That was the first time I heard about there being human slaves in Melromarc. Father's wisdom was everlasting!

Hm? But why would Father know that now?

"So?" Father suddenly pointed at one of the slaves in the cage. "How much is this one?"

"This slave . . ." The monster trainer explained the price.

"Okay, I got it."

Father fell into deep thought.

"That's a lot more than the market price," he said.

Oho? I had never seen father buy a slave before. So how could he possibly know what the market price for a slave was?

Keel

Naofumi's slave

A demi-human with the ears and tail of a dog. She was owned by the same aristocratic family that mistreated Raphtalia. At first glance she seems to be a boy, but she's actually a tomboy. She can transform into a Siberian husky-like therianthrope.

ABOUT KEEL

 Keel really can cheer everybody up, can't she?

She always wore a loincloth. She's a crepe-loving loincloth dog.

Not just crepes. She loved everything you cook, Naofumi.

 She would be great as a peddler. With her lively personality, she'd have no trouble going around selling things.

Chapter Sixteen: Bluff

"I believe this is a fair price," the monster trainer was saying. "It is my personal motto to operate by the market price. Yes sir."

"I'm not so sure about that," Father said.

I started to see what Father was doing here. He didn't actually know about a cheaper store, but he was going for a bluff, I say! He had already set it up well with his comments about human slaves from before too! Father was as clever as ever.

"However, I must say that I'm surprised that the heroes are so interested in slaves. Yes sir."

"I have no chance of making any companions of my own in this country," Father said bluntly. "I need people who I can use. That's all." Then he swallowed and continued. "If I don't have a companion I can work to the bone, I won't get strong enough."

At Father's response, the monster trainer's face lit up in excitement.

"Depending on the situation," Father continued, "I might have the Spear Hero help me out . . . so if you need to eliminate someone, just say it. He'll dispose of anyone for cheap. And in return, you can sell me a good slave for cheap."

"If it is the command of Father, I, Motoyasu Kitamura, will assassinate any rival merchant you so desire!"

The monster trainer snickered. "You didn't look like such good customers at first glance, but it seems that I misjudged you. Yes sir. This changes things. Yes sir."

I never saw the monster trainer in this good of a mood before.

I only remembered him seeming uncomfortable. What had changed? Of course, Father had managed to hit the nail on the head with these negotiations.

"What kind of slave would you be looking for? If you can provide me with a price range, I can better assist. Yes sir."

Father turned to me and whispered in my ear.

"What should we do? Should we buy his recommendation or ask for something in particular?"

Hmmm. It was a good question. For a seller, charm had to be the most important quality. If we bought an unfriendly slave, there'd be no point.

Perhaps there was something from the first go-around that I could use here. It would be logical to simply try to buy whichever slave had been in charge of the peddling in Father's village.

. . . Which was who, exactly?

I tried to remember which slave had been especially good at selling. The filolials had been talking about one person in particular. Of course, since they had Father to guide them, I was sure all of Father's slaves were successful peddlers, but I seemed to remember that there was one individual . . .

That's right—it was a dog-like demi-human named Keel! She was a pig who could transform into a dog, if I wasn't mistaken.

I whispered my answer back to Father.

Yes, I remembered her now! Like big sis, Keel was a demi-human who had been living on land that Father reclaimed as the village. The original population of that area had ended up in slavery due to the waves of destruction. The filolials and other slaves told me about it.

"Is there a slave named Keel here?" Father asked. "From one of the villages ruined by the wave?"

The monster trainer pulled out a list and inspected it.

A while later, he spoke up. "Unfortunately, that slave is not present. Yes sir."

Oho? I had heard that Father got his slaves from this very monster trainer, but could that have been wrong? The same thing had happened with Filo-tan as well.

"Shall I send for a slave with the same profession? Yes sir."

Father folded his arms and fell into thought.

"So you're just trying to charge us the same price for a cheap copy?" he said. "That won't do."

"How dare you—we sell our products in good faith," the monster trainer said. "Yes sir. However, thanks to the wave, there are plenty of new slaves available, and so I could try to find the one you are looking for. Yes sir. Of course, the price would have to increase for our efforts. What would you like to do?"

Father turned to me. "So how about silver?"

I confirmed the amount in the purse with Father.

"Up to 50 silver pieces," Father told the monster trainer. "I wouldn't go a cent above that. You better not try and stick us with a different one either. And if you try to up the bill later, when we're settling it, don't even think about it."

"You heroes drive a frightening bargain. Yes sir."

The monster trainer counted the money with a series of clinks, keeping one eye sharply trained on Father.

If the time loop reset again, I'd make sure I got to see Father's remarkable bargaining ability on display again, I say!

"Please come back here again tomorrow," the monster trainer said. "By tomorrow I should know how long it will take me to get the slave you requested. Yes sir."

"Understood. All right, let's go."

Father tapped my shoulder and we walked out of the tent.

For a while, we stood in the back alley outside the tent. Father shuffled his feet nervously.

Eventually Father spoke up. "Even though I haven't had anything to eat, I feel like I'm going to throw up," he said. "To sell demi-humans, even human slaves . . . I'd seen it before in video games and novels, but in real life . . . it was just so depressing." He shivered.

"Are you all right, Father?"

"Yeah. Yeah, I'll be fine, but I'm not sure if I'll be able to eat for a while."

I supposed he was unhappy because Yuki and Kou were in gloomy moods after our visit to the monster trainer. That monster trainer's tent was truly a terrible place.

"So if it goes smoothly, we'll be able to meet Keel tomorrow, I suppose," Father said.

"Yep."

"So what do we do now?"

"If you're not feeling well, Father, why don't you take a rest?"

"No, I'm fine. If I stopped just because of that, well, I wouldn't be able to make it very far in this world."

What a remarkable attitude! I had caught a glimpse of the true strength of Father's heart!

"So even if we try to make me as strong as we can under the current circumstances, we'd have to stay hidden, right?" Father asked. "In that case, can we even level me up now? It seems like it could be difficult to do."

"That's no problem at all!" I declared.

I lowered my voice. You never knew who could be listening, I say.

"In order to level you up, we need Yuki and Kou's help first," I told him.

"Yeah, but . . ."

"Don't worry about it. We can escape from any pursuer using my portal skill, which allows us to go anywhere I've registered before!"

"Right—I don't think running away is the problem. In the last go-around we managed to escape to Siltvelt, right? But if we were to suddenly disappear now, it would be awfully suspicious to suddenly come back with powerful companions, wouldn't it? We have to be really careful. We can't afford to make a mistake."

Father appeared lost in thought. I hadn't thought that much about it, I say. I was focused on making sure Father was strong enough to prevent any assassination attempts. Of course, if Father suddenly got a lot stronger, it did mean that Melromarc might send stronger attacks against him. Compared to the first go-around, the reason why we had so many assassination attempts in the previous go-around is likely because I had shown off how strong I was.

"How about this? You act as if you only rescued me and wanted nothing else to do with me—" Father explained to me his plan.

It was a good idea. If we followed it, we just might be able to deceive whoever was watching us.

"So I'll go steal some medicine from a well-to-do pharmacy in the castle town and run off into the countryside," Father said. "The monsters are weak there, so I should be fine."

"Very well," I said. "Let's get started then."

Father nodded. "Yuki and Kou, do your best!"

They chirped on my shoulder, cheerful as ever.

"Thank you, Motoyasu!" Father called loudly, as if on purpose. "I'll be fine alone, so go ahead and save this country!" He pushed me ahead.

I waved to him. "Goodbye! I hope we meet again someday!"

Yes, Father was right. Because we were working together, Melromarc would be suspicious of us. So for now, remaining separate was the best way to keep us safe. Father asked me to remember this plan in case the time loop reset again.

I couldn't tell if Father's plan would lead to good luck or bad, but nevertheless, we parted ways.

I left the castle town and went to the next village over. Yuki and Kou kept on chirping the whole way there.

Next up, procuring food!

Normally, I would start by feeding Yuki and Kou soft food and switch over to hard food as they started to level up.

The stomach of a filolial was like a black hole, I say. It was far past time to satisfy their empty stomachs!

But I couldn't go too crazy with feeding them either.

I bought some soft food and started feeding it to them bit by bit.

"Chirp!"

I smiled, watching them as I slowly walked around the village. I had left the castle town a little after noon, so by the time I arrived at the second village outside the castle town, the sun was setting.

Because I hadn't been too pushy in going to the guild or anything like that, I figured Melromarc was unlikely to send any assassins. I couldn't go to Father directly as that would only cause him trouble, and he requested that we go separate ways, after all.

I took a room at an inn in the second village, ate, and went to bed. Yuki and Kou hadn't grown much yet.

But they would soon!

I took a nap for a few hours.

"All right!"

I woke up in the middle of the night. I stuffed the bed with pillows so it looked like I was sleeping there. I then activated Cloaking Lance to hide myself and tucked Yuki and Kou into my pocket.

I slid the window open quietly, leapt outside, and shut it.

"Portal Spear!"

In an instant, I was flung to that castle town that never sleeps—none other than Siltvelt!

Now that I was there, there was no more need for all the precaution, I say! I gallantly dashed across the town!

I was headed to the heart of the surrounding mountains to

fight the powerful monsters there. On the way there I attracted a number of strange looks, but who cares!

Once I got to the mountains, I declared my level to the surrounding monsters and lit up the night with a magic flame as I started to sprint toward them. All of the monsters here were different types from the ones in Melromarc.

I decided to clear the whole area for land to raise filolials in search of my beloved Filo-tan. Soon, this mountain would become a paradise!

"Shooting Star Spear!" I shouted, slaying monsters left and right. "Brionac! Gungnir! Aiming Lancer! Hahahaha, take that, weakling! Too weak, I say!"

The monsters roared, shrieked, screamed, and cried out in terror as I destroyed them all.

I looked up in excitement as an enormous dragon began to storm across the area, heading toward me with a vicious growl.

"No matter how strong you are, you'll never stop me and my precious filolials, I say!" I proclaimed. "The weak are meat, the strong do eat! This is my mountain now!"

The dragon must have judged me as a threat, as it started breathing scorching flames and attacking me with all its might. I rushed toward it, waving my spear, and the dragon suddenly started to fly away as I chased after it. I spun my spear, aimed it carefully, and leapt straight for the dragon's heart.

"Shooting Star Spear X! Die!"

I launched the attack, stabbed my spear through the dragon's chest, and used Burst Lance. The dragon let out a long howl, unable to bear the might of the attack, and fell dead. As it crumpled to the ground, it looked like it died without regrets.

What a cowardly dragon. Fighting requires true resolve. And I would fight for Filo-tan, for Father, and for all filolials!

To air out my frustrations, I kept on fighting those monsters all night long.

Hm? The next dragon I took out dropped some flashy armor. But I had no need for it. Should I lend it to that weapon shop owner we visited to pay him back for his kindness?

And what should I do with all these ingredients that I was collecting from the monsters? I supposed I'd give them to Father later, although I would have to be careful with the timing so no one would suspect us.

Or I could hide everything here in the mountains. It wasn't a big deal even if someone stole it.

"Chirp!"

"Oho? Did you wake up now?"

"Chirp!"

Yuki and Kou had woken up and started to chirp and peck at the monster I had just killed. I couldn't help but smile as I watched them.

I must say, protecting Father while ensuring that there would be no war was incredibly annoying.

Couldn't there be some way to just kill off the crimson swine, the high priest, and Trash?

While I thought about such matters, I went on hunting monsters all through the night.

"Phew! I almost forgot about the time difference." I returned via portal to my Melromarc inn. Things could've gotten sticky if the pillows I left under my sheets had been uncovered, I say.

"Chirp!"

Yuki and Kou had evolved to their second stage. They were around level 28. As expected, leveling them up only at night would prove to be tricky. But if I was out fighting for too long, I would attract Melromarc's attention, so this was the best and only way.

"Chirp! Chirp!"

"Are you hungry now? Leave it to me!"

At least Yuki and Kou were happy to feed on the monsters I had hunted.

In order to meet up with Father again, I headed back up the road toward the Melromarc castle town. Along the way, I found some more monsters to give to Yuki and Kou for another meal. I picked up their drop items and ingredients to pass along to Father as well.

"Oh, Motoyasu. What a coincidence!"

Just as we had planned, I found Father in front of the Melromarc castle town pharmacy.

"Chirp!"

"Wow! Are those the filolials from yesterday?" Father asked. "They got a lot bigger."

"They have much more to grow," I told him.

"I bet. They have to get pretty big to pull carriages."

Father leaned in closer as we talked.

"So?" he asked. "Did it go well?"

"No problem at all," I informed Father. "Yuki and Kou got to level 29."

"Nice!"

"I also found some good armor for you. I can show you it later."

"That's great. Oh, also, by watching the pharmacy I learned a little bit about what kind of medicine they have here, so I went looking for materials out in the fields."

Father showed me the herbs he had collected.

"Chirp!"

"You want some too, don't you?" Father said to Yuki and Kou. He split off a little piece and fed it to them.

But Yuki quickly spit it out with an unhappy sneeze. Apparently, it didn't taste very good. They do say that the best medicine tastes bitter, but chick filolials weren't likely to understand that.

"They don't mean it," I said to Father.

"Oh, I get it. When I started collecting them in my shield, I boosted my harvesting skill and the quality of the herbs started to improve, so I ended up picking too many. Besides that, I was mostly hanging out and fishing at the river there. I'm going to try mixing the medicine later."

"Did they send an assassin?" I asked.

"No, not yet. I'm being careful with what I eat though."

We didn't know how things might change this go-around, so it was good that he was being careful.

Then came another chirp.

"Oh, yeah. Look, it's Sakura!"

Father pulled a little round filolial out from his breast pocket and showed me.

"She just hatched, a little before I got here. Take a look!"

"Of course!"

"Chirp!"

Father raised her up so I could get a better look as she chirped. Oho?

"Her eyes are blue, aren't they?" I asked.

"Huh? Yeah, what's wrong?"

Had I mistaken the color of Sakura's eyes? They had definitely been pink, the same as the rest of her body. That's why we had named her Sakura, after all. But the Sakura that Father showed me definitely had blue eyes. Was it a different filolial?

I did get a good whiff of the smell, and it was certainly Sakura's. That same scent that was preciously close to my beloved Filo-tan's!

Could the past somehow be influencing a different course

of events here? I guessed that the fact that Father had hatched Sakura rather than me ended up changing the color of her eyes. But I had no idea how or why that had happened.

But if the eye color was different from that of the rest of the body, it meant that we had a different filolial on our hands here. Perhaps whoever hatched and raised a filolial really did influence what it became.

It was all very educational.

Well, whatever had ended up happening, Sakura still had the reverse coloring of Filo-tan—white on pink as opposed to pink on white. So I didn't need to rush to figure this all out. If Father or I didn't buy Filo-tan from the monster trainer, someone else would. She could only be on the market for a short period of time. I just had to keep visiting every once and a while and continue to collect more filolials, I say!

"Oh, there's nothing wrong," I said. "So anyways, leave her to me and I'll level her up fast, I say! In the meantime, will you look after Kou, then?"

"That works," Father said. "Okay, Sakura, I'm going to give you to Motoyasu for a little bit, so get stronger and come back!"

Sakura and Kou chirped. "Let's do it," they were saying!

Father tightened his expression. "All right, so should we go to the slave tent now?"

It was time. The monster trainer had said he would know by today how long it would take for him to find Keel.

I nodded. "But I don't think the filolials like the monster trainer very much. So they can wait outside."

"That's fine. We can take our eyes off them for a moment." Father seemed to brace himself. "Okay, let's go in."

I followed Father down the back alley, toward the monster trainer once more.

Chapter Seventeen: An Order

Father took a deep breath and clenched his fists tightly. Mustering up courage, he entered the tent. The monster trainer came to greet us.

"Ah, hello there, heroes. I'm so glad you came back to my humble store. Yes sir."

"So?" Father asked. "Do you have the slave we ordered?"

"I certainly do. Fortunately, a colleague of mine had purchased the slave quite recently, so I was able to procure it immediately."

The monster trainer gave an order to a subordinate, who went to the back of the tent and brought a piglet out toward us.

The piglet oinked several times, struggling against the subordinate's grasp. Could that be Keel? A pig—that wouldn't do at all! I wasn't able to form a clear memory of Keel, so I had no idea if it was even her or not. I certainly wasn't able to communicate with her. Perhaps I would be able to understand her after she transformed into a dog.

"How is she? Yes sir," the monster trainer asked.

Father paused. "How much?"

"Well, we've selected her according to your personality, and the slave registration ceremony is included as well. How about 45 silver pieces? Yes sir."

I saw Father's eyes dart around and he took a deep breath.

I remembered something. I turned to Father and whispered in his ear.

"Father, it's best if we get a little bit of slave registration ink from him too. We can use that to power up her abilities and growth."

I had never had a slave of my own before, but I had used the ink to power up my spear. I'm sure I couldn't do it as well as Father could, of course.

Father nodded. He took a step toward the monster trainer and assumed a haughty expression.

"Hmmm . . . so this is Keel, eh?"

Keel spat out a series of oinks. Father interpreted for me. Apparently, she was talking about how she wouldn't let us tyrannize or mistreat her.

"She seems to have a rather aggressive personality. Yes sir," the monster trainer said, smiling nervously. "Is that a problem?"

Of course, Father's response was right on the mark.

"Part of the point of having a slave is to whip her into shape, isn't it?" Father asked the monster trainer. "A bit of an attitude makes that all the more interesting."

The monster trainer nodded excitedly. "I can tell that you're going places, Shield Hero. Yes sir. Now let's begin the registration—"

"Could you throw in some registration ink too? We'd like to use it on our weapons as well."

"Of course! Yes sir!"

Things had gone as smooth as can be. It was like night and day compared to when I visited this place by myself. Father had even gotten him to throw in extra services for free! I wondered if it was thanks to his haughty attitude.

I explained to Father that in order to complete the registration, he had to add a drop of his blood to the ink. Father cut the same place on his hand as yesterday, where the cut he made to register Sakura was just beginning to heal. A drop of blood fell into place.

The monster trainer's subordinate held the so-called Keel in place and applied the registration seal. She cried out in pain.

She glared at us like we were her oppressors, but halfway through the registration she suddenly went quiet and endured the pain. Naturally, any friend of big sis's would be able to tough it out, I say.

Keel grunted in pain as the registration finally finished.

Father carefully examined the monster seal, checking it all over.

"All done, right?" he asked.

Father handed over the silver pieces to the monster trainer and looked down at Keel.

"From now on, you're mine!" he declared. "Do your best to stay alive, if you can."

Keel cast an angry stare at Father. However, I knew it

wouldn't take long for her to get as attached to him as everyone else did.

"See you next time," Father said to the monster trainer. "I'll come back if I need something else."

"Please come again. Yes sir. I'd be happy to serve you."

Father waved and grabbed Keel by the hand.

"Let's go," he called.

"Yes, Father!"

I followed Father out of the tent. The filolials greeted us with merry chirps.

"We're back!" Father said.

"You waited so patiently," I cooed, petting them and lifting them into my arms.

I could tell the filolials were on the verge of another growth spurt. They were as hungry as could be.

Keel blinked in surprise upon seeing them but quickly looked the other way.

"So what do we do now?" Father asked. "Do you want to take Keel with you so we can have everyone level up together?"

"Not a bad idea," I said. In order to best level up Sakura, I could wait until night, not let her eat anything, and then take her out to the mountains again. We had to make sure that no one suspected that Father and I were working together, I say.

The only problem at the moment was that I had no idea what Keel was saying. This was going to pose a problem, especially considering that the filolials couldn't speak yet either.

"Father, please assist me," I said. "I can't understand the language of pigs, so I don't think I can work with Keel."

"I get that you call women you dislike pigs," Father said, "but what exactly is the problem?"

"Pigs are pigs, I say!" I declared. "They are lowly creatures that squirm in the mud and think of nothing but themselves!"

Father sighed. "I don't know why or how, but you see women as pigs, right? Because of the time loop, maybe? Wait, you're saying she's a girl?"

"Oink!?"

Keel had started to play with the filolials and she quickly turned to Father.

"I thought you were a boy with pretty eyes or something— so . . . so you're a girl?"

"Oink! Oink oink oink!"

For some reason Keel was making a fist and waving it at Father angrily. I had no idea what was going on.

I was merely training filolials to pull carriages for Father! All of us, as Father's servants, had to do our very best to help him, I say.

"Well, if you say so, that's fine with me. Nice to meet you."

"Oink, oink?"

Keel bent her head, seemingly confused. A pig is a pig, but somehow I grasped the gist of her expressions. While words are an absolute no-go, I'm not half-bad with pig expressions.

"So, Miss Keel, since we'll be—"

"Oink!"

"Right, just Keel—since we'll all be working together, meet Motoyasu and Sakura. You, me, and Kou are going to go out and do some fighting to level up together."

"Let's do it!" I proclaimed.

"We just need to make some preparations first," Father said.

But of course! Keel needed equipment from the weapon shop.

Incidentally, it was wonderfully convenient that it wasn't particularly important for filiolials to have any equipment at all. And it was hard for me to comprehend why pigs would need equipment, but since it was Father's idea, I didn't say anything.

We went back to the weapon shop. When the old guy saw Father and Keel, he rubbed his forehead in thought.

"Kiddo . . ." he began.

"No, it's not what you think!" Father said. "Don't look at me like that!" Flustered, Father quickly explained what we had done.

Was the old guy upset that we had a pig with us?

No, he was upset that we had bought a slave.

"I don't know if it's that you're more ruthless than I thought, or if this is just a stain on our country . . ." The old guy trailed off.

"It's the country, I'm telling you," Father said. "I'm the same as I was before! I had no choice!"

The old guy sighed. "Well, if you had no choice, it is what it is. What do you need this time?"

"Can you show me some good equipment for her?" Father asked. He kneeled down in front of Keel and looked her straight in the eye. "We're going to fight together from now on," he said.

"Oink!?"

"I suppose I haven't introduced myself yet," Father said. "My name is Naofumi Iwatani, and I was summoned to this world as the Shield Hero."

Keel oinked quietly.

"Exactly. And the Shield Hero can't fight monsters alone. So I bought you so you could become my offense. It may be a selfish reason, and I understand that you can't trust me yet, but please, from here on, I'd like to earn your trust."

Keel averted her eyes and took several steps back. All I could see was a pig, but she was a demi-human after all. I was shocked that she didn't instantly prostrate herself before the boundless compassion of Father!

"You don't need to trust me yet," Father said. "Trust isn't something that I can just force out of you. But in order to stay alive, you should probably get some equipment."

Father showed the rest of his money to the old guy. I was

holding on to most of the money to buy supplies for peddling, so Father only had a little left.

"I'd like to buy some equipment for her," Father repeated.

"Got it, kid. You have a reason. I'll help you out. Come here," he called to Keel. "I'll pick out some good stuff for you. Can you show me your hand?"

Keel raised her hand.

"I'd recommend a dagger," he said. "They're good as beginner weapons for one, and I think it'll suit her well."

"That sounds good to me," Father said. "We also need some armor that she can easily move around in."

"No problem."

Once the old guy picked them out, Father gave Keel her dagger and armor. But because of her level, they were of fairly poor quality.

"We can't really get around the fact that this is weak equipment," the old guy said. "But you need to be able to use your weapons and armor. Once you get stronger, come back and we'll exchange them for something better."

"Sounds good," Father said.

Keel oinked.

Naturally, having strong weapons alone wasn't enough. I never had to worry about it because I had my spear. But I remembered that even the legendary weapons got gradually stronger as you leveled up, so they worked pretty much the same as if you were buying new, regular weapons—like the old guy was saying.

So was the old guy done talking to Father yet?

"I'm up next," I announced.

"Huh? Do you need something, Spear Kid?"

"I'd like to borrow the back room for a moment," I informed him.

"Again? What are you going to do now?" he asked.

"I'd like you to come with me."

"Well, fine with me. Let's go."

We left Father and Keel in the shop and went to the back room.

"What could it possibly be?" the old guy asked.

"Please allow me to show you something for a moment," I said. I took out all the equipment I had collected as drop items from the monsters last night and emptied it out on the floor. The old guy gasped as they popped out of my spear.

"What the hell!?"

"This is my weapon's drop ability, I say," I announced. "This is what I wanted to talk to about. The next time Father needs new equipment, I'd like you to show these items to him. But when you do, make sure that you tell him that you made them and act like they're weak items."

The old guy nodded. "I don't mind looking after them for you, but why?"

"If I told you," I said menacingly, "I'd have to kill you."

If it became known that Father was in fact strong, then assassins would start coming after us. I had to make sure Father stayed on guard for one, and since the old guy was able to ascertain the weapons' true strength, he had to be in on it too.

"I don't like the sound of this," the old guy said.

"I'll give you your choice of item as a payment," I declared.

"Hang on a second . . ." The old guy took a close look at the drop items. "There's some high-quality stuff in here," he said. "It'll sell well. All right, that settles it. I can take it apart for materials for one, and if it's really helping you kids, I don't mind doing you the favor."

"I thank you from the bottom of my soul!"

"Leave it to me, kid."

With that, I had made arrangements to get Father more powerful equipment. We went out from the back room and I winked at Father.

"Shall we proceed, Father?"

Next up, I had to continue to level up Yuki and Sakura until I could meet Father again.

"See you later. Keel and I are going to go level up. Well, who knows how strong we'll actually get?" he said.

I chuckled. "Do your best, I say!"

"Good luck, kids!"

The old guy saw us off and Father and I went our separate ways. I headed off from the castle town in a direction that suited my whims—toward a different nearby village. I took care of some monsters along the way and fed them to Yuki and Sakura.

My primary objective was to raise Sakura to be as strong as possible. The only problem would be if the Siltvelt emissary were to try to find Father and take him to Siltvelt. But since I already explained all that to Father, he would probably refuse the emissary's offer.

I walked through and out of the castle town with a smile on my face.

Two days passed.

"Gweh!"

Yuki had grown remarkably fast and was about to evolve into her filolial queen form.

"Gweh!"

Sakura was a day behind and had grown into her filolial form.

Today I planned to meet Father "by accident" again. I hopped onto Yuki's back and headed back to the Melromarc castle town.

"Hey, Motoyasu," Father called. "I haven't seen you in a few days."

"Quite so!" I proclaimed. "What an entirely unexpected encounter!"

"Kou really helped me out. Thanks for letting me borrow him."

We acted as if we had found each other by chance at our planned meet-up spot. Kou, like Yuki, was about to change into his filolial king form.

"Want to chat for a few minutes?" Father asked.

"Why not?" I said. "So how much stronger did everyone get?"

Father glanced at Keel and Kou. I didn't see much difference from how they looked two days ago, besides the fact that Keel looked like she had cleaned herself up a bit.

"Oink! Oink oink!"

Unfortunately, I still couldn't understand a word she said. I wished she would hurry up and transform into a dog so I'd be able to at least talk to her!

I suddenly realized that even if a pig could transform into a dog, that didn't necessarily mean it could suddenly speak human language. That would be problematic.

"I'm about level 7," Father said. "Keel is level 8. Kou . . . he's level 10, I think."

Just in case we were being watched, I could tell Father was lying about Kou's level.

"Not too different from Yuki and Sakura," I informed Father.

"So it looks like filolials take on different forms when

raised by heroes," Father said. "I was surprised! They sure can go fast."

"That's filolials for you, Father! Kou, you've done a wonderful job at protecting Father, haven't you?"

"Gweh!"

"Oink!"

"That's right. Keel did a great job too," Father said and patted Keel on the head. Keel looked like she was much more relaxed compared to a few days ago, I noticed. Of course Father, with all of his experience with slaves, was able to calm her down!

"Oh, I almost forgot," Father said. "An emissary from Siltvelt came yesterday."

"An emissary?" I acted surprised. "Why would they come to you?"

"They asked me to come to Siltvelt, but I decided I couldn't trust them and turned it down." He spoke loud for anyone nearby to hear, as if they had tried to force him to come to Siltvelt and it had been quite the traumatic experience. We knew that Melromarc was monitoring Siltvelt closely, so there was a high likelihood they were observing any contact Siltvelt made with Father. Which meant that now Melromarc was probably convinced that Father didn't trust Siltvelt. I'm sure Melromarc's schemers were breathing a sigh of relief, as the last thing they wanted was for Father to make his way to Siltvelt.

There wasn't much upside to going to Siltvelt for us either. They would start sending assassins after us, which defeated the purpose of our whole plan to level up and earn money while tricking Melromarc into thinking that Father was still weak.

Father leaned over and whispered in my ear.

"They want to work with us, so I made a plan to talk again with them today. Do you want to come?"

I nodded.

Then I spoke up again. "Now that you mention it, some emissaries came to me too."

I didn't remember what country it was, but they had invited me to come to their country in the first go-around as well. At the time, the crimson swine had interfered and I wasn't even able to give them an answer.

"But I also refused the offer," I continued. "Shall we take a stroll, Father?"

Back in the first go-around, I had been convinced that Melromarc was the best for me, so I likely would've refused the offer anyways. At the time, I was still being influenced by my knowledge of the online game from my original world, and I thought back then that it would be inefficient to bother working with another country. Ren and Itsuki probably felt the same way.

Based on my knowledge now, I knew that Melromarc was doing everything they possibly could to prevent us from getting our hands on accurate information.

Chapter Eighteen: A Peddling Permit

"So thanks to Keel and Kou, I was able to figure out recipes for mixing most of the medicines. I'll eventually have to make them myself, but that part is fun for me."

Father was chatting casually about what he had been up to for the last few days.

"In that case, Father, could you tell me where you stayed the first night of the adventure? I can't remember."

"Huh? Why?" Father looked uncomfortable.

"Just as a precaution," I said.

Father nodded, guessing my intentions. Yes, it was essential information for me to know in case the time loop were to reset, I say. I had absolutely no idea how I would use it, but it'd be useful to know regardless.

"Well, I have some errands to take care of. Want to come along?" Father asked.

"Sounds good," I said. "Okay, Sakura. Switch places with Kou. You're going to protect Father from now on. Do your best!"

"Gweh!" Sakura went over to Father and nuzzled him.

"Ah, that tickles, Sakura!"

"Gwaa!"

Sakura was delighted to be reunited with Father! The mood had considerably lightened. We set off through the town and passed by an inn.

"That one—and the room is that one, right there." Father pointed and I made sure to remember exactly where he had stayed.

If the time loop were to reset again, this small piece of information could make a world of difference.

"You're the Shield Hero, right?"

"That's me . . ."

On our way to the next meeting place, a demi-human called out to Father.

"What do you want?" Father asked.

"I have something I must ask of you," the demi-human said. "Please, will you come to our nation of Shieldfreeden?"

Oho? Another invitation for Father?

I remembered a group that seemed like they might've been from Shieldfreeden from the first go-around, so I suppose it was them soliciting Father to come there. I stayed quiet while Father paused and muttered to himself, as if carefully considering it.

"Sorry, but I think I have to pass," Father told the demi-human.

Fortunately, I had already told Father all about the events from previous go-arounds! In Shieldfreeden, there was Takt and all of his followers, like the aotatsu girl, I say. Heading there was like jumping right into the fire. There was no need to make our lives more difficult than they already were.

"You don't need to decide right away," the demi-human said. "Why don't you accompany me for just a little? We've prepared something very nice for you, Shield Hero."

"Hmmm . . ." Father glanced at me. "Thanks, but no thanks. I'm pretty busy right now."

"How dare you! I must say, please, come along! If you're worried about the demi-human girl at your side, we can take care of her too!"

"Talk about pushy." Father wrinkled his brow and glared at the demi-human. I wonder if Father had reacted harshly to this incident the first time around as well, right after he had been so cruelly betrayed. "Look, I do things the way I want to, so leave me alone. As the Shield Hero, I'm asking you to leave me alone."

The demi-human looked shocked and clicked his tongue. "Tsk! You'll regret this, Shield Hero!" The demi-human ran off.

I supposed Takt had put his followers up to this. I swore to finish them off sooner rather than later—Takt and every last one of his followers, I say!

"That was uncomfortable," Father said. "The Siltvelt emissary was much more polite than that. He was a little pushy too though."

"Pushy?"

"I said I had things to do and I wasn't going to his country. But he wouldn't give up. It wasn't easy talking to him."

"So now we're going to go talk to him again?"

"Yep. I thought it would be better if you were there, and he finally left me alone when I told him we could talk tomorrow."

And if he didn't leave Father alone, he could simply say it was by order of the Shield Hero. It was very much like Father to have trouble turning down someone's request for help.

"Oink oink oink oink oink?"

"Oh, my bad. Did you want to go?"

"Oink."

Father and Keel were discussing some matter or another, but I hadn't the slightest clue what they were saying. Keel appeared to be shaking her head. Regardless of what they were talking about, it was a bad idea to go to Shieldfreeden.

"All right," Father said. "I guess it's time to go talk to the Siltvelt emissary."

Under Father's direction, we went to meet the emissary. We turned into a back alley and entered a pub full of demi-human adventurers. I didn't know that there were places like this in Melromarc. It wasn't the liveliest meeting spot, but Father appeared to have made plans to meet the emissary here. Yuki and the filolials stood watch outside.

Father pointed out the emissary to me and we went over to him.

"Shield Hero, have you had time to think about what I told you yesterday?"

"Yeah, about that . . . Well, let's introduce ourselves first. This is Motoyasu Kitamura, summoned here as the spear hero."

"It is I, the Love Hunter, Motoyasu Kitamura!" I announced.

"He's a little weird, but we can trust him," Father said.

I am the Love Hunter, and my mission shall last for all eternity, I say!

I wasn't exactly sure why Father called me weird though. Was there something strange about the way I had been acting?

"I've heard about you," the emissary said. "We truly thank you for protecting the Shield Hero."

"I only did what was right," I declared.

No matter how many times the loop reset, I would never be forgiven for my sins from the first go-around, back before I knew the truth. I had to ensure that Father would never again be hurt by the evil schemes of the crimson swine. No matter how many times the time loop reset, I would continue to protect Father with all of my mind, body, heart, and soul!

"So getting back to the main topic," Father said. "Unfortunately, I don't think I'm able to go to Siltvelt."

"Why not, if I may ask?"

"The way they treat demi-humans in this country makes me sick, it really does. I want to do something about it. But we can't just launch an attack. At the moment, I don't intend to go to Siltvelt," Father explained.

The emissary's shoulders drooped in disappointment. I supposed his job was to get Father to come to Siltvelt, after all. But it's not like he was dispatched on the hardest mission in the world, so at least Father did the favor of telling him straight.

"What do you want to achieve in Melromarc?" the emissary asked.

"Since they're keeping a close eye on me, I don't have much choice but to hide, get stronger, and make money by peddling."

"I see . . ." The emissary trailed off. "But do you have a peddling permit?"

"A peddling permit?"

Father glanced at me and I shook my head. I had absolutely no idea. All I knew was that Father earned plenty of money and trust from his peddling in the first go-around. Had he also gotten a permit?

"Peddlers without permits have to pay a large commission to the town," the emissary explained.

"Really?" Father said.

It seemed like we had a problem on our hands. Since Father had done it in the first go-around, I had assumed peddling would be no problem. We would have no choice but to lose part of the profits, then.

"I understand what you want to do, Shield Hero," the emissary said. "At the very least, I'll reach out to Siltvelt. We can make contact with aristocrats amenable to our cause and try to get you a peddling permit."

Father and I were both taken aback by the emissary's goodwill.

"Th-thank you!" Father exclaimed. "I don't know what to say. I still won't be able to come to Siltvelt in the near future, but thank you."

"I understand your intentions," the emissary said. "After the wave, Melromarc will begin to do horrible things. Knowing that you plan to dispense God's punishment to this wicked land inspires us to do everything in our power to help you."

"I'm glad that you at least understand where I'm coming from," Father replied.

Peddling sure seemed like it was going to be a pain. I hadn't heard anything about a peddling permit. I supposed Father was the type to let his actions speak louder than words. Father must not have felt like he needed to explain unnecessary details to me.

"Also, if you're able to hide the fact that the shield hero came to Siltvelt . . . well, in that case, I may actually be able to visit," he added.

"Truly!?"

"Where to begin . . ." Father explained the portal skill to the emissary.

"I've been training over in Siltvelt!" I declared. "Would you like to go in secret, Father?"

"Maybe, especially if it could help everyone class up faster. I'm thinking about it."

The emissary nodded. "Understood. If you wish to come in secret, I have no reason to challenge it. I'll communicate your plans to the Siltvelt leadership."

"Much appreciated."

"I'll reach back out soon," the emissary said. "I'm hopeful that we can get you a peddling permit in the next few days."

With that, we concluded our meeting with the Siltvelt emissary. He bowed politely and hurried off.

Epilogue: Peddling Preparations

"The preliminary arrangements are going smoothly," Father said. "We just need a carriage and the permit. Then we could get going, I think. I've been making medicine with the shield skill, but if I'm going to do it without that, then I think I'll need better tools too."

"If you use a skill, then nothing you make will have any personality, right?" I asked. "For making high-quality products, making them by scratch would be a superior choice, I say."

We discussed the peddling preparations in the pub after the Siltvelt emissary had left.

"Was I selling anything else besides medicine?" Father asked.

"You were. Food, if I'm not mistaken."

"Like meat? Vegetables? Preserved foods?"

"In your village you had plants that grew unusually quickly," I explained.

"Wow. I guess there are plants that ripen more quickly in this world. Did I really have stuff like that?"

"You used the ones from your very own garden."

"Do you happen to remember how I got my hands on those plants?" Father asked.

"Hmmm. As to whether or not I have any idea, I do not know."

"Uh . . . so which is it?"

Back in the first go-around, I had been deceived by the crimson swine and unable to accept that I had lost the battle against the Spirit Tortoise. Afterward, when I went wandering on my own, I was in a village in southwest Melromarc when I heard about how Father had solved an "agricultural disaster" caused by the spear hero—of course, me. In the online game I played, there was some quest about ending a drought, so there must have been some problem with what I had done to end the drought. Every time I had tried to do something in this world using my knowledge of the game I had played, it ended up backfiring. The power-up methods, the Spirit Tortoise, and pretty much everything else too.

"It's not that I don't remember anything at all about it, but not quite enough to try to guess what had happened," I told Father.

"Got it. Well, if we have time, we could try to find out."

"I suppose so. I get the sense that you had told me in the first go-around that it was dangerous if you used the plants incorrectly."

"It doesn't sound like we'll be trying to grow them anytime soon."

"Fair enough. We need to guarantee we do it right, so let's forget about the plants for now."

The more I thought about it, the more I had a fair idea of what had happened. But regardless, we didn't have a place to grow plants. Once we got our hands on a secure location for agriculture, we could revisit the idea.

"So you're working on building up a supply of medicine to sell, correct?" I asked Father. I figured I could help out by thinking up a product that would be a surefire best-seller! "How about a food cart?" I suggested. "With your marvelous cooking skills, we'd rake in piles of cash, I say!"

"Huh? My cooking?" Father frowned. "I'm not really confident about my cooking."

"Your cooking is exquisite! Peerless!"

"Oink?"

All of a sudden, Keel seemed interested in the conversation and said something to Father.

"I'll think about it," Father said. "If I can increase the quality of products with my shield skill, then that's not a bad move."

Whatever Father did was guaranteed to be a hit. Father seemed like he was enjoying the conversation.

"It feels wrong, but this is starting to be a little fun," he said, smiling softly.

"I am overjoyed that you are having fun, Father," I proclaimed.

Father always had a rather sullen expression in the first go-around, I recalled.

"Trying to figure out what to sell and how to sell it is fun," he said. "In a game and in real life too."

"I know how you feel, Father." I could remember well the feeling of launching new ventures with my pig companions. Father and I were enveloped in a similar atmosphere of excitement.

"Once we finish figuring out what to do for peddling, what do you plan to do, Motoyasu?" Father asked.

"Yuki will be ready to evolve into her angel form soon, so I'm going to buy some materials to make clothes for her, I say." Previously I had ordered some materials from the monster trainer, if I wasn't mistaken. So perhaps I'd do the same thing again. At this rate, Yuki would soon be walking around naked if I didn't get her some clothes.

"Making clothes?" Father asked. "You can do that? Impressive!"

"It's nothing compared to your cooking skills!"

"I'm definitely not *that* good at cooking," Father said. "Maybe we could sell the clothes you make."

"If you so desire it, Father. I'll slay pigs and sew together their skins to make beautiful clothes!"

"That's not . . . quite . . ." Father frowned. "Anyways, let's finish making our preparations."

"Naturally, I say!"

Our arrangements proceeded smoothly and we prepared to start our peddling.

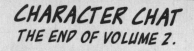

That's all for now. Good work!

Great work, I say! Father, how did I do?

For the most part, you were ridiculous. But I suppose I should've expected you to make life difficult for me.

A struggle, as always. I have to ask though, why haven't I shown up yet, outside of this character chat?

I don't want to think about it. Your situation can't be pretty.

I know . . .

I'm sure you're doing just fine, big sis! Your dauntless courage will get you through it all!

Will it really?

According to Motoyasu, you're quite the hero.

I leave that sort of impression on people, don't I?

I'm worried that Motoyasu isn't even going to find you at this rate.

Yeah. And even if he does find me, I'm concerned that my suffering would only increase.

I'm going to keep my promise to you, Father, and find Filo-tan while I'm at it! I can't wait for you all to see where my unstoppable love hunting takes us next!

QUESTION CORNER
LET'S ASK OUR REGULAR CHAT MEMBERS SOME QUESTIONS!

Q1. What do you want in a lover?

Q2. What do you think about while lying in bed?

Q3. Favorite food?

Q4. How do you spend your free time?

Q5. Who would you swap places with for one day?

Q6. What do think about hot spring baths?

Q7. Do you have a Melromarc shop recommendation?

Q1. Filo-tan.

Filo-tan Filo-tan Filo-tan!

Q2. Filo-tan and filolials.

That way, I can meet Filo-tan and filolials in my dreams!

Q3. Filo-tan's leftover— (Naofumi stopped Motoyasu from finishing.)

Filo-tan's— (Raphtalia covered Motoyasu's mouth.)

Q4. Making stuff for Filo-tan.

It's super fun!

Q5. Filo-tan.

One surefire way to figure out Filo-tan's whereabouts is to simply swap places with her for a day!

Q6. A place for peeping.

Female filolials are more appealing when being peeped at, I say.

Q7. The monster trainer's tent.

You can meet filolials there

MOTOYASU